A Change of Heart
at
The Vintage Dress Shop

About the Author

Annie Darling lives in London in a tiny flat, which is
bursting at the seams with teetering piles of books. Her
three greatest passions in life are romance novels, vintage
fashion and Mr Mackenzie, her British Shorthair cat.

Also by Annie Darling

The Little Bookshop of Lonely Hearts
Crazy in Love at the Lonely Hearts Bookshop
True Love at the Lonely Hearts Bookshop
A Winter Kiss on Rochester Mews
The Vintage Dress Shop in Primrose Hill

ANNIE DARLING

A Change of Heart
at
The Vintage Dress Shop

HODDER &
STOUGHTON

First published in Great Britain in 2024 by Hodder & Stoughton Limited
An Hachette UK company

1

A CIP catalogue record for this title is available from the British Library

Paperback ISBN 978 1 399 71533 1
ebook ISBN 978 1 399 71535 5

Typeset in Plantin light by Manipal Technologies Limited

Printed and bound in Great Britain by Clays Ltd, Elcograf S.p.A.

Hodder & Stoughton policy is to use papers that are natural, renewable
and recyclable products and made from wood grown in sustainable forests.
The logging and manufacturing processes are expected to conform to the
environmental regulations of the country of origin.

Hodder & Stoughton Limited
Carmelite House
50 Victoria Embankment
London EC4Y 0DZ

www.hodder.co.uk

'Life is a party. Dress like it.'

Audrey Hepburn

Dedicated to every woman who knows the transformative power of a really good frock.

PART ONE

Chapter One

After an unrelenting winter and a very wet spring, it was now June and most definitely summer.

'Phew! What a scorcher!' screamed the newspaper headlines, accompanied by pictures of bikini-clad young women frolicking in the waves on beaches from Skegness to Southend.

It was a world away from Cressida Collins's workroom high up in the eaves of The Vintage Dress Shop in London's Primrose Hill.

It was a very well-appointed workroom. One wall was taken up with floor-to-ceiling shelves containing a rainbow of spools of coloured threads. Glass jars and boxes of buttons and beads in every hue and every size. Zips, findings, trims, feathers; not to mention bolts of fabric, even though Cress didn't make dresses, she just repaired them. It never hurt to have a few metres of muslin or silk voile – in various shades, from alabaster white to a deep, dense oyster – on hand for when she was fitting or altering wedding dresses.

At the bottom of the shelves was a small library of reference books. Cress thought of them as her style bibles – they included titles from *The Thirties in Vogue* and *The Golden Age of Couture* to biographies of all the great British fashion designers: Alexander McQueen, Hardy Amies, Zandra Rhodes.

Along the other wall was the workbench where Cress's sewing machine and overlocker lived. There was a pinboard full of tear-sheets and inspiration from magazines, rough sketches of dresses that had been or were going to be altered, and Post-it notes. A hundred or more Post-it notes, all covered in Cress's handwriting, which was illegible to everyone but her, even though the workroom was testament to her organisational skills. Cress was a firm believer that there was a place for everything, and everything should be in that place.

She currently sat further along the bench on a high stool, though she'd much rather be sitting in the plush and very comfortable blue velvet armchair where she did most of her hand-sewing. But the armchair was directly under one of two skylights, through which shone the sun's unrelenting glare. No wonder then that the workroom felt hotter than the surface of Venus, even with two fans going full blast. It meant that Cress had to take regular breaks because her hands would get sweaty – and one didn't sweat on vintage.

She was doing some fiddly alterations on a tiny and fragile 1950s coral, shot-silk party dress with a 22-inch waist. Alas its new owner, a seventeen-year-old girl who was going to wear the dress to her prom, had a 24-inch waist.

Cress straightened up, with a little groan, from where she'd been bent over carefully unpicking a seam. Over the rattle of the fans, she could hear raised voices. Was her need for a cold drink greater than her need to avoid conflict?

She returned to the unpicking but now all she could think about was an ice-cold Diet Coke from the office fridge downstairs. So cold that beads of condensation would trickle down the can as Cress clasped it in her sweaty hand because, despite the fans, her hands were horribly . . . *moist*.

With another groan she stood up. Her dress was stuck uncomfortably to the back of her thighs. She pulled herself free of the damp fabric, then ventured into the fitting room to see what she looked like in the full-length mirror. As she had suspected, she looked as hot as she felt. Her dark curly hair was so frizzy that it was practically triangular and though she'd tanned to a pleasing shade of caramel these last few weeks, her face was red and sweaty. She tugged at her sleeveless pale blue smock, which she'd made herself, and which was still clinging damply to her. Cress peered closer at the glass, ran the tip of her finger over the arch of her eyebrows (even her eyebrows were moist) and poked a tongue out at her own reflection.

She'd much rather look at the shop's most expensive, high-end dresses hanging in the small room next door. Usually the sight of the rails of elegant gowns, by designers who were likes gods to Cress, never failed to lift her spirits, even on days when she felt like a hot sweaty mess.

Cress stepped out into the main salon, its walls lined with wedding dresses – from the palest white through to ivory, cream, champagne, oyster, silver and gold. There was even one black wedding dress, a confection of tulle and silk taffeta, though so far all their brides had shunned it. 'Married in black, you'll wish you were back,' as the mothers of these brides inevitably said.

At one end of the salon, there was a circular raised platform surrounded by mirrors on three sides so that anyone trying on a frock could see how it looked from every angle. There were three cream and gold chintz sofas positioned so that any accompanying entourage had a good view too, and on a side table was a cream and gold decorative box, which was always well stocked with tissues. A lot of tears, both happy and sad, were shed in front of those mirrors.

In the middle of the salon – in pride of place, really – was the shop dog, Coco Chanel, a black French bulldog with an attitude that would make even her famous namesake give pause for thought. She was lying on her back, stumpy legs spread as a fan sent cooling wafts over her lady bits.

'You have no dignity, CC,' Cress muttered, though actually she'd quite like to lie naked on the floor with a fan trained

5

on her undercarriage. She really wasn't a summer person. Cress much preferred autumn or winter, because she liked to be able to wear a cardigan most days. Right now, even the thought of wearing a cardigan made her feel as if she was being boiled alive.

She paused at the top of the spiral staircase that led down to the main shop floor, where she could hear Sophy, her beloved sister-friend, and Phoebe, her slightly less beloved boss friend, having words, as they were sadly wont to do. Very loud words.

'I'm just saying that when I was in Australia, we offered a rental service at Clive's Closet,' Sophy was saying as Cress brushed past her with a weak smile.

'How I wish you'd stayed in Australia at Clive's bloody Closet,' Phoebe hissed back.

To be fair, ever since Sophy, Cress's stepsister, had returned to The Vintage Dress Shop, after a year and a bit in Australia visiting family and working in a Sydney thrift store, she'd become quite one-note about just how differently they'd done things at Clive's Closet.

And to be fair to Phoebe, if Cress wasn't a summer person then Phoebe wasn't a summer person on steroids. She was always impeccably turned out in a chic black dress, seamed stockings and high heels, a full face of make-up including winged liquid eyeliner and deep red lipstick, and a glossy, poker straight black bob with thick fringe. It was a chic, elegant and also quite an intimidating look. But it also wasn't a look that held up well when the temperature was in the mid-30s. Phoebe's fringe kept separating and her eyeliner kept smudging. So, no wonder she wasn't in the best of tempers.

'Cress, don't you think it's a good idea to rent out the dresses as well as sell them?' Sophy called after her, but Cress pretended that she hadn't heard as she took a can of

Diet Coke out of the fridge in the little sliver of a kitchen off the back office.

She quickly stepped through the back door onto the tiny patio, which overlooked the Regent's Canal. On a summer's day, it was picture-perfect. The sun glinted off the water as gaily coloured canal boats chugged past, framed by the rich, green leaves of the trees that lined the path. Though they were a little wilted, a little less green than they had been, and Cress missed the cooling breeze that often carried off the water. Today was devoid of any breeze, cooling or otherwise.

She held the cold can to her heated face and tugged at the thin cotton of her smock dress, which was still sticking to her.

There was a sound behind her and she looked round to see Sophy stepping through the back door.

'Phoebe is *so* annoying!'

Cress held her hand up in protest. 'I can't, Soph,' she pleaded. 'I can't take another speech about renting out the dresses . . .'

Sophy paused from opening her own can of Diet Coke. 'But at Clive's Closet we—'

'I'm going to hurl myself into the canal before you can finish that sentence,' Cress said, punctuating her words with a delicate burp from gulping her fizzy pop too fast.

'I don't mean to be annoying.' Sophy sat down on one of the wrought-iron chairs they kept outside, wincing slightly as the backs of her thighs made contact with hot metal. 'It's just frustrating that Phoebe is so closed-minded. It's like she doesn't even want to grow the business.'

Cress loved working at The Vintage Dress Shop, especially as her previous place of employment had been at the very obscure Museum of Religious Relics in Chelsea, where she'd worked after graduating from fashion college. She'd spent the next nine poorly paid years repairing ecclesiastical gowns and soft textiles until Sophy had wangled her a job here. Cress was very grateful that she got to handle beautiful dresses all day instead of cardinals' robes, bishops' cloaks and a never-ending array of very stained hassocks.

For the last fifteen months, she worked with the dreamiest of fabrics: whisper-soft georgette and chiffon, the fragile paper-thin slipperiness of old silk and satin. Cress especially loved transforming the most stressed woman into the best version of herself with the help of a few strategic darts and tucks, the taking down of hems and the taking in of seams. There was nothing better than helping women onto the dais and watching them take that first nervous glance in the mirror. Then the slow realisation dawning that they were wearing a dress that accentuated everything they loved about themselves. Even the bits of them that they hadn't thought they did love. A slow smile would blossom, even if the woman was tired and on third-day hair, and she became beautiful because she finally understood that she was beautiful.

One could never underestimate the power of a good dress. A good dress and Cress's skilled fingers. So when Sophy or Freddy, who looked after the really boring business side of things, started banging on about additional revenue streams and growing their online receipts, Cress tuned out.

'I need to carve out my own niche,' Sophy was saying now. 'Really make my mark, don't you think?'

'I thought you were only here until you found something else?' That was what Sophy had claimed when she returned from Australia a couple of months ago, and it was the only reason that Phoebe had unwillingly given her her old job back. Well, that and the fact that Sophy's dad, Johnno, owned the business. But he'd gone back to Australia with Sophy and, though he'd lived in London for over thirty years, he was now happily ensconced on the family sheep station and had no immediate plans to come back.

'Well, let's just see how things pan out. While I am here, I want to be productive, rather than just filling up space. It might even turn out that renting is so successful that . . .' Sophy paused and looked around as if she suspected Phoebe of having the patio bugged. 'Well, it might turn out to be a business in its own right. That would show her!'

'Please, Soph. I don't want to hear about your plans for vintage dress world domination. I mean, yay you, but it's probably best that I don't know,' Cress tried to explain in a way that wouldn't cause Sophy to take offence.

Sophy just grinned. 'So, Phoebe can't force the details out of you. I mean, you've got all sorts of torture devices upstairs. Pins, pinking shears, that overlocking machine.'

'Phoebe would never torture me. I'm her favourite,' Cress pointed out, though really Coco Chanel was Phoebe's favourite and all Phoebe had to do, all anyone had to do, was fix Cress with a stern glare and she'd tell them anything they wanted to know, even her pin number. 'Australia has changed you.'

'That was why I went away. Because I was so fed up with where I was, who I was . . .' Sophy tailed off. 'I needed to change. Before I went to Australia, I'd been stuck in the same boring rut for the last ten years.'

It was true that Sophy had come back from the Antipodes with an entrepreneurial spirit that she'd never had before. She even looked different. She still had the same silky-smooth, fiery red hair that Cress has always envied because she herself had a mop of dark, unruly curls that got larger as the weather got hotter. Sophy had pale skin to go with the red hair, but she'd come back from Oz with an actual suntan. 'It got hot and even with sunblock on all my freckles kind of joined up,' she'd said by way of an explanation. 'Turns out I'm a redhead who tans.'

With the suntan and the entrepreneurial spirit had come a new confidence that probably came from bushwalking and sheep-shearing and being treated like some kind of oracle of vintage fashion at Clive's Closet. The confidence showed in how Sophy carried herself, shoulders back, face tipped up to meet the world head on. She'd even changed her wardrobe, which had previously consisted of many shapeless dresses in a muted colour palette. She'd had to be coaxed into a vintage dress when she'd first come to work at The Vintage Dress Shop but now, right at this minute, she was wearing a vintage playsuit in a cool, crisp blue-and-green floral print on white lawn cotton, with her legs and shoulders bare. The playsuit looked fantastic on her.

It was very disconcerting. Cress knew that she herself was one of life's plodders. That was OK. The world needed plodders just as much as it needed go-getters and those annoying people who swore that they got by on four hours' sleep a night, which left them more time to attain their goals.

But it had felt more acceptable to be a plodder when your best friend and stepsister was sort of a plodder too. Now, Sophy was definitely more of a go-getter. Before Sophy had gone to Australia, she'd freed herself from the shackles of the high-street fashion chain where she'd worked for years, and a stagnant long-term relationship. Then she had reconnected with her absent father, Johnno, taken a job at The Vintage Dress Shop and fallen in love with Charles, who dealt in semi-precious gemstones and sourced some of The Vintage Dress Shop's more high-end frocks. Cress had even wondered if Sophy would ever make it to Australia, because she couldn't seem to tear herself away from Charles, but she had, and now that she was back, she still hadn't returned to her formerly ploddy ways.

She'd moved into a cool houseshare in King's Cross with Anita, who also toiled away at The Vintage Dress Shop, and generally Soph was having lots of adventures. Spontaneous adventures. The other weekend she'd gone to Paris, just like that. She'd already had Saturday booked off work, and on Friday lunchtime she'd noticed there was a sale on Eurostar seats. By ten o'clock that night, she and Charles were in Paris and staying at his friends' apartment in Le Marais. Charles was the kind of man who had friends in exotic locations.

So now Cress was plodding along on her own. Still living at home with her parents. Still dating Colin, her school sweetheart. Still saving up for a deposit on their own place. But as Cress trudged back up the stairs she remembered that, in the last eighteen months, she had changed jobs, which was a huge thing. Major.

Plus, Cress had a successful side hustle. She scoured charity shops, bargain bins and eBay listings for damaged vintage dresses, then lovingly restored them to something of their former glory. In some cases, all she had to do was insert a new zip or replace some buttons. Then she sold them in her Etsy shop, along with her hand-embroidered tote bags.

Cress had stuff going on. She lived a fully rounded life. But for what was left of the day she felt restless and irritable, though she couldn't pinpoint the exact reason why. Maybe it was the heat. Maybe it was all that seam-unpicking. Maybe it was too much Diet Coke.

It was just as well that she was seeing Colin tonight. That was sure to improve her spirits.

Chapter Two

When you've been in a relationship with someone for fifteen years, it often felt like you knew everything about that person. That there were no surprises left, nothing to shock you. Which was just how Cress liked it.

She and Colin might have been dating since they were sixteen, but they weren't joined at the hip. They both had their own passions and interests. While Cress lived for unearthing a pristine-condition 1950s Marks & Spencer dress or a circa 1960s *Vogue* from an unpromising selection of clothes and magazines in a charity shop, Colin had a similar enthusiasm for music.

In fact, his collection of vinyl records was so vast that it dominated three-quarters of his bedroom and had even colonised his parents' garage, which had been weather-proofed before the reinforced shelving had been assembled. When he wasn't cataloguing his vinyl, Colin was at record fairs, or pub pop quizzes, or talking to his fellow vinyl lovers on internet forums.

They had such different interests, but, when Cress and Colin came together, it just made sense. They had a shared history that was so long, so deep, that they knew everything about each other. Colin had loved Cress and Cress had loved Colin through bad haircuts, exam revision, job woes and a week in the Lake District when it had rained solidly for the entire time they were holed up in a self-catering cottage with a leaky roof. There had also been so many good times; celebrating everything from graduations to first jobs and birthdays in their favourite restaurant, a little Italian in East Finchley. They were also adept at combining their individual passions into mutual pastimes – whether it was a film that combined good music and good fashion like Baz Luhrmann's *Elvis* or the David Bowie retrospective at the V&A museum. Last year, Cress had even persuaded Colin to go to the ABBA hologram show. He'd totally cried to 'Chiquitita' and then sworn her to secrecy.

But mostly they did what they were doing on this Thursday evening. Hanging out.

As Cress unlatched the gate and walked up the garden path of a modest three-bedroom semi-detached house just round the corner from the almost identical house that she called home, she put a hand to her tummy to see if it was fluttering.

Sophy had remarked that whenever she saw Charles – and she saw Charles *a lot* – she always got a 'fluttery feeling' in her stomach. Cress didn't. Her stomach was gurgling a bit but that could have been the three cans of Diet Coke, plus it had been too hot to eat anything for lunch except a Magnum. After fifteen years, the flutters had gone. That wasn't a bad thing. It was just how it was. The flutters gave way to familiarity. Which was why she had her own key.

'It's only me,' she called out as she opened the front door.

'I'm in the kitchen, love!'

Cress walked down the hall to the kitchen, where Mary, Colin's mum, was red-faced as she peered into her air fryer.

'Can I do anything to help?' Cress asked, hooking her tote bag strap to the back of a chair. She looked past Mary to the large window by the sink, where she could see Roy, Colin's dad, watering his flowerbeds.

'No, you're all right. Nothing fancy tonight. Managed to get some salmon on special offer and we're having that with salad and new potatoes. Too hot for our usual Thursday-night sausage casserole, isn't it.'

Mary and Roy were creatures of habit. Until the mercury in the thermometer was edging into the high 30s, apparently.

Cress took a glass down from the cupboard and filled it with water from the filter jug in the fridge, making sure that she then refilled the jug before putting it back. Those were the house rules.

'Shall I take a glass out to Roy? He looks very hot.'

Mary glanced out at her husband. 'It's the hosepipe ban. We're having to save our bathwater and then rig up a hose-pipe from the bathroom window down to the garden.' She lifted her eyes to the heavens. 'Honestly, Cress, you should have heard him effing and jeffing.'

Cress had heard Roy effing and jeffing countless times. When she'd first started seeing Colin, she'd been terrified of his father. Her own dad, Mike, was one of the mildest men you could ever hope to meet, while her stepdad Aaron was easy-going and laid-back. But she'd soon (well, after a few years) realised that Roy was quick to anger and after shouting a bit it would all be forgiven.

Cress carried a glass of water out to Roy and listened again to the tale of the bathtub hosepipe. When she was finally able to make her excuses and head back to the house, Colin had arrived home from work.

'Don't come near me,' he warned, holding his hands up as Cress approached for their usual hug. 'The Northern line was like a sweatbox. I smell like ripe cheese. Time for a shower before dinner?'

'Be quick,' Mary said, as Cress took cutlery out of the drawer so she could lay the table. 'We're eating outside. Though I said to Roy that I'll probably be eaten alive by midges. That bloody pond of his!'

Ten minutes later, they were seated around the durable green plastic patio table. Colin was freshly washed, his light brown hair wet and pulled back in its customary ponytail. He was wearing an ancient Queen t-shirt and combat shorts, his feet bare, although Roy said it was uncivilised to eat without shoes on. Roy didn't see the wink that Colin gave Cress, otherwise they'd never have heard the end of it.

Luckily, Colin took after his mother rather than his father when it came to looks and temperament. The two of them could sulk like it was an Olympic sport.

Roy was florid, especially in the heatwave, and, though he didn't have much hair left on his head, what hair he did have seemed to have migrated to his beetling eyebrows and ears. As a concession to the heat, he was wearing a short-sleeved beige shirt, but not even the heatwave could come between Roy and what he and Mary called slacks and Cress called chinos.

Although Mary was a tiny woman and Colin was just shy of six feet, he had inherited his mother's finer features and her pale blue eyes. In fifteen years, Cress had never seen her in a pair of trousers, or whatever you wanted to call them. Her honey-blond hair was cut in a practical bob that wouldn't dare to frizz, and she was never seen without mascara and her nails immaculately painted in a pinky-beige that she'd never deviated from in all the time that Cress had known her.

They were both so traditional and yet, especially when she'd first crushed on him in a crowded school dining hall, Colin was very much his own person. Most of the boys in their year were either wearing jeans slung so low that you could see their pants and pretending that the suburban streets of Finchley were actually the urban jungle, or were emos with long fringes poking out from their hoodies, carrying skateboards everywhere with them but never actually getting on them.

But Colin danced to his own beat. Well, not danced. Colin didn't dance. But he kept himself to himself, ear-buds always in, head always down. But occasionally Cress would catch him looking at her. No one had ever looked at Cress like that before. As if she was someone worthy of being looked at, rather than a shy girl who didn't like to stand out from the crowd.

It wasn't until they'd found themselves forced to sit next to each other, on a school trip to see *As You Like It* (which they were studying for GCSE English) at the Globe Theatre, that they actually spoke to each other. They both liked the play, though it was very hard to learn anything in their particularly rowdy study set and they both hated Kai Rowlands, main culprit of the rowdiness. From such tiny acorns had grown a relationship that was fifteen years long and still going strong.

Now, the four of them talked about Roy and Mary's upcoming holiday. They always went to St Ives in Cornwall, where Mary's sister lived, the second week in July, before the schools broke up. And they wanted to know whether Cress and Colin might come with them, as they'd done in the past.

'Maybe,' Cress said. 'Although the shop is so busy. We're in the middle of wedding season. I might be able to come down for a weekend.'

'But then we'd have to get the train,' Colin pointed out. Neither of them drove. Not when they were saving up and it was so expensive to run a car or even drive in London. 'Also, a mate of mine has got a spare ticket to Latitude Festival that weekend. Though I don't think much of the line-up.'

Colin never thought much of the line-ups of any of the music festivals he attended with his friends.

'Let's see a bit nearer the time,' Cress suggested.

'It's only three weeks away,' Mary said. 'It would be lovely to just have you, Cress, even if our Col can't make it.'

'It would,' Cress agreed, even though she didn't really enjoy holidays with Colin and his parents. Let alone just Mary and Roy. That would be very . . . *trying*.

If she went away with friends or with her own mum, the vibe was always a lot more relaxed. It was all right to chill in your pyjamas for half the day, or spend hours on the beach just glorying in the sun on your skin and the gentle lap of the waves. Cress was always mindful that she was saving up for the deposit on their own place, but when you were on holiday it was all right to treat yourself. To maybe have a spa day. Or buy a piece of jewellery that was mostly shells and would be consigned to the back of a drawer once she got home. That was the whole point of a holiday.

Mary and Roy had a very different idea of holidays and treats. They always had a jam-packed itinerary of local places of interest that actually weren't interesting at all. The North Devon Maritime Museum had been a particular low point. Also, they wouldn't even stop at a service station for lunch but packed their own sandwiches, which were to be eaten in the car park of the service station after you'd had a wee and stretched your legs.

They packed their own sandwiches for the beach too. For days out. For days in when it was too rainy to go out. Not even fancy holiday sandwiches, with several fillings on exotic bread. No, it was ham or cheese on sliced brown bread and either mustard or mayonnaise. You weren't allowed to have both.

The rule was only relaxed on the final night, when they'd go out for fish and chips and Roy and Mary would exclaim over how expensive it was. 'Ten pounds for a tiny piece of fish!' 'I can't believe how stingy they were with the portions.' It took all the pleasure out of haddock and chips and a side of mushy peas.

So, Cress just smiled vaguely and refused to be drawn in on more definite plans for Cornwall.

After they'd cleared away the dinner plates, they sat in the garden until the midges really did start to bite and Cress couldn't take any more talk about the hosepipe ban or Roy's ingrown toenail.

She and Colin retreated to his bedroom. Familiarly, comfortingly, it hadn't changed much in the last fifteen years. Still the grey walls with the red woodwork, still the same red and grey duvet cover. Still the neatly folded pile of laundry on the bed, because Mary did everything for Colin. She'd even replenished his snack drawer and restocked the drinks in the mini-fridge under his desk. Although, unlike when he and Cress were sixteen, now they didn't have to keep the door open or have Mary regularly intruding to make sure they weren't getting up to anything. Which they never had been.

It had taken three months for them to work up to kissing with tongues. Two years before they lost their virginities, in a static caravan in Cromer that belonged to Cress's step-gran.

They weren't getting up to anything this evening either. Cress flopped on the bed, limbs akimbo as Colin switched on his fan. Then he sat in his gaming chair and caught up on his Reddit forums. Cress took her laptop out of her bag and updated the stock in her Etsy shop. It was an evening well spent.

It wasn't until just before ten that they both looked up from their computers.

'Are you staying the night?' Colin asked, swivelling round to look at Cress.

'I could,' she said. For the last year or so, after Mary had made Colin cull some of his holiest t-shirts, she had had her own drawer. She lay back on the bed. Even with the fan going full blast she could feel a rivulet of sweat trickle down her neck. 'But I don't know . . . I think it's too hot to share a bed.'

'It is,' Colin agreed. 'And I have to get up really early tomorrow. We've got a new shipment of motherboards coming in and I said I'd be there to sign for them.'

Colin worked in IT for a private bank in the City of London. That was about as much as Cress knew about his job. She found the intricacies of computer programming and malware attacks about as riveting as Colin would find it if she gave him a detailed breakdown of how to put in an invisible zip.

'But I'll see you Sunday,' Cress reminded him, because they took it in turns to do Sunday lunch at each other's houses.

'You will.' Colin stood up from his chair and stretched. His t-shirt rode up to uncover a sliver of pale belly. Cress averted her eyes, because it always made her feel weird when she saw bits of people that they didn't realise she was seeing. Only the week before, she'd stood behind a man on the tube who had a huge boil on the back of his neck and she'd been tormented by the idea that he hadn't known it was there and might accidentally spear it while he was combing his hair.

'What was that?' She realised that Colin had asked her something because he was looking expectantly at her.

'I said, do you want me to walk you home?' he asked in a very tired voice, like the five-minute stroll would finish him off.

Cress took the hint. 'No, you're all right. You said you had to get up early.'

Colin shot her a grateful smile. 'But message me to let me know you got home safely.'

'Of course,' Cress said, as she packed up her bag. Then she hurried downstairs, because Mary and Roy liked to lock up on the dot of ten.

The streets of Finchley were deserted. Cress's walk home was disturbed only by the occasional dogwalker, and, a little further up the road, a fox, which stared boldly at her until a car came and it disappeared between two hedges.

The lights were still on at her house, and, when she opened the front door, her mum called out, 'Have you watched *Love Island*?'

Cress poked her head round the door of the living room, where her mum, Diane, was sitting in a swimsuit with her feet in a washing-up bowl full of cold water. Her stepdad Aaron was working lates that week.

'I haven't and I hope you didn't watch tonight's episode without me.' At the beginning of each new season they agreed that they weren't going to watch *Love Island* because it was always full of gaslighting and terrible behaviour and it wasn't fair that the girls had to wear bikinis that showed their bottoms and their side boobs, underboobs and pretty much all their boobs, while the guys got to swan around in long shorts.

Then, every time, they got suckered in and were emotionally over-invested in at least one couple by the end of the first week.

'Of course, I haven't. It's no fun without you.' At fifty-five, in a good light – and even under the big light in the living room – Diane could easily pass for a woman twenty years younger. She and Cress were often mistaken for sisters, which Diane put down to slathering herself in Palmer's Cocoa Butter at every opportunity and her twice-weekly Zumba class. Cress could only hope that some of it was down to genetics too, because she'd like to still look youthful in her fifties without having to take up Zumba. Diane piled a handful of black curly hair on top of her head and blew out of her mouth to direct a weak stream of air towards her chin. 'Be a love and go and get me a Calippo out of the freezer and we'll watch it now.'

Cress did as she was told, nabbing a pineapple Twister for herself. Then as Diane fast-forwarded the SKY box to the start of the show, she remembered to message Colin.

Home safe and sound. Sweet dreams. See you Sunday. C x

She waited for him to message her back, but he must have already gone to sleep. But it wasn't until one of the *Love Island* couples had their first kiss outside of a challenge that Cress realised that neither she nor Colin had even touched each other all evening. Not once.

Chapter Three

It was still hot the next day. Like it had been hot all night, so Cress had barely slept.

Maybe that was why she still felt so irritable and restless that morning. She was even short with Sophy when they met, as they always did, at Chalk Farm station. Cress usually liked to think that she wasn't the sort of person who was short with other people, and especially not Sophy.

But then Sophy hadn't even said hello. Instead she'd launched straight into her usual patter. 'I spent all of yesterday evening working out what we'd need to launch a rental service. Definitely some extra stock. I'm still waiting for all those vintage dresses I shipped from Australia to arrive, and sorting out insurance, but—'

'No!' Cress was wearing her big sunglasses just like the ones Audrey Hepburn wore in the opening sequence of *Breakfast at Tiffany's*, so Sophy couldn't see that she was rolling her very tired and puffy eyes. 'I'm not going to have another day listening to you and Phoebe arguing.'

'But it's a brilliant idea to offer a rent-a-dress scheme. That's what we did in Australia . . .'

Cress also didn't want to spend the day listening to Sophy bang on about what she'd done in Australia. If Sophy hadn't gone to Australia, then maybe she wouldn't be having all these unsettling notions. Cress didn't mind that Sophy had had a major boyfriend upgrade from the often oafish Egan to the elegant and always exquisitely dressed Charles, because

Charles made Sophy very happy. But everything else, the new-found confidence, the plans to expand the business, even the wearing of another very cute playsuit, seemed to Cress like portents that maybe Sophy had outgrown her. 'We both know that Phoebe is never going to rent out her precious dresses . . .'

'But they're not actually *her* dresses . . .' Sophy said as they reached the counter of their favourite café. They had both agreed that it was too expensive to get a coffee every morning, especially from cafés in Primrose Hill, where they were twice as expensive than coffees in a less exclusive postcode. But they both conveniently forgot that agreement as summer had become hotter and hotter and neither of them could successfully make the iced coffee that they were both addicted to. 'Two iced lattes with coconut milk and one pump of caramel sauce, please. No, Cress, put your money away. You got them yesterday.'

Cress was only slightly placated. 'She thinks of them as her dresses though, so you might as well just give up now . . .'

'Never! Which is why I've gone over Phoebe's stupid head and pitched the idea directly to Freddy, who loves it. I mean, it's using the same inventory but getting a second revenue stream from it.'

'Well, let Freddy deal with it,' Cress advised, but when they got to the shop, Phoebe was at the door all ready to make sure that not one particle of iced coffee went anywhere near the rainbow array of dresses.

'Quickly! Straight out onto the patio with both of you, though you know full well we open at ten and it's nearly five to,' she said sharply. This made Sophy stick out her chin, which meant that she was spoiling for a fight.

That was why Cress gulped down her coffee in record time so she could disappear to the sanctuary of her little workroom. She'd kept the blinds drawn overnight – sadly she couldn't keep the skylights open, on account of burglars – so the room wasn't quite as stiflingly hot as it had been yesterday.

She turned on her fans, then settled down for a morning of hand-stitching. She put in her AirPods – a Christmas present from Colin, who got some kind of tech-person discount with Apple. She had several episodes of her favourite vintage fashion podcast, Preloved, to listen to. Five minutes in, Coco Chanel entered, positioned herself in a shaft of sunlight and promptly fell asleep.

Very soon Cress forgot that she was restless and irritated, even though she could hear Coco Chanel's cacophonous snores over the voices in her ears. There was something about the slippery-smooth perfection of white satin, her hands moving deftly and swiftly as she hemmed metres of the fabric with tiny, precise stitches, that sent Cress into a Zen-like state. She was one with the dress.

She was on the homeward strait with the hem when the last podcast episode finished and she was suddenly aware of a lot of chatter coming from the salon, even though she was pretty sure that no one had booked any appointments for wedding dresses or occasion-wear that morning. Phoebe would rarely grant admittance to the atelier, as she grandly called it, without an appointment.

But when Cress emerged from her workroom, she was greeted by an atelier full of people. Not their usual clientele either.

There was no blushing bride. Or grimly determined mother of the bride trying to surreptitiously look for a price on one of the wedding gowns hanging up. Not that they had prices on any of the dresses in the atelier. Phoebe said that it lowered the tone. She also said, when she was being really impossible, 'If they have to ask the price, then they can't afford it.' But really, it was very hard to price a wedding gown, especially if you had to factor in the cost of alterations.

Not that the people assembled seemed unduly worried about letting out the seams of a 1930s fit-and-flare wedding dress.

There were three women. One of them was middle-aged, her platinum hair cropped and quaffed, wearing an effortlessly chic ensemble of black wide-legged trousers and an impeccably cut white silk blouse. She was accompanied by two younger women. One of them was in a strappy khaki sundress and Birkenstocks, her bleached hair lilac at the tips; the other in a pair of white linen dungarees and a thin vest underneath, which showed off her toned arms and an exquisite pair of collarbones.

Cress immediately summed them up as Very Cool. She always shied away from the Very Cool as she herself was Very Uncool. She'd made her peace with that years ago. The older woman was tapping away on an iPad as the woman in khaki ticked something off on a clipboard while the third held up a dress for inspection. Not a wedding dress, but one of their high-end vintage pieces from the room next door.

It was an early 1960s, bright orange wool, short-sleeved, A-line dress designed by Courrèges. Cress didn't even want to *look* at wool dresses, much less handle them, but the woman with the iPad now seemed to be filming it, which was a huge no-no. People had been banned for life from The Vintage Dress Shop for lesser crimes. Phoebe was going to have a fit – but Phoebe, who'd just emerged from the designer room with two more dresses, had a smile on her face. Not even the fake smile she used when she had to suck up to awful but spendy customers and really, she was gritting her teeth. No, this was a genuine Phoebe smile, which made her look almost approachable.

'You know, I sold a Mary Quant dress only two weeks ago,' she said to the older woman. 'If only I'd known you were coming then. It's getting harder and harder to find Mary Quant in the wild. I blame the V&A for doing a retrospective on her.'

It was then that Cress saw that there was one other person in the salon.

A man.

Men didn't frequent the salon. Apart from Johnno, the owner now ensconced on an Australian sheep station, and Freddy, who handled the business side of things, men very rarely came into the shop. Occasionally someone would accompany a wife or girlfriend into the downstairs shop. But up here in the more rarefied climes, they didn't dare venture.

After all, it was bad luck for the groom to see the wedding dress, or twenty-five prospective wedding dresses. This also seemed to extend to the father of the bride. And, though they very occasionally had a bridal party that included a man – a bridesman, rather than a bridesmaid – they tended to understand their assignment. Which was to keep the compliments coming and offer a male perspective only if it was asked for.

They certainly didn't lie full-length on one of the sofas. Not like this man, dressed all in black. His tousled hair was so dark that it was almost black too. He was very, very pale and wearing dark glasses and reminded Cress of a young Bob Dylan because she'd seen *Don't Look Back*, a 1967 documentary about the nasal-voiced protest singer, almost as many times as she'd forced Colin to watch *Breakfast at Tiffany's*.

Occasionally one of the younger women would approach him with a dress but he just waved it away with an impatient hand.

Cress couldn't even begin to imagine what was going on. Phoebe was now halfway through one of her favourite rants about how Instagram influencers were appropriating all the good vintage, with no respect for its provenance and history, and were generally ruining it for everyone else.

No wonder that she didn't notice as Cress edged her way out of the atelier then quickly beetled down the spiral staircase.

The shop was empty of customers – they were always quiet before lunch on weekdays – and Sophy, Anita and

Beatrice were taking advantage of Phoebe's absence to have turns standing in front of the big fan behind the cash desk.

'What on earth is going on upstairs?' Cress asked, which made Anita, who was entertaining Sophy with an impersonation of Marilyn Monroe in *The Seven Year Itch*, jump.

'Oh my God! Don't creep up on people,' she snapped, because the heat was making all of them tetchy. 'I thought you were Phoebe. You nearly gave me a heart attack.'

Cress tried again. 'There are people upstairs filming the dresses and Phoebe is just *letting* them.'

'They're something to do with a film,' Bea said with a shrug. 'That's all I can tell you because that's all Phoebe told us. You know how she likes to play her cards very close to her chest.'

'We were hoping that they might have some famouses with them, but no,' Anita said sadly, then sighed rapturously as the fan lifted the hem of her black 1950s circle-skirted dress. 'Don't suppose you're going out for an ice cream?'

'I wouldn't eat ice cream before lunch,' Cress said, because she'd been raised better than that. 'But I am going to make some tea if you're interested.'

'It's too hot for tea,' Bea said, as she slumped against the back of one of the shocking-pink sofas that were a much-Instagrammed feature of the shop. Today she had her long blond hair twisted up in Princess Leia side buns and looked splendid in a halter-neck, sarong-style dress in a tropical print, but was sadly stuck in a small, stuffy shop and not on a Caribbean beach or Hawaiian island.

'Actually, you're meant to drink something hot in a heatwave,' Sophy said. 'It regulates your body temperature. When I was in Australia . . .'

Those magic five words had Cress scuttling to the back office because she really couldn't take any more tales of all the things that Sophy had done in Australia.

While Cress waited for the kettle to boil, she stepped out onto the patio, though it was hotter outside than it was inside. She heard the kettle click off and stepped back into the office to get her favourite red and white striped Cornishware mug (a Secret Santa present from last Christmas, which had the words Sewing Queen painted on it) down from the cupboard. She was just wondering if Earl Grey might be more thirst-quenching than her usual Yorkshire Tea when there was a cough from the doorway.

She turned round to see that the black-clad *man* from the salon had managed to lever himself upright and get down the stairs and was now leaning against the door frame as if it were the only thing holding him up.

'Tea,' he said. There was a significant pause. 'Please.'

They weren't meant to make tea for the customers, although there was champagne upstairs for the high rollers and the big spenders in a special fridge that Cress wasn't allowed to use for her Diet Coke because it set the wrong tone. Film people probably counted as high rollers.

Cress nodded. 'Milk? Sugar?'

'Honey,' he rasped. Cress supposed that being difficult was very on-brand for a film person.

She had a rummage in the cupboard and managed to find a half-empty jar of honey. It had granulated with age but she successfully squeezed a couple of generous dollops into a mug and gave it a good stir.

He made no move to come into the office, so Cress was forced to take the tea to him like she was a servant. He was quite a bit taller than she was, so she had to look up, only to see her flushed face reflected in his sunglasses.

He grunted something that didn't sound anything like 'thank you', then turned to go.

Cress sighed, because this was beyond both her pay grade and her personal remit. 'I'm sorry but you absolutely can't have hot drinks anywhere near the dresses,' she told him sternly. 'You'll have to drink it there.' She gestured to the open back door. 'We have a very nice patio with a view of the canal.'

He shied away from her gesturing hand like he was a vampire and the merest hint of sunlight would see him disappear in a puff of smoke and a cloud of dust.

Instead, very awkwardly, so that Cress would squirm when she thought about it later, they both stood there with as much distance between them as the small back office would allow, gulping down their hot drinks. Which actually did nothing to regulate Cress's body temperature. She wished that she'd had a Diet Coke instead.

He drank his tea so quickly that Cress was surprised that he didn't burn his oesophagus, then he put the mug down on the nearest desk and quickly retreated as Sophy advanced.

'You know, I think I will have a cup of tea,' she said.

'I wouldn't bother. I'm even hotter than I was,' Cress told her. 'Do you know who that man is?'

Sophy shrugged. 'Apart from being one of the film people, I don't. And also, who wears all black in this weather? Madness!

'Only very pretentious people,' Cress said.

Sophy looked at her in surprise. 'It's not like you to be so bitchy.'

'It's the heat. It makes me really scratchy and also, he didn't even say thank you for his tea. Just left his empty mug on that desk for me to fetch like I'm his skivvy or something,' Cress said as she snatched up the offending mug and proceeded to wash it with quick, angry movements.

Even Sophy's gentle hand on her shoulder in a sympathetic gesture made Cress want to snap, snarl and shout, 'Don't touch me!' – and it wasn't even like she was premenstrual.

By the time she gathered herself and went back upstairs, the man had resumed his original position and was prostrate on the sofa once again while the two younger women fluttered around him. Coco Chanel came lumbering out of Cress's workroom and made a beeline for the sofas, which were her favourite nap spot, but she was snatched up by Phoebe.

'Not today, my darling,' she cooed as Coco Chanel tried to wriggle out of her arms. 'You'll have to snooze somewhere else. Oh, Cress! There you are! How are you getting on with hand-sewing the hem on that wedding dress train?'

'Nearly finished,' Cress said. 'Though I swear that the train gets longer and longer every time I turn my back.'

Phoebe was standing next to the older woman, who smiled kindly. 'I hate hand-sewing. It must be hell in this weather,' she commiserated in a warm Scottish accent, which sounded familiar. It wasn't just her voice, either, Cress could have sworn she knew the woman from somewhere, but she couldn't place her.

There was a slightly tense pause and then Phoebe stopped nuzzling Coco Chanel's wrinkly neck and remembered her manners. 'What am I like? This is Cressida, our absolutely amazing restoration and alterations goddess. She's done miraculous things with dresses that I thought were damaged beyond repair – and, Cress, this is Jackie Coulter . . .'

'Oh my goodness . . .' Cress breathed, sure that she was doing a good impersonation of the heart eyes emoji.

'. . . who's a very well-known film costume designer,' continued Phoebe, who was practically heart-eyed herself. 'You know that emerald-green 1930s dress that Florence Pugh wore in that Amy Johnson biopic, well, Jackie designed it . . .'

There were no words to describe the utter perfection of the dress in question, so Cress just clasped her hands together in supplication. 'Big fan,' she gasped. 'Huge fan. Massive. The outfits in that adaptation of *The Cazalet*

Chronicles. I wanted *all* the dresses and I adored that yellow tartan Vivienne Westwood trouser suit you wore when you won your Oscar.'

'Thank you,' Jackie said, and didn't back away so she could immediately call up her lawyer and ask them to take out a restraining order. 'I'm sure we're going to have many interesting conversations about fashion.'

'I'd love that,' Cress said, her bad mood melting away like butter on a hot griddle. 'I'd love that more than anything in the world.'

'But first you need to finish that hem,' Phoebe said crisply, because Cress was standing still with a gormless smile on her face and would probably stay there gurning indefinitely if she wasn't ordered to disperse.

Sadly, the film people left quite soon after that.

Cress was planning another Magnum lunch but Sophy staged an intervention with a tub of tuna salad. 'I'm worried that you're going to get scurvy,' she said as she coaxed Cress to take a full hour's break.

They decamped to Primrose Hill along with what seemed to be half of London. When they eventually found a spare patch of grass, it was dry and parched and felt itchy against Cress's legs as she confessed to Sophy that Mary's idea of a salad was two lettuce leaves, a whole tomato and half a hard-boiled egg.

'She means well,' Sophy said, digging around enthusiastically in her own tuna salad, which had far more exotic ingredients, like rocket, pine nuts and feta. 'So, are you going to St Ives with them this year?'

Cress knew she was being uncharitable as she pulled a face at the prospect of St Ives. 'Maybe. Maybe not. I haven't decided.'

'That was actually a rhetorical question,' Sophy said, pushing her sunglasses up so she could scrutinise her stepsister's face. 'You *always* go to St Ives.'

'Not always,' Cress grumbled, because there was that year when she'd had shingles and, although she liked a routine, a certain balance and rhythm to her life, no one wanted to be thought of as boring and predictable. 'Anyway, Colin is going to Latitude Festival that weekend.'

'Oh, so you're going with him. That will be nice. A little romantic getaway.' It was one of Sophy's most endearing qualities that, even though they both knew that she wasn't one of Colin's biggest fans, she never voiced that opinion. Instead, she was a reliable hype man for their relationship.

Even though . . . 'There's nothing romantic about sleeping in a tent. Or queuing to use the loos, which are absolutely foul by the end of the first day. Or having to see a load of whiny guitar bands when I'd much rather just . . . not.'

Sophy gently nudged Cress's arm. 'Are you and Colin all right? You can tell me if you aren't and I won't judge or take sides. I'll just be a sounding board or a shoulder to cry on. Whatever you need.'

'Me and Colin are fine,' Cress insisted, because they weren't *not* fine. They were the same as they ever were. 'But I was wondering, the last time you saw Charles, what did you do?'

'Nothing special. We just went to a little rooftop tiki bar he knows in Soho and drank daiquiris and then we went back to his place and well . . .' Sophy allowed herself a small but very cat-that-had-got-the-cream smile at what might have occurred when she was back at Charles's place. But a secret little rooftop restaurant with daiquiris, then a diplomatic fade to black, was much more romantic than anything that had happened to Cress last night at Colin's house. In fact, it was much more romantic than anything that had happened to Cress in the last calendar year. Maybe her entire life. 'You know, we're in the first flush of . . . well, whatever.'

'Does whatever mean— are you *in love* with Charles?' Cress didn't know why she sounded so surprised. It had been obvious that Sophy was in love with Charles before she'd even gone to Australia. Why wouldn't she be when Charles always gazed at Sophy, when he thought she wasn't looking, as if she were some divine goddess come to Earth and he couldn't quite believe that she wanted to spend her mortal days with him?

'Well, when you count up the time that we've actually been in the same time zone, then it's only been a few months. So it's far too soon to be talking about love.' Sophy whispered the word like she didn't want to tempt fate. 'But I really, really like him.'

'He really, really likes you,' Cress said. She couldn't remember the last time that Colin, or indeed anyone, had gazed at her with the same rapt expression.

'Anyway, come on, let's not be those women who can't talk about anything other than their menfolk. Far more important things we should be discussing, like how are we going to get Phoebe to spill the beans on the film people?'

It was a very welcome change of subject. Also, it was good to talk tactics, because Phoebe could be very secretive. Cress had known Phoebe for more than a year, and would even say that she was quite a good friend when she wasn't being a very officious line manager, but she didn't even know where Phoebe lived or if she was dating anyone.

'Compliments and bribery?' Cress suggested. They gathered up the debris from their lunch, then walked very slowly back to the shop while they exchanged more and more ludicrous examples of just how far they'd go to wheedle information out of Phoebe.

'I'm going to offer to walk Coco Chanel every day,' Sophy said as they entered the shop.

'You can't walk Coco Chanel,' Phoebe exclaimed from halfway up the stairs. It was like she had bat sonar where other people had ears. 'It's too hot and she's brachycephalic,

33

poor darling. Do you want her to keel over before you've even reached the corner? Do you, Sophy?'

'I really don't,' Sophy said. 'My bad.'

'And how's the job hunt going?' Phoebe asked with real eagerness to her tone.

Cress had a very strong suspicion that Sophy didn't plan on going anywhere, hence her plans to expand her temporary role to cover summer leave into something more permanent.

'It's going,' Sophy said vaguely, then hurried in the direction of the back office so she wouldn't have to meet Phoebe's gimlet gaze any more.

Cress offered Phoebe a weak smile. She very definitely wasn't going to be trying to winkle out any information about the film people.

'Come on, Cress! No dawdling.' Phoebe actually clapped her hands to chivvy her along. 'We've got an afternoon full of appointments. Have you finished hemming that train?'

Chapter Four

Cress *had* finished that hem, in time for the bride-to-be to have a fitting at four.

Josie was as indecisive as ever but she'd remembered to bring the heels she was going to wear on the day, along with her matron of honour, her older sister Emma, who was very firm in her opinions.

'It looks fine, Josie. You look fine,' she snapped after Josie had spent fifteen long minutes on the dais in the dress staring at herself in the mirror, then taking a step one way, then the other, to see if the hem was too long or even too short, the train swirling around her like ice cream in a cone. 'Bloody hell, I'm losing the will to live here.'

Josie gathered her curly blond hair up in a loose ponytail. 'Do you think I should have my hair up or down?'

Cress didn't have an opinion either way. 'Um, could you just keep still while I pin . . .?' She finished pinning the right-hand side seam. The dress was still a little too loose. 'And like a statue as I do your left side.'

'Maybe we should just cut the bottom off entirely,' Josie suddenly said, lifting the train that Cress had literally just sweated over to above her knees. 'A long dress with a train . . . is that too old-fashioned? If it was shorter then I'm more likely to wear it again.'

'Just ignore her,' Emma advised and, although Cress liked to be a champion for their customers and always wanted them to have the dress of their dreams, she'd rather stick

35

her own pins in her own eyes than have to do any more hemming.

Phoebe was usually on hand to deal with these problems, but she was downstairs as they'd suddenly been overrun with late-afternoon browsers and three women who had a wedding to go to this coming Saturday and had left it to the last minute to find outfits.

'You look lovely,' she assured Josie. 'Just a couple of minor adjustments and the dress will be perfect. You'll be perfect. Please trust me on this.'

Eventually they left, Josie now wondering if she should get a second dress for the reception, but that was nothing that Cress could help her with.

She scribbled some notes to herself about the alterations on a Post-it then stuck it on the garment bag and hung it up on the rail in her workroom. She really hoped she was done with interacting with customers for the day.

Then she rearranged a couple of the wedding dresses that had been put back on the wrong hangers. Everyone knew that mushroom went next to taupe, not cream. Cress would have liked nothing more than to sit between the two fans she had going and maybe do some very light repair work on a lurex 1960s minidress that needed a new zip.

But here was Phoebe coming up the stairs with someone in tow. 'You really should have made an appointment,' she was saying. 'You're lucky that I could fit you in.'

Phoebe was great with the dresses. Not always so great with the dress-wearers.

Cress attempted a welcoming smile to make up for the way that Phoebe was rolling her eyes like the woman coming up the stairs behind her was just too much.

She didn't seem too much. She was in her late forties, with a harried expression that seemed to turn to despondency as she took in the wall-to-wall wedding dresses.

'Oh God, I'm not getting married,' she said in a voice that was more Essex than Primrose Hill. 'Chance would be a fine thing.'

'As I said before, we keep our premium dresses up here,' Phoebe explained shortly, gesturing at the small room just off the main salon. She turned to Cress. 'This is Tina . . .'

'It's Tanya actually . . .'

'Here for something to wear for her fiftieth birthday party,' Phoebe continued, fixing the other woman with an assessing stare as she shied away from Phoebe's laser eyes.

'I'm not a size eight,' she said apologetically, tugging at her white t-shirt, which was far too big for her, though her cropped jeans looked too small. It was as if Tanya wasn't on first-name terms with her own body. It was a phenomenon that Cress had experienced with quite a few women, who'd all been surprised that they were being guided into dresses for the body they had and not the body they thought they had. 'You probably haven't got anything I could get into, but I saw a piece about you online and I was in the area and I thought there was no harm in popping in.'

'We really do prefer people to make an appointment,' Phoebe said again. 'When's your birthday?'

'It's October.'

'And what size are you?' Phoebe had no problem in coming right out with the difficult questions.

'A size fourteen?' Tanya ventured with a wince. 'On a good day. If I've had food poisoning or a stomach bug.'

'Oh, October is ages away. Plenty of time to— Ow! Thanks for treading on my foot, Cress.' Phoebe glared at Cress, who had indeed just trod on her foot before she could tell Tanya, who looked like she was regretting ever stepping over the threshold, that she had plenty of time to lose some weight between then and now.

'We're going to find you your dream dress and you're going to look absolutely beautiful.' Cress stared pointedly at Phoebe, who finally got a clue. They'd had many similar occasions with similarly fearful customers and, every time, Cress refused to toe Phoebe's line, even though she'd much prefer a quiet life.

Yes, Cress could be a pathological people-pleaser. But then she could also be as stubborn and as intractable as Phoebe herself.

'Of course, of course,' Phoebe now agreed. 'Why don't you take a seat and I'll pull some frocks for you.'

Tanya sat down with a grateful sigh and eased one puffy foot out of one sandal.

'I'll get you some water,' Cress said, and just as she returned from the water cooler in the kitchen Phoebe came back too, with the only two dresses that they had in a size fourteen.

It was very hard to find good-quality plus-size vintage. Hard but not impossible, though Phoebe didn't try very hard to stock anything bigger than a size twelve. It was another thing that always sat rather uncomfortably with Cress, who was a size fourteen. It didn't matter how much she ate or didn't eat. Or how much she exercised or didn't exercise. She was a size fourteen because that was what nature intended her to be.

One of the dresses was a wiggle dress in a very unforgiving bronze satin. 'It won't do up,' Tanya called out from the changing room. She sounded close to tears.

'Can we see how it looks?' Phoebe asked with another eye-roll.

'No!' came the anguished cry.

'Maybe the other dress?' Cress suggested. This was a gorgeous chiffon caftan in a melange of blues and greens.

Cress and Phoebe waited in silence until Tanya emerged from the cubicle. The dress was on. She was in the dress. But she didn't look very happy about it.

'Those are great colours on you,' Cress exclaimed. 'You have the bluest eyes.'

Phoebe didn't say anything for five agonising, awkward seconds. Then: 'Let's get you up on the dais,' she said.

'Let's not. It's too tight under the armpits and I can't do up the zip,' Tanya said, yanking at the filmy fabric in a way that had Phoebe hissing.

'It's fine,' Cress said gently. 'Let's get you back into the cubicle and out of the dress.'

Usually she wasn't so hands-on with the customers. But the only way to get the dress off was to ask Tanya to put her arms straight up and then Cress tugged for all she was worth.

Once Tanya was back in her loose white cotton top and jeans, she looked even more frazzled than she had when she first arrived. 'Let me have another look for you, or maybe we have something downstairs. We've got some stock in the basement that we haven't had a chance to sort through.'

'You haven't got anything that's going to fit me,' Tanya said flatly.

'I'm sure if we regroup . . .'

But it was too late. Tanya had burst into tears.

'Oh no! Oh dear!' Cress put her arm round the older woman. It was too hot for hugging but, unlike Phoebe, she couldn't ignore a human being in pain. 'This is an us problem, not a you problem.'

She led Tanya out into the main atelier and parked her back on one of the sofas while Phoebe stood there wringing her hands.

'It's not worth crying over,' she said helplessly.

'You know, the average British women is a size sixteen,' Tanya hiccupped through her sobs. 'So, why is it that when I want a nice dress in a size sixteen – because yes, we all know that I'm not really a size fourteen – I'm made to feel like a freak of nature?'

'It's just not cost-effective for us to stock plus-size vintage,' Phoebe explained. 'And a lot of it is handmade, and a vintage size sixteen is the equivalent of a modern size twelve, so you see . . .'

'I've spent my whole life waiting to get to the good part. But the good part never gets here.' Tanya sniffed. '*When I lose weight, it will happen. If I get my teeth fixed. If I win the lottery.* If I do this, if I do that, everything will be different. But nothing is ever different and now I'm going to be fifty and I'm trying to accept that this is my life and this is the way things are, but for one night I want to feel like a queen. Is that too much to ask?'

'Of course it isn't,' Cress said, even as she felt a warning twinge right in the gut, because Tanya's words resonated with her in a way that she really didn't want to explore right now. Or maybe ever.

Tanya was crying again. Not that she'd ever stopped. But these were big, noisy tears that sounded as if they were being ripped out of her. Cress tightened the arm that she already had round Tanya's shoulders and Phoebe . . . Phoebe looked absolutely horrified.

'You know how I feel about people crying on the dresses,' she hiss-whispered at Cress, then shook her head. 'I'm going to get Sophy.'

Usually it made Cress smile to herself, the way that Phoebe, unable to handle any displays of raw emotion, would always absent herself and get Sophy to deal with it. 'Sophy's a people person,' she'd say in much the same way that anyone else would describe someone as a 'serial killer', or an 'abuser of animals'.

But Sophy *was* a great people person. She arrived in the atelier with another glass of cool water and a sympathetic smile and, within five minutes of soothing words and rubbing circles on Tanya's back, the woman had quietened down to just the odd hiccup.

'A dress size is just a number,' Sophy said. 'Digits on a label. It doesn't mean anything. It's not a judgement and it's not validation. It's actually false information. I'm anything between a size eight and a size eighteen depending on which high-street shop I'm trying jeans on in. You know?'

Tanya nodded and blew her nose. 'I've made a complete fool of myself.'

'You haven't!' Cress and Sophy assured her in unison.

'It's just, I haven't had a great life. I've had an OK life. I let things happen to me instead of taking charge and now I'm going to be fifty and I'm looking back and taking stock and it's all just been kind of disappointing.'

'But you're talking as if your life is over when it isn't. It's just a new chapter,' Sophy said. 'Fifty isn't old. My mum's fifty-three and I can hardly keep up with her.'

'My mum too,' Cress murmured. 'And I bet you've done loads of amazing things in your life.'

'Well, I did used to sing on cruise ships,' Tanya said with another sniff. 'While I was waiting for my big break, which never happened.'

'But still, you were in the entertainment business and you got to travel the world,' Sophy pointed out. Everything that Tanya had achieved, which she then negated because she'd been waiting for something better, Sophy was able to turn into a positive.

'And I've been in love with the same man for thirty years, waiting for him to put a ring on it, and I'm still bloody waiting. Two kids, a dog, a bloody mortgage and he's still coming up with reasons why he doesn't want to make a commitment to me.'

'But you've loved and you've been loved . . .' Sophy was clearly struggling now.

'I'm not sure that he does love me. We just rub along and it's easier and cheaper to stay together than to break up.'

Tanya took a deep, shuddering breath. 'I've never had a day when it was all about me. Never got married. I was seven months pregnant on my twenty-first birthday. Didn't have a big thirtieth birthday because my mum died that week. Spent my fortieth birthday having an emergency appendectomy. But this year even though I'm dreading the thought of being fifty, I had this stupid idea that instead of hating getting older, I was going to celebrate me. And now I can't even get a stupid dress that fits.'

'Did you have a particular dress in mind?' Cress asked. 'I'm guessing you like the vintage style.'

Tanya nodded, then got to her feet. 'Something like that?' she said hesitantly, pointing at a wedding dress that had been hung up face-out. It was a 1930s ivory silk gown, cut on the bias, with tiny cap sleeves. 'But with proper sleeves. No one needs to see my bingo wings. But I couldn't even get that dress over my head.'

It was a tiny dress, and Tanya looked like she was about to cry again as she contemplated the frock and then her own reflection.

'I can make you that dress!' Cress heard herself say. 'Maybe not *that* dress, but I can make you any dress you want.'

Tanya turned away from the mirrors. 'You can?' she asked tremulously.

'She absolutely can. I did ballroom dancing when I was a teenager and Cress made all my costumes,' Sophy said with a fond smile. 'She can do amazing things with a length of tulle.'

'Why don't you go home and have a think about what you'd love to wear? Maybe put some ideas on a Pinterest board and then come back and we'll have a chat. I'll take some measurements and work out the cost,' Cress said, like she made bespoke dresses all the time, even though that wasn't what she was employed to do and oh my God, Phoebe was going to kill her.

'A dress just for me? A one-off?' Tanya didn't sound tearful any more but wistful, hopeful.

'Your dress of dreams,' Cress confirmed because maybe Phoebe never had to find out. Or if she did, Cress would already be in a witness protection scheme.

As she travelled home on the tube that night, sweaty and bookended by even sweatier businessmen, Cress couldn't help thinking about the two very different women she'd met that day.

There was Jackie Coulter, who very clearly followed the beat of her own drum. Who'd succeeded on her own terms and was doing something she loved. Then there was Tanya, who, although it sounded as if she had had a full and interesting life, felt as if she'd never really got off the starting blocks. She'd wanted stardom and she'd wanted the happy ever after but somehow had only got an approximation of both.

Cress guessed that she was somewhere between the two of them. She wanted to follow the beat of her own drum, but most days she couldn't even hear it. She loved working at The Vintage Dress Shop (and she wouldn't even have been doing that, if Sophy hadn't rescued her from the Museum of Religious Relics,) but she didn't want to be doing alterations and repairs for the rest of her working days. And she definitely wanted the happy ever after, but she'd been with the same man for fifteen years and they didn't seem any closer to moving in together, never mind getting married.

Well, something had to change.

As soon as Cress got off the sweaty hell that was the tube, before she'd even left the platform, she dialled Colin's number.

He didn't pick up because he never picked up. He hated talking to people on the phone, so Cress sent him a voice note, which was probably easier than actually having to chat this one out.

43

'We've been saving up for ten years, Col. We must have enough money by now to put down a decent deposit on our own place. So, um, can you book next Wednesday as holiday? It's my day off, and we'll go and look at some places. Let me know if you have an area that you prefer. OK? OK. Let's do this! Love you.'

Chapter Five

Colin didn't reply, though Cress knew for a fact that he wasn't out that evening.

The next morning, it was clear that he'd listened to her voice note, but his silence was deafening. Also, very annoying.

Phoebe was also being quite annoying and had decided to call one of their very sporadic staff meetings, mostly because the absent Chloe, the other full-time member of staff, currently sunning herself in Mykonos, had decided to extend her holidays. 'It will be unpaid holiday,' Phoebe said sternly from the second stair, where she liked to address her minions. Coco Chanel sat on the fifth stair to supervise the proceedings. 'We only get four weeks paid holiday and it needs to be requested in advance. This is very unprofessional of Chloe.'

'It's just as well I'm here to cover,' Sophy said. 'I can cover indefinitely.'

'I'm sure it won't come to that,' Phoebe insisted, but she looked unsettled at the prospect of having Sophy around for an indefinite amount of time. 'Anyway, happier news. The film people are coming back.'

'What are the film people doing with us anyway?' Anita asked.

'They're going to be making a film about a sixties fashion designer and of course we *are* London's premier vintage shop,' Phoebe said, which wasn't strictly true. 'Between you and me, I'm sure they'll probably ask me to come on board as a consultant.' She sighed a little longingly. 'That would be amazing. Getting to work with Jackie Coulter. Talking about vintage dresses all day.'

Phoebe seemed to be forgetting that she already talked about vintage dresses all day, every day.

'Who was that man?' Cress asked, because, when she hadn't been thinking about Jackie and Tanya or being annoyed with Colin, she'd allowed herself to feel a little irritated every time she thought about that very rude, very black-clad man with his stupid sunglasses.

'He's called Miles,' Phoebe said, but didn't seem to know much beyond that.

'He seemed a bit pretentious,' Anita noted, which made Phoebe rear back on her stair like Anita had insulted her own mother, or, worse, Coco Chanel.

'Oh, Anita, he's a very creative person,' she scolded, though usually Phoebe was the first person to be uncharitable about someone else. 'When someone is that artistic, so caught up in their own vision, then they're allowed to be a little, a little . . .'

'Up themselves?' Sophy suggested. 'Difficult? Well, Cress is the most creative person I know and she's not the least bit difficult.'

'Yes, Cress is creative but I'm talking about that special magic that you get when people have very artistic tempera-ments. You can't expect them to live by your own boring, basic rules,' Phoebe said smugly, as Sophy bristled at the implication that she was boring and basic. Cress was low-key bristling too. Sophy wasn't boring or basic; she was the sort of person who went to Paris on a mere whim.

But did people think that *she* was boring and basic?

It was something to ponder but, before she could, the shop door opened, and, eager for the distraction, everyone looked round, ready to rush to the aid of a customer and end this boring meeting.

There was a universal sigh of disappointment that it was only Freddy.

'I hope you don't greet paying punters with the same lack of enthusiasm,' he said with a grin.

Freddy said most things with a grin – when he wasn't arguing with Phoebe, which happened a lot. He wasn't particularly tall, but he had such energy and charisma that he always filled any room. With his moptop of unruly brown hair, green eyes, which were usually creased up what with the grinning, and the tattoos that covered his arms, he looked like Harry Styles's older, cheekier brother. Today he was wearing a pair of slim-fit Sta-Prest grey trousers and a black Fred Perry short-sleeved shirt (he liked the mod look, did Freddy) that highlighted the fact that, when he wasn't working, he was putting in some time at the gym.

'Suns out, guns out,' Cress heard Anita whisper to Bea as the muscles in Freddy's arms flexed rather beautifully when he folded them.

He was a solicitor by trade, though Cress could never imagine Freddy studying law, but as far as The Vintage Dress Shop was concerned he sorted out the business side of things. No one else, not even Phoebe, was cut out for dealing with rates and VAT and Camden Council. He'd been Johnno's right-hand man, and now that Johnno was gone, Freddy was even more hands-on.

'Glad you're all here,' he said now. 'Pheebs, Soph, why don't the three of us sit down and thrash out this new rental scheme?'

'Sounds great,' Sophy agreed, while Phoebe stiffened where she stood.

'Don't call me Pheebs, you know I don't like it. And I don't understand why you're acting like this stupid rental idea is a done deal. It very much isn't.'

It was time to be somewhere else, Cress thought. 'I've got a ton of alterations to get through,' she mumbled, squeezing past Phoebe as she heard Anita saying something about putting the kettle on and Bea muttering about going down into the basement to stock-take.

Even from the safety of the workroom, Cress could hear raised voices. Mostly Phoebe's raised voice, to be fair.

There were a lot of minor repairs that needed to be done. Nothing too engrossing. Replacing a button or a hook and eye. Mending a ripped seam and a dropped hem. So Cress didn't have to concentrate very hard and could think about how Colin still hadn't replied to her message.

When that thought started making her cross, she turned her attention to Tanya, who *had* just messaged her.

> Thank you so much for yesterday. I'm so excited about having a dress made just for me. Have spent all morning on Pinterest!

Cress wondered what Tanya's dream dress might be. Also, there was no way that she could make the dress on the quiet, unless Tanya came round to her house, and that felt like it would be quite a deceitful thing to do.

She was just going to have to come clean and confess, even though Phoebe would be furious. But if Phoebe was in a bad mood anyway . . .

Cress waited until the voices downstairs were a little quieter, then crept down the stairs.

'It's ridiculous to have dresses hanging here, taking up space, when they could be earning money,' Sophy was insisting, her chin and chest stuck out the way they did when she was determined to win an argument.

'It does make good business sense,' Freddy added as Phoebe put a hand to her heart, like they'd both jointly stabbed a dagger through it.

'I'm not having my dresses snatched away for a night or a weekend by people who won't take proper care of them, because they're not financially or emotionally invested in them. They won't treat them kindly.' Phoebe now put a hand to her forehead like she was about to have an attack of the vapours – or maybe she was really having an attack of the vapours. 'They'll come back ripped or stained, maybe they won't come back at all.'

'Yeah, well, that's why we have insurance,' Freddy said in a bored voice like he'd seen Phoebe's attack of the vapours many times before and was now immune to it. 'I mean, we charge what? A hundred quid to rent a dress for a week. I don't know, I'd have to work out the exact costings. But by the time it's been rented out a couple of times, we've more than covered our costs and then we could still go on to sell it for full price.'

'Especially as retail's down at the moment,' Sophy chimed in like she read the *Financial Times* every morning.

'You two . . . you know the price of everything and the value of nothing,' Phoebe snapped, and she didn't seem to be getting any less angry, so now was as good a time as any . . .

Cress leaned over the banister. 'Sorry to interrupt but while you're here, Freddy, Phoebe, I've agreed to make a customer, Tanya, who came in yesterday, a special-commission dress . . . um, from scratch. That's OK, isn't it?'

Freddy shrugged like he really couldn't care less. 'That's fine. I don't see what the problem is.'

Unfortunately and inevitably, Phoebe could see many problems. Her eyes narrowed. 'What do you mean, *from scratch*?'

'Well, she's going to tell me what her dream dress looks like and I'm going to make it for her?'

'From what pattern?' Phoebe demanded.

'I'll probably have to make the pattern myself, or maybe use one of our dresses as a template . . .'

'Stealing the design and copyright more like,' Phoebe said, because her blood was well and truly up and she was beyond any reason.

'Being inspired by,' Cress insisted. Everyone did it. Cress knew for a fact that one of the country's leading designers (she'd been at Central Saint Martins with him) blatantly ripped off at least one vintage dress in every collection.

'Where are you getting the fabric? Who's paying for the fabric?'

'I was going to cost it all up and then obviously what Tanya pays over that would go to the shop, I wouldn't be skimming anything off,' Cress said in a hurt voice because, even though Phoebe was angry, she didn't need to cast aspersions on her honesty.

'If Cress is making a dress for a customer, then I don't see why she shouldn't get some commission,' Freddy said. 'Once you've got more details, let me know and I'll work something out. Now, so this rental scheme is agreed in principle, me and Sophy just need to sit down and hammer out the final details. Maybe we could set up a Zoom with the legendary Clive of Clive's Closet fame?'

'It's not agreed in principle by me—'

'So, get me up to speed with the film people,' Freddy said quickly. He was clearly not going to give any more attention to Phoebe's profound and very noisy unhappiness. 'I spoke to the producer last night. He said that the meeting went well?'

'I suppose,' Phoebe said because she was still on the sulk setting. 'Jackie, that's Jackie Coulter, said we had a very good curation of dresses.' Her bad mood was melting away in front of their eyes. Phoebe flicked back the edge of her razor-straight bob. 'She said I had *exquisite* taste.'

'I've never been in any doubt about that, Pheebs,' Freddy said softly, and she melted a little bit more.

'Just don't forget it,' she grumbled, but then couldn't resist preening a little. 'Are they coming back then? I said they could come back and that I'd be happy to help in any way I could. Maybe as a fashion consultant.'

'They would like to come back,' Freddy agreed. 'Would you be happy to liaise with them?'

'I would.' Phoebe nodded, a pleased smile threatening to break through. 'And I said that if they needed to, they could borrow some of the dresses. For a retainer fee, and they'd have to sign something.'

'You mean, they'd be renting them?' Sophy actually cracked her knuckles in glee, and Freddy was grinning again.

'You're monsters, the pair of you,' Phoebe said hotly, and that was Cress's cue to make her excuses and flee upstairs again.

Chapter Six

They didn't have to wait long for the film people to reappear. They were back the next day.

Or rather one of the young women, the one with the lilac tips, returned, along with the black-clad Angel of Celluloid. Cress glimpsed them as they disappeared into the designer dress room with Phoebe, but she was putting the finishing touches to a wedding dress that a courier was coming to collect before lunch, so she didn't pay them much attention.

The dress was finally finished. Cress was in the middle of packing it away in one of the elegant heirloom boxes they used for their special occasion dresses, between layers and layers of acid-free tissue paper, when she sensed someone lurking in the open doorway of her workroom.

'Is the courier here?' she asked, not raising her head, as she selected a long length of their trademark Wedgwood-blue silk ribbon to tie round the box. 'I'll be two minutes.'

'Not the courier,' said an amused voice and she looked up to see him – what was his name again? – slouched nonchalantly against her door jamb.

Cress didn't know why but she could feel her cheeks heating up, but her hands refused to be flustered. She expertly tied the ribbon round the box and fastened it with a pretty bow.

'Cress, the courier's here!' Phoebe bustled past *him* and dared to tap her foot impatiently as Cress placed the box in their biggest bag, made of stiff white card, again with their lovely blue ribbon handles. 'Excellent. Good work. Didn't mean to be crabby before, but Freddy . . .'

She didn't finish the sentence but took the bag and bustled out again. All the while the man was standing there, still with his sunglasses on.

Cress unwillingly looked up in time to see him take his sunglasses off and hook them into the collar of his black t-shirt, to reveal a pair of deep blue but very red-rimmed eyes. 'It's Cressida, isn't it?'

Nobody called her Cressida. Not even Diane, who'd been reading Georgette Heyer's *False Colours* when she'd been in labour and, as a result of a lot of gas and air and an excess of hormones, had decided to name her daughter after the heroine. But now she was always . . .

'Cress.' Her eyes widened as he stepped into her workroom, because it was forbidden territory to all but staff. But still, he came at her, with his hand outstretched.

'I'm so sorry about the other day,' he said, in a voice that was more than a little husky. 'And I wanted to introduce myself. I'm Miles, I'm the assistant director on *Beat!* I was suffering from terrible hay fever the first time we met. It felt like my head was twice its usual size and my throat was so swollen, I could hardly speak.'

Well, that did explain a few things. 'Sounds dreadful,' Cress said, shaking his proffered hand. He had lovely hands, she noticed, and a very firm, but not punishing, handshake. The handshake went on just a moment too long. Long enough that it was almost like holding hands. 'No wonder you wanted honey in your tea.'

'You must have thought that I was a pretentious jerk. Every cliché about people who work in the entertainment industry rolled into one,' Miles said with a shudder and a conspiratorial smile.

'Oh, not at all,' Cress said, even though she and Sophy had thought exactly that. 'You seem to be feeling better now?'

'I had a steroid shot and I've got to have an antihistamine shot once a week for the next six weeks too.' Miles ran long fingers through his dark hair, which was almost as unruly as Freddy's. 'Apparently normal over-the-counter antihistamines won't cut it. Anyway, I would have bought you some flowers as a peace offering but I was worried that I'd relapse. So, I bought you the next best thing.'

The next best thing would have been a copy of *Vogue Italia* or some lovely vintage buttons, but the pink and white striped paper bag that Miles presented with a flourish was easily the third best.

'Pick 'n' mix?' Cress said in surprise, taking the bulging bag from Miles. 'I love pick 'n' mix.'

'Who doesn't?'

He came to perch on the edge of her workbench as Cress investigated the contents of the bag. All her favourites were present and correct, from fried eggs to fizzy cola bottles and jumbo jazzies.

He was probably used to the kind of women, film women, actresses, who never ate anything that had even come close to some sugar, but it had clearly been obvious that Cress was not one of those women. She was suddenly self-conscious of her, well, her everything, but especially her legs and arms.

It was odd. Usually Cress was all about the body positivity. She'd had so many brides in tears in the atelier after putting themselves on ridiculous crash diets because they thought that was what they should do before getting married. Then, instead of enjoying the run-up to their weddings, they spent most of their time very, very hangry.

Cress liked to think that she was quite pragmatic about what she looked like. She was more interested in what her body could do – whether it was whipping up a simple skirt in half an hour or walking up the escalators at tube stations when she was on one of her very rare health kicks. And Colin seemed happy with how she looked. Whenever he was passing her favourite bakery, he always remembered to buy her her favourite caramel éclair. He wouldn't do that if he thought she should lose weight.

But now, in front of Miles, who, despite the bloodshot eyes, was good-looking in a very cool, very film-person kind of way, Cress felt like she wasn't enough. Or rather, she felt like she was too much.

During the cooler months, Cress wore one of her handmade work smocks with unfeasibly large pockets over a black jumper and trousers. But that wasn't an option when it was hot, so today she was wearing one of her summer smocks, which were a bit longer but sleeveless, and now she was aware of her thick legs and even thicker arms. No wonder Miles thought that she was the sort of woman who'd be happy horsing down a huge bag of pick 'n' mix. Because that was precisely what she was.

She realised that she'd lapsed into an uncomfortable silence, not that Miles had noticed. He was too busy looking around her workroom with interest. His gaze came to rest on her well-stocked shelves.

'Would a fashion designer work in a room like this?' he suddenly asked.

'Gosh, I don't know.' Cress thought about it. 'If they were quite a well-known fashion designer then they'd probably have a much larger workspace for their whole team. Pattern cutters, seamstresses, that sort of thing. What kind of fashion designer were you thinking of?'

'Well, our film is set in the sixties. It's about a fashion-obsessed girl who starts off as a model but really wants to make it as a fashion designer in a male-dominated industry.'

'Believe me, it's still a very male-dominated industry,' Cress muttered as she pulled several books down from her shelves. A couple of friends from her Central Saint Martins days had studied fashion design, rather than fashion conservation as Cress had, then moved to Paris to work with a world-renowned designer. The stories that they had to tell had shocked Cress to the very core. 'This is about Hardy Amies. He wasn't a very cutting-edge designer, certainly not in the sixties, he dressed the royal family a lot, but it has great pictures and even a floorplan of the house in London where he worked.'

Miles took the book from her. 'I hardly know anything about fashion. And, to be honest, I felt so rotten the other day that I didn't take much in when Phoebe was talking. But it seemed quite advanced chat and I'm still mastering the basics.'

'The sixties is quite a varied decade when it comes to fashion. People think of the Swinging Sixties and imagine that it was all mini skirts and bell-bottom jeans, but that wasn't what was happening in the early sixties,' Cress said, the alleged thickness of her limbs now forgotten as she piled more books on the counter. Autobiographies of both Mary Quant and Barbara Hulanicki, founder of Biba, and a great book on the fashion of Liberty's department store during the sixties.

'The dark underbelly of swinging London is what we're aiming for,' Miles said. 'Our heroine gets swept up in all manner of seedy goings-on. Oh! Now, even I've heard of Mary Quant.'

They had a lovely chat about Mary Quant, Jean Muir and Zandra Rhodes. Or rather Cress talked and Miles asked the kind of questions that showed that he was actually listening to her. Even Sophy, who loved her a lot, would get a glazed look in her eyes when Cress started having what she called 'nerdgasms about fashion'.

Talking to Miles was like talking to one of her friends, but there seemed to be a flirty edge to it. Cress wasn't the sort of woman who imagined that men were coming on to her even when they were just having a perfectly ordinary conversation. Unlike Anita. Pity the poor man who happened to sit next to her on the bus because there were no other seats free. 'Way to make it obvious. I could tell he fancied me,' was something that she'd actually said after that very scenario.

But even with red-rimmed eyes, Miles had a gaze that seemed to penetrate right through Cress's outer layers. As if he liked the look of her outer layers. And when she lifted a hand to push the heavy weight of her hair back and refasten it with a scrunchie, he licked his lips. Not in a gross, sketchy way but in a way that made Cress want to lick her lips too.

Cress didn't know how long they talked but suddenly Phoebe was at the doorway, with a bridal party in tow, which meant that Cress had been yammering about famous female fashion designers all the way through her lunch hour.

'I'm so sorry for keeping you,' Miles said, straightening up from the counter that he'd been leaning on. He touched Cress's arm and, despite the heat of the day, it felt as if goosebumps had instantly sprouted in that spot just below her elbow. 'Would you mind if we swapped numbers and would you mind if I needed to pick your brains again?'

'No, that would be fine.' Cress had to remind herself that, despite the searing glances that seemed to see into her soul, and the lip-licking, Miles was only interested in her fashion nous. Which actually made a refreshing change because, even though she'd been with Colin for fifteen years, she doubted that he even knew who Mary Quant was.

Later that night, as Cress was sorting through her vintage dress patterns to see if she had any designs that might suit Tanya, her phone chimed with a WhatsApp.

'At last!' she said out loud, because Colin still had her on read-only and she was low-key fuming at him.

But it wasn't from Colin, it was from Miles.

So great to meet you properly today. Really
looking forward to working with you.

And Cress was sure that the only reason she got a sudden
swoony, swoopy feeling in her stomach was the huge quantity
of pick 'n' mix that she'd consumed that day.

Chapter Seven

Colin had finally, very grudgingly to Cress's mind, agreed to book a day off and spend it looking at properties.

'We're only looking,' he'd said. 'Like, a fact-finding mission. I won't commit to anything more than looking. I don't want you impulse-buying a four bedroom house.'

'That's not how house-buying works,' Cress had said.

'But we're not buying. We're only looking.'

That very unsatisfying conversation had happened only after Cress had phoned on the landline and Roy had taken the portable phone up to Colin's bedroom so he *had* to talk to her. It was like being sixteen again, though at sixteen Cress had yet to discover some of Colin's more unappealing character traits.

But fifteen years down the line, she knew everything about Colin, good and bad. He'd sounded so unenthusiastic about the prospect of this new chapter of their lives that Cress had actually gone round to his house to pick him up rather than meeting at Finchley Central tube station. Colin had a very inconvenient habit of 'forgetting' about things that he didn't want to do.

Cress might not like it, but she was used to it. Colin was always resistant to any events, outings, experiences that needed some forward planning, everything from holidays to trying a new restaurant for the first time. Then once Cress had done all the forward planning, he'd reluctantly agree to come, and usually had a good time.

She didn't even want the additional emotional labour she'd take on when they did actually buy their first home, but still she had a delicious flutter of butterflies in her stomach as they set out on this adventure.

'This is exciting. New beginnings and all that.' Cress pointed out as they changed at Euston on to the Victoria line. 'Also, we can't live at home for ever.'

'Yeah, but this is really out of the blue,' Colin said, even though it wasn't. They'd both been saving up for a deposit for the ten years since they'd started full-time employment. That was a lot of saving up.

Cress wished that Colin had made more of an effort. He was wearing a very old, very faded Genesis t-shirt with even older jeans and a pair of greying plimsolls that were starting to come away at the sole. It wasn't going to make a good impression on the estate agent.

But when they got out of the tube at Tottenham Hale and made their way to the estate agents, Jaxon 'with an x', looked about twelve and was more interested in staring at his phone than critiquing Colin's outfit.

'So, yeah,' he said, his eyes on his screen and his thumbs moving at lightning speed as he messaged someone. 'We can see three of the properties that you emailed me about, Chrissy.'

'Um, it's Cress.'

'Cool, let's get going.'

'I can't believe that you think Tottenham is somewhere you want to live,' Colin hissed as they followed Jaxon round the corner to where he had his estate agent-branded Mini parked. 'They've had actual riots here.'

'That was years and years ago,' Cress said firmly. 'More importantly, it's in Zone Three and property here is still relatively cheap.'

'This first flat is nearly three hundred thousand pounds! That's not cheap!' Colin's voice was so shrill that it sounded like he'd done something painful to his vocal cords.

'It *is* cheap for London.' Because she'd been looking on RightMove for the last few days, Cress was used to how expensive property was. Shocked. Appalled. Panicked. But also, resigned. Considering that neither of them had ever had to pay rent – Colin getting room and board for free while Cress just gave Diane some housekeeping money – they'd both squirrelled away quite a considerable sum of money over the last decade. Enough for a very generous deposit and mortgage repayments that should be doable.

However, the first property, the cheapest, was a one-bedroom flat in a dingy street a good mile away from the tube. The mildew and the damp seemed to be the only things that were holding the walls together.

'Great opportunity to put your stamp on the place,' Jaxon said as the three of them tried really hard not to breathe in so they wouldn't be asphyxiated by the spores from the mould.

The second place was the most expensive, an actual house, nearer the tube; but that wasn't enough to mollify Colin, who was in a very definite sulk now. 'Be murder on match days when Spurs are playing at home. Good luck being able to get anywhere,' he sniffed, even though he didn't drive so it wasn't like he had to worry about the traffic being gridlocked.

'You could try to be more open-minded,' Cress said as they stared at the house, which looked tired and in need of updating with its stone cladding, grimy UPVC windows and weed-strewn front garden.

'So, this property has been in the same family for fifty years,' Jaxon said as he wrestled with the front door. 'It's turnkey, ready to move in right away. Just needs a little refresh.'

It smelled like the family who'd lived there for fifty years had also died there and it had been weeks before anyone discovered their bodies. Cress's eyes hurt from the garish, swirly orange and red carpet, which didn't match the floral wallpaper or the curtains, which were in an entirely different floral print.

The house was basically a two-up two-down with a bathroom on the ground floor, beyond the peeling Formica units in the kitchen, featuring an orange bathroom suite.

Whoever had lived here before had *really* liked orange. They peered out at what Jaxon optimistically called a back garden, but was really a yard with cracked paving slabs and a shed that looked like it might fall down in the next moderate puff of wind.

'This is right at the top of our budget,' Cress said apologetically, because Colin had already exited the premises and was sitting on the front wall. 'Then we wouldn't have enough money to do it up until we've saved all over again.'

'Just as well I've kept the best to last,' Jaxon said. Cress was relieved that he wasn't taking it personally that she'd rather live at home until she was ninety than ever set foot again in the first two properties.

Still, Cress's expectations were low, so low that they were pretty much on the ground as Jaxon drove them through the very mean streets of Tottenham until they were in what he called: 'South Tottenham and you're a minute's walk from Seven Sisters tube station. That is a literal minute not an estate agent's minute, which really means you'll have to walk fifteen minutes through an industrial estate. You feel me?'

Cress was definitely warming to Jaxon, and, once they were standing outside a pretty Victorian property with sash windows and a door painted a cheerful and sunny yellow in what seemed to be a very quiet street, she wanted to hug him.

It just got better and better as they toured the two-bedroom ground-floor flat and Cress exclaimed happily over the property, which had original fireplaces and wooden floors but a modern fitted kitchen and a bathroom with teal-coloured metro tiles. The back garden was small, but it had a lawn and a tiny bit of decking where 'we could sit out in summer,' because Cress could already easily see herself living here.

'But where are my records going to go?' Colin demanded. 'And all your sewing shit?'

To call her prized collection of vintage dresses and fabrics, findings and buttons shit was horrible. So horrible that she had to blink back tears. Cress would never be so rude or mean about Colin's bloody record collection, though why he needed five different editions of the same virtually unlisten-able prog rock album, she'd never know.

'There's a basement cellar for storage, guys,' Jaxon said as they crowded into the narrow entrance hall. 'Could also apply for planning permission to get another bedroom down there.'

'Then we'd be adding value on,' Cress said because both her dad, Mike, and her stepdad, Aaron, had said that they needed a property that they could add value to so it would be a proper investment.

'If I were you, I'd think about making an offer today,' Jaxon advised. 'A place like this is going to get snapped up asap. If you came back to the office now, then I think our mortgage advisor has a free slot.'

Both dads had also warned against using a mortgage advisor attached to an estate agent and Cress already had an appointment lined up with the woman who looked after Mike's pension and his ISAs. 'We need to have a chat,' Cress said with a pointed look at Colin, who had his back to her. 'But I'll be in touch very soon.'

Cress knew that people often thought that she was very mild-mannered and timid, and she could be both of those things. But when she was with Colin and he was in one of his moods – and honestly, he could sulk for England – she felt very much like the grown-up in their relationship. Worse! Sometimes, like now, with Colin sullen and silent as they retraced their steps to the main road, she felt like the parent dealing with an absolutely impossible toddler.

She exclaimed over the cafés they passed and the library and how 'the tube really is very close,' until Colin ground to a halt. 'OK, I get it,' he groused. 'The area is . . . all right, I suppose, but that flat is still too small and too expensive.'

With some more cajoling, Cress convinced him that they should get some lunch and have a chat.

Once he was looking a bit happier with a grilled chicken panini in front of him, Cress wiped the smile off his face by handing him the information sheet she'd put together. Bullet-pointed and double-spaced and everything.

'OK, so that's everything we need to apply for a mortgage, including statements from both our current and savings accounts,' she said brightly. 'Might as well have that all sorted before we sit down with the mortgage advisor. It will save time.'

'I don't want some stranger poring over my bank state-ments.' Colin scowled and managed to take a bite of the panini at the same time.

'But that's how it works. They need to know that we've got enough for a deposit and that we'll be able to afford the mortgage payments,' Cress said through gritted teeth. She felt a lot like screaming instead of eating her tuna baguette. 'Is something bothering you?'

'No,' Colin said and refused to elaborate on that.

'Well, there obviously is. Do you not want to move in with me?' Cress couldn't keep the hurt out of her voice. They'd been together for so long and yet so rarely got the chance to be alone together – Sophy was always teasing her about it – and she'd often imagined what it would be like to be living just the two of them. 'I thought you'd be happy about this.'

Colin put down his panini. 'Why would you think I'd be happy about this?'

'You don't want to be with me any more?' Cress choked out.

'No! Of course I want to be with you, but moving in together . . . Where has all this come from?' He gave a short, sharp bark of laughter. 'It's Sophy, isn't it? She's giving you ideas. Well, she's not moved in with that fancy new boyfriend of hers, has she, so she can just mind her own business.'

'That's because they've only been dating for a few months – but she moved in with Egan when they'd only been going out for a couple of years,' Cress said of Sophy's ex, whom she'd never liked – in the same way that Sophy didn't like Colin. Difference was that Sophy never ran Colin down to Cress; it was a pity that Colin didn't give Sophy the same courtesy.

'Yeah, well, look how that turned out. They broke up, didn't they?' Colin pointed out triumphantly. 'We're fine as we are.'

'We can't just stay the same for ever, Col.'

'Don't see why not.' Colin picked up his panini again and would not discuss moving in together, mortgages or looking at more flats. He didn't actually stick his fingers in his ears and chant, 'La la la, I can't hear you,' but he came pretty close.

When they said their goodbyes at Euston station, Cress changing on to the Northern line to go home and Colin heading into the West End so he could visit one of his favourite record shops in Soho, their parting was extremely frosty.

Chapter Eight

'I was so cross that I didn't even kiss him goodbye,' Cress told Sophy the next day as they walked from Chalk Farm station to the shop. 'Then I didn't even send him a goodnight WhatsApp.'

'That will show him,' Sophy said but, when Cress glared at her, she assumed a more sympathetic expression. 'I'm sure he'll come round. This all feels a bit out of the blue, you suddenly deciding to move in together . . .'

'I'm just fed up with life happening to me, instead of me happening to my life,' Cress said. 'Look at how much everything changed for you after you got made redundant from Belle Girl. In eighteen months, you've changed everything, and you seem much happier for it.'

'I am,' Sophy agreed. She nodded for emphasis so her red hair looked like fire as it caught the morning sun. 'And at the time I didn't even realise I was unhappy. So, is this your way of telling me that you're planning to move to Australia for a year?'

'Nothing that drastic,' Cress said with a shudder, because she'd never survive the flight and, even if she did, she didn't want to come face to face with a snake like Sophy had.

'This is just a minor blip with you and Colin, we both know that, but if the worst happens then I do recommend hooking up with a foxy new boyfriend. If nothing else, and this isn't a dig at Colin, he's the only guy you've ever kissed. You must have wondered what it would be like to kiss someone who isn't Colin.'

'But I don't want to kiss anyone else,' Cress protested. Sophy shrugged because they'd reached the shop, but she muttered under her breath, low enough that Cress almost didn't hear, 'Don't knock it until you've tried it.'

But Cress really didn't want to try kissing anyone else. Not that there was a whole queue of likely candidates all desperate to know the touch of her lips. Because she'd been with Colin all of her adult life, Cress had never looked at other men in that way. Well, apart from Timothée Chalamet, Harry Styles and Austin Butler. Cress was in a fifteen-year relationship, yes, but she wasn't dead.

Anyway, she'd always been so engrossed in her sewing and associated projects that she was pleased that the relationship part of her life was already ticked off.

That didn't mean that she was going to cave and get in touch with Colin first as she usually did. He'd been churlish and unpleasant yesterday and he owed her an apology.

It wasn't until halfway through the morning, as Cress was steam-pressing a very wrinkled silk dress and trying not to sweat into her own eyes, that her phone chimed. Cress was not the sort of woman who dropped everything for a WhatsApp ping. So it wasn't until she'd finished her steam-pressing that she picked up her phone to discover that, even if Colin had gone radio silent, there was another man who wanted to make contact with her.

Hey Cress. Me again!
Is it hard to learn how to make a dress? Like, the designing and cutting and stuff?
How long did it take you to figure it out? Did you do sewing at school? This is Miles by the way.
(Your biggest fan.)

Cress couldn't help but blush as she replied.

Flattery will get you everywhere! My grandma taught me to sew when I was about six when I wanted to make new dresses for my dolls. By the time they were teaching us how to make tote bags at secondary school, I already had my own sewing machine and could follow a pattern.

But yes, anyone can learn how to sew. Maybe not the designing, but everything else is just following instructions.

Why? Is this for the film?

Miles messaged back mere minutes later.

Is that how the great designers learned to sew?

Everyone knew how to sew back in the olden times, I think.

It was quite hard to get any work done with Miles messaging her every few minutes and wanting to chat about everything from the evolution of the minidress to her three favourite designers from the sixties.

Cress was always happy to chat about fashion and sewing, but Miles had Jackie Coulter, Oscar-winning costume designer, on hand to answer all his questions. Cress was surely a very poor substitute.

It was nice though, validating even, that someone like Miles thought that someone like Cress had opinions worth knowing. So even though she was very busy, every time her phone chimed she felt a small but powerful thrill that Miles had nothing better to do with his time than message her. Especially as she knew full well that Colin had lots of downtime at his job (he'd once told her that he spent half his day pretending to be busy rather than actually being busy) but was just sulking. Yet again.

It was nearing the end of the day. Cress was tidying up her workroom and getting things ready for her first job tomorrow when her phone chimed again.

> Hope I haven't been a pain in the arse today. But you've been an absolute star. I really appreciate it.

Yes, it was very good to be appreciated, rather than ignored. Especially when Miles messaged her again.

> I definitely owe you a drink or two, if you're free in the next few days?

There was that small but mighty thrill coursing through her again.

> Maybe?

> I'm sure you're busy doing all sorts of exciting things but I don't suppose you could do tomorrow? I know it's short notice but I'd really like to see you.

Cress put her hands on cheeks that were suddenly hot in a way that had nothing to do with her furnace-like working conditions. Was this . . . not about work? Was this actually . . .

> We could meet at my club in Soho. I've got a proposition for you.

> That sounds great.

It didn't just sound great. It sounded intriguing. Illicit even, Cress thought as Miles messaged her back with a time and a location pin.

It probably wasn't anything of the sort. There could be a perfectly innocent reason why the very good-looking Miles wanted to meet Cress outside of work in a Soho drinking den. But she couldn't think of one.

Maybe that was why Cress didn't tell anyone. Not even her mum or Sophy, though there wasn't much that she didn't share with them.

It was pleasing to think that maybe she had layers. A bit of mystery to her, instead of being an open book. Not even an interesting book but probably an easy-to-follow-instruction manual.

The next day, on the dot of six, Cress unplugged her sewing machine, overlocker and steamer, which was her way of clocking off. Then she slipped into the atelier's changing room so she could swap her shapeless smock for a pretty summer dress in a flattering fifties style of nipped-in waist and swishy skirt. It was in a crisp white lawn cotton with tiny white flowers embroidered on it, which gave the dress texture.

Apart from when it was hot and all Cress could bear to wear was one of her longer smocks, the other ninety per cent of the year she rarely ventured from her tried and trusted black trousers and black top ensembles. Which was odd, considering how many vintage dresses Cress owned. She loved to pore over them and considered it to be like having a collection of paintings that gave you immense pleasure when you looked at them.

You needed to have a certain disposition, a certain confidence, to wear vintage clothes. Cress knew that she didn't really have it. You were marking yourself out as different, as a free spirit who couldn't be contained by whatever fashions were on the high street. You were inviting people to look at you and Cress didn't want to be looked at. She'd never been one of those people who longed to be famous, as she couldn't imagine anything worse than being under constant scrutiny. To have the whole world looking and judging you? No thanks! Especially with her frizzy hair and her features that always seemed a bit too large for her face. Sophy and her mum both said that Cress was beautiful, but they were contractually obligated to say that. Cress had never felt truly beautiful, not even for one day.

But as she looked at herself in the mirror, Cress thought that she looked all right. She threaded some smoothing serum into her hair so that it separated into curls. The sun had kissed her skin to the same colour as a Werthers Original, despite her religiously applied SPF, so she just needed a bit of mascara and a tinted lip balm and she was good to go.

Steeling herself for an interrogation as she presented herself downstairs looking gussied up, Cress was relieved to discover that Charles had arrived to take Sophy out on yet another thoughtful and surprising date. Sophy only had eyes for Charles, who was wearing a cream-coloured suit with a blue floral Liberty print shirt and matching pocket square, and a besotted expression as he gazed down at Sophy, who was gazing up at him with the same goofy grin.

'We're going to the seaside,' Sophy announced.

'Isn't it a bit late to go to the seaside?' Cress asked as she headed for the door, still a little anxious that Sophy would want to know where she was going and in a proper dress too.

'Traffic allowing, we'll be in Whitstable in ninety minutes,' Charles said, curling a strand of Sophy's hair round his fingers. 'Just in time for fish and chips on the beach and a quick spin on the waltzers.'

That sounded lovely. Cress longed for a cooling sea breeze but instead she said a hurried goodbye and then decided that, rather than getting on a stuffy tube train, and as she had an hour, she'd walk through Regent's Park to get to central London.

Cress tried to be at one with nature. The Japanese called it forest bathing. But while Cress appreciated the trees and the (very dry, very bleached) grass, Regent's Park on a hot summer evening was as crowded as Piccadilly Circus just a couple of miles away.

She also felt quite giddy with nerves. Even though she'd met Miles twice now, exchanged countless WhatsApp messages, and knew that he was more interested in her fashion smarts than anything else, she also knew that he had a proposition for her – that sounded kind of flirty and a little bit dirty. Like *Indecent Proposal*, one of Diane's favourite films, where Robert Redford offers up a million dollars to have sex with the very much married Demi Moore. 'Decent proposal, more like,' Diane would always say when she watched it, which was a lot.

Not that Miles wanted to give Cress a million dollars – and she would have been astounded and shocked to the very core if he wanted to have sex with her. Also, the guilt was kicking in now. She and Colin hadn't spoken for a couple of days and here Cress was, sneaking off to meet another man.

Then Cress got lost in Soho, as she always did, and had to keep reminding herself of the mnemonic Going For Dinner With Billie Piper, to remember the order of Greek Street, Frith Street, Dean Street, Wardour Street, Berwick Street and finally Poland Street where she eventually found what she was looking for; a discreet black door with the name of the club, Hookhams, etched on a small brass plaque.

She was ten minutes early – Cress *always* arrived ten minutes early, to everything – so tried to slowly walk up a narrow twisty wooden staircase to a very minimalist reception area.

She gave her name to the sleekly intimidating man behind the desk and was directed to a room that was painted entirely black, walls, floor and ceiling. However, the chairs and tables were a hotchpotch of different styles, from floral, shabby chic, overstuffed armchairs and velvet banquettes to modernist, Danish teak G-plan tables, along with some rustic scrubbed pine and even some very modern glass and tubular steel chairs, which didn't look at all comfortable.

'Hey! Over here!' Miles had already bagged a tan leather chesterfield sofa, and waved at Cress so she didn't have to stand, flustered and slack-jawed, in the doorway.

She felt inexplicably shy as she walked over to him, but he smiled broadly as if he were very pleased to see her.

'Hi. Hello,' Cress muttered, thinking that she was going to take Miles's hand and shake it, but he was already leaning forward to brush his cheek against hers. 'Oh!' She took a step back, but he was still leaning forward to brush his other cheek against her other one. 'We're doing two. I always get confused.'

'In France, they do three, which completely throws me,' Miles said, finally taking a step back himself, but then catching hold of Cress's hand. She hoped it wasn't too hot and clammy, but if it was Miles didn't seem to notice, because he smiled at her again. 'I'm so pleased you could make it.'

He wasn't wearing sunglasses, although in the corner there was a table of noisy young men, with designer hair-cuts and designer jeans, all still wearing their sunglasses and bellowing at each other. Miles's eyes weren't red and puffy either, and for once he wasn't wearing all black but a quite retro Hawaiian-style short-sleeved shirt in red adorned with black palm trees and skulls and crossbones, the details picked out in gold. He had good arms, toned arms, like he worked out but hadn't made working out his religion. And, Cress hadn't noticed this before, he smelled amazing. Of sea salt and limes.

All in all, he was quite the snack, as Anita would say. And then Cress realised that she was just standing there gazing at him with, no doubt, a moony expression on her face.

'Sorry,' she said with an apologetic little cringe. How she wished that she hadn't been intrigued and had just stayed home and watched *Love Island*. In fact, if she could just make her excuses and leave, she could probably make it back to Finchley in time for *Love Island*.

Miles frowned a little bit and didn't say anything. But he looked as if he was trying to think of something to say. 'Why don't you sit down,' he suggested finally. 'I'll get you a drink. What are you having? They have a great gin and tonic menu, I think there's about twenty different variations of a g and t on there.'

'Oh, I don't drink. I mean, I drink. I'd be totally dehydrated if I didn't. But um, I don't drink alcohol,' Cress said, and she wished that the black walls would just swallow her up so she'd stop making an utter fool of herself. Not that she was embarrassed that she didn't drink – but then again, there was no way that she was going to tell Miles that once a week, on Sunday nights, she did partake of a cocktail in a can, usually a mojito, and that was her absolute limit.

'I'll order you something long and refreshing then,' Miles said, and he seemed unperturbed that Cress was just ridiculous, the very opposite of cool, because he shot her another smile, then went to the bar.

Cress was grateful of the five minutes to gather herself. She patted down her hot face and fussed with her skirts, then looked at Miles's back as he stood at the bar. He was long and lean. Almost as tall as Charles, who was even longer and leaner. Whereas Colin was only a couple of inches taller than Cress, and, when they weren't in a fight, they'd joke that it was just as well that Cress never wore heels.

The thought of Colin made Cress even more nervous. She felt as if she was vibrating at such a high frequency that she might float off the sofa altogether, but when Miles returned with their drinks, she was still sitting there and trying to keep her face calm.

'I got you a virgin Tom Collins with a splash of elderflower in it,' he said, and Cress didn't know what a Tom Collins was, but the drink was delicious and thirst-quenching.

'So, really appreciate you meeting me like this,' Miles said after he'd taken a long pull from his bottle of lager.

'Oh, that's all right. It's fine.'

'Just trying to get my head round all the moving parts on this film, while the director is in Belfast scouting locations,' he explained. 'It's much cheaper to film there and there's all sorts of grants and incentives.'

'I'm sure it's lovely but I never really thought of Belfast as being a glamorous sort of place where they made movies,' Cress said.

'You'd be surprised. They shoot a lot of TV shows there. Like *Line of Duty* and *Game of Thrones*.'

Colin had loved *Game of Thrones*. Cress shifted uncomfortably on the sofa. Miles was sitting next to her but there was a respectable gap between them, though he turned so he was facing her.

He smiled at her. Cress smiled back but it felt more like a grimace. This was so awkward. She couldn't think of anything to say but was in an agony of expectation waiting for his mysterious proposition.

She looked around the room for inspiration, her gaze settling on one table after another. Each one full of interesting-looking people all gabbing nineteen to the dozen. Miles must be used to a place like this and people like these, being a film person.

'So what does an assistant director actually do?' she asked, relieved that she'd thought of something to fill the silence, and also she genuinely wanted to know the answer.

Miles smiled again like he was pleased that Cress was interested in his world and, to be fair, they had previously talked a lot about fashion.

'I guess the easiest way to explain it is that I bridge the gap between cast and crew, between technical and creative, but most importantly between the director and everyone else working on the production. Which means soothing a lot of egos, putting out a lot of fires,' he said with a wry smile. 'I also sort out budgets, shooting schedules. You name it, I probably do it.'

It sounded a lot like Miles was the Freddy of *Beat!* Cress nodded. 'It sounds very stressful.'

'Yeah, it can be but it's usually worth it when all the different elements and egos come together to make something magic,' he said, his face soft as if he was imagining some faraway sound stage and a perfectly in-sync and choreographed troupe of dancing girls.

'Like in a Busby Berkeley musical,' Cress said, her own face wistful, as she could easily picture a typical 1920s Busby Berkeley routine, the dancers shot from above so it looked as if they were in a kaleidoscope as they made intricate, per-fectly choreographed patterns with their arms and legs. 'I always think how perfect those are.'

'Yes! But then I always feel a little sad when I watch those exquisite dance sequences and I think about all the hopes and dreams the dancers must have had. I'm sure most of them never made it past the chorus line and now they're dead and no one knows who they were but they're still immortalised on the screen, high-kicking for all eternity. It kind of breaks my heart,' Miles said in a husky voice like his hay fever was about to put in a reappearance.

As it was, Cress's heart experienced a little pang of sorrow for those now long-gone dancing girls. 'I know just what you mean,' she said.

'Oh God, I didn't mean to get so deep . . .'

'It's fine,' Cress assured him.

'I'm not always so emo.'

Cress didn't mind a man who was in touch with his emo-tions. It made a nice change. Not that Colin was devoid of emotion. Far from it. But he didn't talk about his feelings, preferring to go silent so that Cress was always the one who had to work out what he was upset about and then fix it. It could be exhausting. 'There's nothing wrong with talking about your feelings,' she said a little earnestly.

'Getting emotional about dead dancing girls is one thing but I wouldn't subject you to a lot of chat about my feel-ings. I hardly know you.' Miles took a sip of his lager, then grinned. 'Though let's see where we are at the end of next week.'

'Well, I look forward to that,' Cress said, and she was out of her depth here and way out of her comfort zone but it seemed like there was a flirty thing happening again. Miles kept maintaining eye contact, though sometimes his gaze would drop to Cress's mouth, making her wonder if she had a smear of chocolate on her face left over from her lunchtime Magnum.

Now the silence didn't seem awkward, but rather charged. As if the things they weren't saying were more important than the things they had said.

Cress stared back at Miles. His eyes – so blue, but a dark and stormy blue – were truly extraordinary, but then he looked away because there was a commotion at the entrance to the bar.

The commotion was caused by a statuesque blond woman poured into a tight white dress, who caught sight of Miles and waved.

'Darling!' she cried as she glided languidly towards them so that Cress couldn't help but think of Jerry in *Some Like It Hot*, describing Marilyn Monroe's sensual walk as 'Jell-O on springs.'

She reached her destination, their table, and Miles's arms as he stood up to greet her and enfolded her in a hug. Then she freed herself, only so she could kiss him. Briefly. *But right on his lips.*

'Darling!' she said again. 'It's been *too* long.'

'I literally saw you yesterday,' Miles said with an exasperated but indulgent tone as the woman dropped elegantly into the armchair opposite them and crossed her long legs.

'Well, yesterday seems like an age away.' She had a low, husky voice that was as sexy as the way she walked. 'I'm absolutely gasping for a drink.'

The barman was already on his way over, although up until that point there didn't seem to have been table service. 'Can you make me your most delicious gin and tonic?' she asked him. 'Your best one ever?'

The barman, who was chiselled and cut and covered in more tattoos than even Freddy, agreed, with a slight stutter and a dopey look, that he could.

78

'Are you two ready for another one?' she asked Miles and Cress, and Cress could only shake her head because she was sure that if she tried to speak it would come out as a squeak.

How was it that they could both be women wearing white dresses and yet in front of Cress was a goddess, and while Cress also had arms and legs and a face, it was as if they were two different species?

The barman was despatched and then Cress felt the full weight of the other woman's appraisal. From the top of her head, and she was sure that her hair had gone frizzy again, to the tips of her toes in her white Birkenstocks, which were very comfortable to walk in but were not a pair of strappy silver sandals that looked like new-season Gucci.

'So, who is this gorgeous creature that you've been keeping all to yourself?' she demanded of Miles, which was so far from the truth that she had to be taking the piss.

'Ella, this is Cress, who's my go-to source for all things fashion and also, I hope, a new friend,' Miles said gently, as if he realised that Cress was now so far out of her comfort zone that she'd need a tracking device and night-vision goggles to find her way back there. 'Cress, this is my friend Ella, who's playing the lead in *Beat!* and who also needs to dial it down just a little bit.'

'Oh God, am I turned all the way up to eleven?' Ella asked in slightly less grand tones. 'I've just come from an audition and I'm still in work mode.' She shot a friendly smile at Cress and rolled her eyes. 'What must you think of me?'

It was the oddest thing. Ella shifted in her chair and, right in front of Cress, she transformed from goddess into mortal woman. Still a very beautiful, very elegant woman, but she was no longer radiating quite so much star power.

And now that Cress could look at her without being blinded, she realised that Ella's face was very familiar, and her surname was just on the tip of her tongue but she couldn't think what she'd been in. It probably wasn't very polite to get her phone out so she could have a quick look on IMDB.

Cress also realised that she was sitting there with no doubt a gormless look on her face, but Miles put his hand on her knee for just one fleeting but quite glorious second as if to comfort her, ground her.

'So, Cress here has been the most generous help even when I'm bombarding her with stupid questions on WhatsApp. She also has a sewing machine that looks more complicated than the flight desk of a space shuttle,' he said to Ella. 'But I wanted to wait for you before I asked her the big question.'

Ella clasped her hands together and shot Cress a beseeching look. 'Please say yes.'

'You said you had a proposition for me?' Cress said slowly and now that Ella was here, and they were improbably talking about sewing machines she had a suspicion that there was going to be nothing illicit or intriguing about the proposition.

'The film's about a fashion designer, right? Someone who knows how to make clothes . . .'

'Well, yes, that's what a fashion designer does,' Cress said.

'The thing is, darling, I can't even sew on a button. Thanks ever so,' Ella added to the besotted barman, who was back with her bespoke gin and tonic.

Cress forgot to be nervous or suspicious in favour of being aghast. 'You can't sew on a button?' Even Aaron, her stepdad, could sew on a button.

'Well, I've never needed to. There's always been someone from the costume department to do it for me,' Ella explained.

'So, we were hoping that you'd agree to mentor Ella, let her shadow you at the shop for a little while,' Miles said, his startling blue eyes focused completely on Cress again. 'Like how Renée Zellweger interned at a publishing house when she got the part of Bridget Jones.'

'That way it would be convincing when I have to do the sewing stuff. I promise that I wouldn't get in your way. You'd hardly know I was there,' Ella said, which Cress very much doubted.

Should she have been flattered? Maybe. But all she felt was a cheek-scouring embarrassment that she'd entertained even the vague notion that Miles might be interested in her *in a non-work, non-sewing stuff* sort of way. Obviously he wasn't when he mixed with women like Ella. Besides, Cress had Colin, she didn't need to have her head turned by anyone else, and now she felt even more guilty.

'I'm very busy with wedding season,' she said, because she could only imagine their poor brides and mothers-of-the-brides and bridesmaids and wedding guests in need of a posh frock having all their thunder stolen by Ella. 'Also, you'd have to clear it with Phoebe.'

Phoebe would never agree to it . . .

'I'll get Jackie to take Phoebe out for lunch, sweeten her up,' Miles said, so Cress supposed it was a done deal.

Then Ella wanted to know all about Cress and as Cress reeled off her tragic biography of working at the Museum of Religious Relics for most of her career, it was just more humiliation.

Eventually she was able to make her excuses and flee, when a party of people suddenly descended on them and it was more 'Darlings!' And 'It's been too long's!' Cress didn't think that anyone even noticed when she slipped away.

But the worst was yet to come. Though initially her heart soared when she saw she had a voice note from Colin.

About bloody time, she thought as she stood in a Soho doorway with her phone to her ear.

'Yeah, so I know I was a bit of a dick the other day. I mean, like, the whole house thing threw me. Bit out of the blue. Some warning would have been nice. Anyway, I'm really sorry. Don't

be mad at me. Oh God, I know you're going to be mad at me.'
He took a deep breath and Cress, a sense of mounting dread
overpowering her, wished that he'd get to the point. 'The thing
is . . . I always intended to, but the thing is . . . I meant to but
well, I never got round to it.

'I don't have the money saved up, Cress. I should have. But
whenever I planned to, there was usually some record that I
wanted. And it's not like I could just buy it some other time.
That's not how it works. Like, if I didn't buy, say, a test pressing of Thin Lizzy's debut single when I saw it, then it wasn't
going to be there next time. So, I don't have any money for
the deposit. I'm really sorry. Please, don't be angry with me.
I feel bad enough as it is. So, can you call me? But only when
you've had a chance to calm down. OK? Also, Mum wants
to know if you're going to St Ives with them this weekend.
Says it's a bit rude that you haven't confirmed yet. Anyway,
love you. Bye.'

PART TWO

Chapter Nine

It was obvious, after his world-shattering revelations that he hadn't saved up a single penny, that Colin wouldn't be picking up his calls. Of course he wouldn't! So, once she could see past the red mist and hear something beyond the roaring in her ears, Cress left him a voice message.

'You're coming round mine on the dot of seven thirty tomorrow morning and you're going to look me in the eye and explain what's going on. It's the very least you can do,' she instructed, her voice low and intense with barely repressed emotion. 'Otherwise I'm coming round to yours and I'm going to lean on the doorbell until you let me in.'

Colin was not one of those people who thought that morning was the best part of the day, but Cress needed to hear the devastating news straight from the source.

Colin wasn't the only one who hated getting up early. His mother Mary could barely speak before nine o'clock and two cups of strong coffee and wouldn't be best pleased to have Cress kicking off on her front path long before then.

So Cress wasn't entirely surprised that at 7.29 a.m. Colin was on the doorstep, a haunted look in his eyes. Maybe it was from the ghosts of all the money that he hadn't saved.

'Oh, Colin, love, it's a bit early for you, isn't it?' Diane said as she came down the stairs to see the two of them standing awkwardly in the hall. 'Have you had breakfast yet?'

'Not yet,' Colin said forlornly like he was some kind of having-to-get-up-really-early-in-the-morning victim in this scenario. 'I'd love a—'

'He doesn't want breakfast,' Cress said in the tight voice that made anyone who knew her, really knew her, back the hell away.

So Diane, with a fixed smile, skirted around them to hurry to the kitchen, and Colin scowled but didn't say anything as Cress ushered him into the lounge then shut the door behind them.

'Start talking then,' she said, sitting herself down on the edge of an armchair, her arms wrapped round her.

Colin sat down on the sofa and then shrugged. 'I kind of covered it in the voice note I left you.'

'I want to hear you say it.' Cress could feel that her eyes had gone very wide, very starey. She wasn't sure that she was even blinking any more. 'Go on.'

'I haven't saved any money,' Colin said in a very quiet voice.

'You haven't saved any money in ten years.'

'Yeah, but, did you really think that I was going to save money when I first started working and was on a low salary?' He pouted, his lower lip jutting out, his forehead scrunched up like he was in some deep kind of existential pain. An existential pain that was entirely of his own making.

'Yes, I did, because that was what we agreed.' Oh, the injustice of it all! 'Especially as even at your first job out of university, you were still earning twice what I was at the museum, and I pay my mum housekeeping while Mary doesn't charge you any rent.'

When you'd been going out with each other for half your lives, you didn't have any secrets from each other. Apart from the fact that Cress had believed that, like her, Colin was saving three hundred pounds every month and whacking it into a high-interest savings account.

'I always intended to and I thought that I'd make the shortfall up when I got a pay rise but, you know, record collecting is a very expensive hobby.' Colin was starting to sound a little peevish.

'Yes, because you just have to have umpteen different editions of the same bloody record!' Cress could feel the first warning prickle because she was a rage crier. She was also a sad crier. An anxiety crier. And a cute-kittens-in-a-Dodo-video crier, but she was absolutely determined to get through this without any tears.

Colin scoffed in disbelief. 'Says the woman who spends a fortune on eBay buying tatty old sewing patterns and moth-eaten dresses.'

'But I make money from it. Because it's not just a hobby, it's a side hustle.' Cress could feel herself puffing up with indignation like an angry pigeon. 'Some months I even saved up *more* than three hundred pounds.'

'It's not my fault that I'm not good with money. I'm just not a material kind of person.' Colin tried another tack, which might have been convincing if he didn't have a state-of-the-art stereo system, which he was constantly adding to. Plus God knows how many computers and techy bits of kit and not to mention the records, the bloody records.

Cress's jaw was clenched so tightly, she could barely force the words out. 'Do you want to try that one again?' she demanded but, as she said it, she realised this interrogation about how Colin hadn't saved any money wasn't the important thing. What was important was . . . 'Why though? Why . . .'

'I said I was sorry last night,' Colin said in more conciliatory tones. 'Come on, Cress, it's just money.'

The prickle had become a throbbing behind her eyes now. 'But it's not just money. It's our future. Everything that we've been planning for years. You lied to me—'

'No, I didn't lie to you! If you'd asked me how much I'd saved, asked to see my bank statements, then . . .'

'You know that I thought you were saving. You lied by omission . . .'

'I mean, that's semantics, really,' Colin said, trying to verbally wriggle out of his crimes. 'Technically I never lied.'

'You deceived me. Buying a first pressing of *Sgt. Pepper's Lonely Hearts Club Band* was more important than saving up for a deposit. More important than us buying somewhere to live. More important than moving in with me.'

All this time Colin had been looking at Cress, mostly with a hangdog expression on his pale face. But now he averted his gaze and stared down at his hands.

'You don't want to move in with me.' It wasn't a question. It was a statement of fact and one that made Colin flinch as if Cress had struck him.

'Not really. Not right now,' he muttered, his voice so low that Cress had to lean forward to hear him. Outside the door, she could hear Diane going upstairs. 'I love you . . .'

'But you don't want to live with me . . .'

'It's not that. It's just . . . I don't know why things have to change. I like living at home,' he said, because he was a 33-year-old man whose mum still did all his cooking, cleaning and laundry, replenished his snack drawer and his mini-fridge and didn't even ask him for a nominal house-keeping fee. No wonder he liked living at home. 'You've got to admit that we both have it pretty good.'

Cress did do her fair share of the cooking and the cleaning. Yes, she paid Diane and Aaron a monthly sum that was far below market rent, though she'd offered to pay them more, and often splashed out on a takeaway or a nice bottle of wine or other treats. So, of course she loved living at home, but she'd also loved planning the life she'd have when she had her own home. How she could decorate it any way she wanted, and not in the various different shades of grey that her mother favoured. She'd have her own kitchen and her own bathroom and she could use all organic cleaning products and not have Diane and Aaron's friends around when she just wanted to chill out on the sofa in her pyjamas.

She hadn't minded the lack of privacy or having to hide her favourite snacks from Aaron because when he came home ravenous after a night shift he'd eat anything that wasn't nailed down. Or the fact that the light on the upstairs landing hadn't worked for years because it was too high to get a ladder up to change a bulb. None of that had mattered because, one day, Cress would have her own place.

It seemed to her now that most of her adult life had been spent in saving up and waiting for the day that they had their own home, and then *everything* could start. 'All these years I've been living a half-life . . .'

'You what?'

'We had a plan, Col,' Cress said, her voice thick with tears now because the crying was inevitable. 'I was working towards us having our own life. I mean, what did you think was going to happen? That we'd have kids and still be living with our parents?'

Colin didn't say anything because the face he pulled, more of a disgusted grimace really, said things more clearly than words ever could.

'Oh my God, you don't want kids!'

'We never talked about having kids,' Colin pointed out, which wasn't strictly true.

'We didn't talk about *not* having kids either.'

They might not have had an explicit conversation about exactly when they were going to start a family, but they had talked about children. That Colin thought that Lennon would make a perfectly acceptable name for their first child, whether it was a boy or a girl. They'd talked about the kind of parents they didn't want to be, like their old school friends Raj and Sandy who micromanaged their three kids to the extent that they even scheduled their toilet time.

'Cress, babes, this is just minor stuff,' Colin said in a wheedling tone. 'We're on the same page about the important stuff. That I love you and you love me and we give each other space and we're not one of those sad couples who have to live in each other's—'

'No! No! No!' It started as a hoarse whisper and ended up being very loud shouting. 'We are not on the same page about the important stuff. You've been lying to me for ten years. Actual lying! We want different things. You want to be waited on hand and foot by your mum like a gigantic man-baby – no wonder you don't want kids – and you love your boring records but you don't love me and also, I think your record-collecting is stupid and ridiculous . . .'

'No, it's not!' Colin didn't mind that Cress had just called him a gigantic man-baby, but God forbid she should diss his precious records.

'I hate the Beatles. I always have!' Cress shouted, which was a lie. She actually liked the Beatles quite a lot, but she couldn't stand the way that Colin went on and on about them in the most boring, trainspottery way. But the thing was that Cress was very slow to lose her temper – tectonic plates had moved across glaciers faster than it took Cress to get angry – but once she had lost it, all bets were off. 'And I hate you!'

'Don't be stupid.' Colin never lost his temper. He just sulked. Got more and more sullen until he became silent, and Cress was sick of that too. How she always had to be the one to give in when they were having a fight. Or say sorry to make the peace, even when it wasn't her fault.

Well, not any more she wasn't. 'I must have been stupid to waste so much time on you!'

'I can't deal with you when you're being like this,' Colin said, his face paler. Even his eyes seemed sunken in an effort to look everywhere but at Cress, who couldn't be contained by an armchair any more.

She jumped to her feet, all the better to stand over Colin with her hands on her hips and glare at him. 'Fifteen years we've been together, and nothing has changed. I'm sick of it. Sick of you!'

'Stop being so aggy, Cress. I've said I'm sorry and we both know that we're not going to break up over . . . basically, when you look at it rationally and stop being hysterical, it's just a misunderstanding.'

'A MISUNDERSTANDING? A MISUNDERSTAND-ING!'

Colin flattened himself against the sofa cushions. 'You need to calm down.'

Cress had left calm several minutes ago. 'I don't need to do anything and never mind breaking up with you, actually, I never want to see you again.'

'That kind of is breaking up with me,' Colin pointed out, then looked as though he really wished he hadn't when Cress threw her head back and screamed, 'Get out!'

Colin was already on his feet. 'You're completely over-reacting about this,' he said. 'And the things you've said to me are way out of line. Like, the Beatles—'

'Why are you still here?' Cress demanded, fists clenched, toes curled, fight face firmly on. 'I told you to get out!'

He got out, Cress hard on his heels. Once he'd stepped through the front door, he turned to say something, but Cress didn't care to hear it. She slammed the door so hard that the house shook, the letter box rattled and the In This House We . . . framed poster fell off the hall wall.

Cress stared down at the saccharine pronouncements. 'In this house we do forgiveness' certainly wasn't high on her list of priorities right now.

'Goodness me, what was going on down there?' Diana poked her head over the banister. 'Aaron's on lates this week. He's trying to sleep, Cress.'

The red mist was slowly dissipating. Cress's fists unclenched. She swallowed hard. Her throat was sore from all the shouting. Though what was truly amazing was that she hadn't cried.

Yet.

'Darling, what's the matter?' Diane had come down the stairs by now and all it took was one gentle and loving hand on Cress's arm. 'What's wrong?'

Cress burst into tears.

Chapter Ten

After crying in Diane's arms for quite some time, Cress stumbled up the stairs to her own room.

Even though they were in the middle of a heatwave, she got into bed fully clothed and pulled the covers over her head. Then she got out of bed to go back downstairs and retrieve her phone, shying away from Diane's offers to make her a cup of tea.

Then it was back to bed and, with shaking fingers, Cress sent Phoebe a message to say that she was ill and wouldn't be in.

It was the first time that Cress had ever skived off work. Although it wasn't exactly skiving. Heartbreak was an illness and she was crying so hard that, at one point, she thought she might throw up.

She spent all day in bed. Eventually she stopped crying but she didn't stop being a curled-up lump of sheer misery.

She kicked the covers off and starfished on her bed, the bright summer sun bursting in through the window and making a mockery of her emotions, which were dark and stormy.

How could you know someone for so long but not really know them at all? This was the second time this had happened to Cress. Sophy's hopes and dreams had been as familiar to Cress as her own and were just as small and as manageable. A job that paid the bills, a steady, comfortable relationship and small joys, be they a Saturday-night takeaway, a trip to the cinema or a weekend's minibreak (usually with each other.)

Then Sophy had changed everything about her life and those small and manageable dreams, even dragging Cress along with her to start a new work life at The Vintage Dress Shop. She'd been to Australia and had big adventures and she had a new relationship that was full of passion and excitement (God knows, there'd been enough times that Cress had walked in on Sophy and Charles snogging like teenagers), and now she wasn't afraid of making waves and taking no prisoners, especially at work.

Yet she still remained the same sister-friend that Cress loved. But how could Cress still love Colin when he wasn't the man she'd thought he was?

He'd lied. He'd cheated. He'd betrayed her. Not even with another woman but with shelves and shelves of vinyl records. So many of them that there wasn't room for Cress. Or the life that she'd been planning and dreaming about for over ten years. A little home, just for the two of them, where they could grow together and have a family. Every time he'd bought another record, which he just *had* to have, he'd been stamping all over Cress's dreams.

Eventually, Cress managed to get out of bed and take a cool shower, which did nothing to soothe her fevered emotions or sticky skin. When Aaron emerged from his bed, she made him a mug of tea and took it out to him in the garden, where he gave her a keen look from his recumbent position on the sunlounger.

'You all right?' he asked. 'Do you want to talk about it?'

Aaron had been in Cress's life since she was twelve. Her dad, Mike, was very much her dad and she could tell him and her stepmother (Sophy's mum) Caroline anything, but Aaron was also her dad in a different but just as profound way. While Mike was mild and quiet unless you went near his computer – Cress very much took after him – Aaron was also fairly laidback, but he didn't suffer fools at all. Also, he never

94

minded speaking up or wading in when injustice was afoot. In fact, he seemed to enjoy it.

'I can't,' Cress said, her voice wobbling alarmingly although she'd been sure she was all cried out.

'Well, you know where I am,' he said lightly, the sun glinting off the top of his bald head, which was as shiny and brown as a conker. When Cress joined him on the neighbouring sunlounger and pointedly passed him a bottle of suncream, he obediently applied it. Then they lay side by side and still Aaron didn't press her for any details like her mum would have but gently manoeuvred Cress into a long, meandering chat that took in the deafening party that next door but one had had the previous Saturday, climate change, what to get Diane for her birthday and who'd eaten the last Calippo.

It was much the same when Diane came home from work. She took one look at Cress's puffy face and red eyes and gave her a quick hug but didn't ask her any leading questions. It was enough for Cress that later, when they were watching *Love Island*, she lay with her head in Diane's lap while her mother stroked her hair.

When Cress woke up the next day after a fitful sleep, she was tempted by the whole crying and staying in bed thing that she'd done the day before. But among the many messages on her phone, including five from Sophy and one from Mary wanting to know if Cress was coming to St Ives that weekend, there was also a voice note from Phoebe.

She was obviously trying to be supportive, though that didn't come naturally to her.

'Do hope you're feeling better. Completely understand if you're not, but I'm just worried about all our brides who need the most important dresses of their lives altered.'

Cress emerged from Chalk Farm tube station in her biggest, darkest glasses, to find Sophy waiting for her with a huge cup of iced coffee and her very favourite pistachio cream and chocolate croissant.

Sophy didn't say anything at first. Just looked at Cress, who was head to toe in black, her gaze lingering on the dark glasses and trembling lips.

'Oh, sister-friend,' she said, her own voice catching. 'I'd ask you if you were all right, but you're very clearly not all right.'

Cress had vowed to be strong and to keep her own counsel but this was Sophy and her resolve melted like the ice cubes in her coffee. They didn't even go straight to the shop, though they were officially ten minutes late, but detoured to the banks of the canal, where they found a bench and Cress could tell Sophy everything.

'And then I think we broke up,' she said finally.

Sophy did a cartoon double-take. 'Just back up a second, please. This is the first time I can even remember you and Col having a fight. Like, a proper fight. That doesn't mean you've broken up.'

'I told him that I never want to see him again,' Cress pointed out though she understood why Sophy was having a hard time processing this information.

Cress and Colin had been absolute. Together for fifteen years. They never really argued. They definitely weren't one of those annoying couples who were always breaking up and then getting back together every five minutes. Yes, Colin was famous for his sulking, but they were as together as salt and pepper.

'Wow, this is like the ravens leaving the Tower,' Sophy said, taking Cress's croissant-crumby hand. 'I can't even imagine how you must be feeling.'

Cress steeled herself for Sophy to finally confess that she'd never liked Colin, but Sophy just shook her head, her attention fixed on a gaily coloured barge that chose that moment to gently glide past them. Then she turned back to Cress.

'I'm sure this is just a temporary thing with you and Col. Maybe he could get a loan to cover his share of the deposit, or take on a greater share of the mortgage payments. There has to be a solution.'

'Maybe,' Cress said unenthusiastically, though she was already resigned to having to live by herself in some tiny shoebox in Zone Eight.

'Or you could find a new dream,' Sophy said with forced brightness. 'You have all that money saved up. You could start your own business. Open a rival vintage dress shop. Ha! Phoebe's head would explode, which would be an added bonus . . .'

'Even then she'd make sure it didn't explode anywhere near the dresses.' Was that a smile trying to force its way on to her face?

'Goes without saying.' Sophy grinned and nudged Cress with her arm. 'You could even go wild and run away to Monte Carlo, find the roulette tables and put all your savings on red. Just for the sheer hell of it.'

'I'm definitely not going to do that,' Cress said. When she'd been filling in mortgage questionnaires, it had been very quickly established that she was risk-averse. Then she remembered that Colin hadn't filled his in, and she'd been meaning to nudge him about it. Then she thought of all the emotional labour she'd always done on Colin's behalf, from reminding him of his own mother's birthday, even buying the present and cards, to sorting out planes and accommodation and travel insurance whenever Cress had managed to persuade him that they should go on holiday. Even then, he'd only agree if there was a gig or music festival on that he wanted to go to.

Her thoughts must have been flickering across her face, because Sophy gave Cress's hand another squeeze. 'It's OK to be sad,' she said.

'But I'm not sad,' Cress said through gritted teeth and tightly clenched jaw. Nobody seemed to understand exactly what she was going through. 'I'm absolutely bloody furious is what I am.'

'Oh . . . I see,' Sophy said, but then both their phones chimed with the same message from Phoebe demanding to know where they were.

Usually, Cress would be inwardly cringing at the thought of incurring Phoebe's wrath. But not today, Satan.

She was waiting for them at the door of the shop, her perfect bob seeming to quiver in the mid-morning heat haze. 'About time,' she said, but all her ire was focused on Sophy. Sometimes there were benefits to being Phoebe's favourite. 'If I knew how to do payroll, I'd be docking your wages.' She turned a less angry face to Cress. 'And how are you?'

Cress sighed. 'I'm all right, I suppose.'

'It's a thing with Colin,' Sophy said so that Cress didn't have to. 'They've maybe broken up and Cress will be taking no further questions at this time.'

'Oh, Cress, I'm so sorry.' Phoebe took hold of Cress's hands so she could awkwardly pull her in for a very stiff hug. 'Most men are absolute trash. You're better off without him. This is why there's very little room in my heart for anything other than vintage dresses and Coco Chanel.'

This was more than Phoebe had revealed about her inner landscape than ever before. Though it seemed as if her inner landscape was quite barren.

'But I'm glad you're all right,' Phoebe continued with a shuddering breath, as if she were maybe remembering the man who had made her conclude that almost every one of his species was trash. 'Now can we talk about the terrible thing that's happened?'

'Oh my God, what?' Sophy asked, stroking Phoebe's stiff arm. 'What's going on?'

'It's awful . . .' Phoebe staggered from the door to one of the shocking-pink sofas in the middle of the shop floor and collapsed on it, like her legs weren't capable of holding her up.

Cress knew a moment of genuine alarm as Phoebe really did seem quite distraught. Maybe she'd had a devastating medical diagnosis and only had months to live? But then Cress looked beyond Phoebe to the back of the shop where Bea was sitting behind the art deco-inspired desk rolling her eyes and mouthing something that Cress couldn't decipher.

'It's Chloe,' Phoebe said at last.

'Has she extended her holiday again?' asked Sophy, who'd also caught Bea's eye-rolling and was now looking less sympathetic.

'She didn't even tell me. She told Freddy.' Phoebe sniffed. 'She's not coming back from her holiday. She's decided to have a career change and train as a social worker. How selfish!'

'Such a terrible person to want to help other people,' Sophy muttered, but Phoebe was too deep into her misery for it to register.

'Right when we're at our busiest,' she said, gesturing with both arms at the shop, which was still devoid of customers at just gone ten and wouldn't start filling up until past eleven. 'How will we cope?'

'It's just as well that I'm here for the foreseeable,' Sophy said cheerfully and with a gleam in her eye as she bustled past the prostrate manageress. With Chloe gone, they were a full-time employee down, so it stood to reason (and probably Freddy) that Sophy could stay on. No wonder Phoebe looked like she was about to go into a full decline.

'It will all work out,' Cress said, and the great thing about Phoebe making this very minor inconvenience all about her was it had really taken Cress's mind off her own heartache. Now, she was itching to get upstairs and get started on her work rather than staying down in the shop and mouthing platitudes at Phoebe.

In fact, she was in the mood for some really intricate repair work that would require all her concentration. They had a thirties wedding dress that needed a lot of beadwork replaced. That would be just the ticket.

'Also,' Phoebe said, as Cress placed her foot on the first step. 'Those film people!'

Cress turned round. In all the drama of the last thirty-six hours, she'd completely forgotten about Ella – hadn't even told Sophy that she'd met her – and Miles, and their hare-brained scheme to have Ella shadow her. Why had she agreed to it?

'What about the film people?' she asked, a tiny flame of hope flickering to life because Phoebe would never agree to it.

'I have to say that sort of request would have been better coming from Jackie Coulter and not some random production assistant . . .'

Hope fizzled on.

'Yeah, about that . . .'

'They seem to think that you're free to simply drop everything and I had to tell them you weren't in no uncertain terms.'

Rather than feeling sorry for herself, now Cress was feeling very sorry for the poor random production assistant who'd had to deal with Phoebe. Still, she was relieved that she wasn't going to have to spend long days with the woman who'd claimed Miles's heart. Not that she wanted Miles's heart herself.

Plus, she wasn't in the market for a new man. Cress didn't know if she was still with her old man, though Colin was going to have to do something pretty bloody spectacular to get back in her good graces. 'I really appreciate that.'

'I said to them, I said, "I'm not having my brides messed around. And I don't care if this actress has been nominated for a BAFTA, she can fit in with us and not the other way round,'" Phoebe recalled grandly.

'Oh, so she is coming in then?' Cress clarified. She hoped that she didn't sound as bitterly disappointed as she felt.

'Tomorrow morning and the first sign that she's getting in the way, then she's out,' Phoebe said, and Cress made a mental note to stay out of Phoebe's way too. There was only so much stress she could cope with.

Chapter Eleven

The day passed in a blur of bridal fittings and beadwork repairs, though it couldn't pass fast enough for Cress. Every bride whom she ministered to, each of them giddy with nerves and expectation, was like salt *and* vinegar being poured directly into her wounds. Plus, she still had plenty of time to think and brood and for her stomach to lurch in dread every time her phone chimed with a message.

The messages were never from Colin, who, true to form, would be in sulk-mode by now. His mother, however, was not.

> Col is so upset about the way you spoke to him. You know how sensitive he is. No point in being too proud to say you're sorry

Obviously Colin had given her a very biased account of why they'd split up. Also, in Mary's eyes, Colin could do no wrong, which actually explained a hell of a lot.

> Now, are you coming to St Ives this weekend?

> Won't be coming to St Ives

Cress had messaged back, fingers trembling, heart racing, at the daring terseness of her reply. She also wanted to say, with every fibre of her being, that she wasn't sorry at all, but she wasn't that brave.

Her heart was still a bit skittish as the day drew to a close and she had just one appointment left. Tanya was coming in for her first session, with her moodboard and also with, Cress hoped, a positive mental attitude, because if Tanya cried again then Cress was sure that she too would cry, possibly while lying full-length on the atelier floor.

But when Tanya came up the stairs, she had a nervous smile on her face, which had to be a good sign. Her blond hair was newly highlighted, she was wearing a pretty blue and white summer dress and lipstick and she generally looked much happier and pulled-together than when Cress had last seen her.

Cress ushered Tanya into the changing room to take her measurements and run through a few ground rules.

'So, this is a safe space,' she said as she wrapped a tape measure round Tanya's waist. 'A place of trust. What happens up here is between you and me. Also, there will be no talk of crash diets or diets of any kind. I'm going to make you the dress of your dreams, not a dress that you'll fit into only if you spend the next few months avoiding carbs and being hangry. OK?'

'OK!' Tanya repeated with an emphatic nod. 'I'm so sorry about what happened last time.'

'Honestly, the amount of tears that have been shed up here, you wouldn't believe,' Cress said. Some of those tears being her own. The week when Sophy had definitely decided that she was going to Australia, possibly for ever, had been a particularly soggy one.

Once she'd taken Tanya's measurements, she led the other woman back into the salon. 'Now, let's sit on the sofa and you can talk me through your moodboard.'

'Yeah, so about the moodboard . . .' Tanya pulled an iPad out of her bright yellow tote with the words My Other Bag Is A Louis Vuitton printed on it. 'When I thought about how I wanted to look at my party – the dress that, in my head, is the perfect dress – well, there was only one contender. Look!'

She handed the iPad to Cress so she could see Tanya's dress of dreams, which looked very, very familiar.

'It's one of the most beautiful dresses in the world,' Cress said with a little sigh as she looked at a picture of Audrey Hepburn in the opening sequence of *Breakfast at Tiffany's*. Audrey was wearing a timeless, elegant, black satin, full-length, sleeveless sheath dress, with cut-outs that gave it almost a racer back. 'You know, Hubert de Givenchy designed two versions of this dress but they both showed a lot of leg and when Audrey Hepburn took them to the studio, Paramount decided that they weren't suitable and they got Edith Head to redesign the lower half.'

'They auctioned one of the three Givenchy versions of the dress in 2006,' Tanya said. 'It went for just shy of five hundred thousand pounds, and as for the other two, the original hand-stitched prototype is in the Givenchy archive and the other one is . . .'

'. . . is on display in a museum in Madrid. Oh, Tanya!'

They clutched each other's hands because it wasn't every day that you met a kindred spirit.

'You get me. You really get me,' Tanya said, raising Cress's hand so she could kiss it. 'Except, I can't go sleeveless. That's an absolute deal-breaker.'

'Audrey did have those black gloves that went past the elbow.'

Tanya held out her arm and shook it. Then slapped the underside of said arm. 'It's the bit past the elbow that I'm worried about. My bingo wings don't feature too highly in my plans for my fiftieth birthday party,' she said, and Cress wasn't going to argue. She longed to be full of body positivity and most times she was, except when she was having a weak moment and contemplating her own upper arms.

'I could do you a sleeve in black gauze, but you've got gorgeous shoulders so I think we should still have the cut-outs at the back,' Cress decided, gazing at the iPad screen and then at Tanya.

'As long as I can wear a bra. Most of the dresses I've tried on were completely backless. Who are these people designing for?'

They both shook their heads. 'I haven't been braless since I was thirteen,' Cress said with a shudder at the thought of being forced into a backless dress. She opened her sketch pad and uncapped her favourite Muji black fibre tip pen. 'Now, what are your legs like? They look pretty good to me.'

Tanya raised the hem of her dress to reveal toned calves and very shapely ankles, one of which she now rotated. 'Well, people do say that they're my best feature.'

'I love the opening sequence of *Breakfast at Tiffany's* but Audrey Hepburn was really having to hobble in that skirt. So I say that we honour Monsieur de Givenchy's original design by flashing a little leg. After all, there was a very elegant side slit in the version Audrey wore in the film poster,' Cress said as she began to sketch out the black dress that was going to make Tanya the belle of any ball that she attended.

'The thing is though that Audrey Hepburn was tiny and ...' Tanya gazed down at her figure, which to Cress's eyes was very trim ... 'And I'm not tiny.'

'I'm designing this dress for you, not for Audrey Hepburn,' Cress said firmly. 'You have to trust me. You're going to look amazing.'

It was odd. Cress had so much doubt and uncertainty in so many other aspects of her life but when it came to patterns and cutting out fabric and stitching the pieces together, she always had faith in herself.

'Actually, I do trust you,' Tanya said, sounding surprised. 'Which is weird because I have serious trust issues. Though who wouldn't if they'd been with my fella for as long as I have.'

'Hear hear! Men will always let you down, but a little black dress will always be there for you.' They hadn't even heard Phoebe come up the stairs but there she was suddenly, standing over them and looking down at the iPad and Cress's sketch pad. Coco Chanel had managed to clamber onto the sofa next to Cress and was also casting a critical eye over her very rudimentary design.

Now Cress was suddenly seized with uncertainty. You could never get away with an inferior little black dress on Phoebe's watch – but, miracles of miracles, she was nodding in approval.

'Very nice. It's a pity that your budget won't stretch to a pearl and diamond necklace like that,' Phoebe said a little wistfully.

'My stepsister, her boyfriend deals in costume jewellery. I'm sure he can sort something out for you,' Cress promised rashly and ten minutes later, when Tanya left, it was with a wide smile that could no longer be described as nervous.

Cress had been dreading the end of the day with nothing to look forward to but going home to brood, but, as soon as she'd shut the door behind Tanya, she was waylaid by Sophy.

'Any plans for tonight?' she asked as she vacuumed under one of the sofas.

'I'm going to drown my sorrows with a Calippo or three,' Cress replied because there was no point in pretending otherwise.

'Or, just a thought, I have an absolute craving for dim sum, turns out my mum and Mike do too. I'm going to meet them at that fancy new Chinese place off Parkway in half an hour if you fancy it,' Sophy said very, very casually, but with a shrill top note so that Cress knew that there was nothing casual about this sudden excursion for dumplings and spare ribs. 'Because, you know, when I'm feeling down, there is nothing like a hug from your dad.'

This was very true. Cress's dad, Sophy's stepdad, Mike gave the best of hugs. There was no way that you could be in his arms and not feel safe and secure.

'I could be tempted by a steamed pork bun,' Cress said just as casually.

'Great, I'll buy you ten of them,' Sophy said and it was a done deal.

Half an hour later, Cress walked through the door of the Happy Bun and straight into her dad's arms. She'd sworn that she wouldn't but, as soon as he was squeezing her tight and she got that comforting scent of Old Spice and Imperial Leather soap, she started crying all over again.

'It will all come out in the wash,' Mike murmured in Cress's ear as he stroked soothing circles on her back.

There was no point in trying to do anything with her face, not even put her big black sunglasses back on, because it was hard to use chopsticks if you couldn't see what you were doing. So Cress sat down, still sniffing, Sophy and Mike on either side of her and Caroline, her stepmum, sitting opposite.

Caroline had her lips pursed tight, in the exact same way that Sophy did when she was about to sound off about something.

'I'm going to say it,' she announced, though Cress couldn't imagine what she was going to say. Knowing Caroline, it was bound to be an unintentionally amusing rant about someone who'd dared to displease her. She was in a two-years-and-running feud with the people who lived opposite them because they'd once tried to nick their wheelie bin.

Frankly, Cress could do with the distraction, but Sophy rolled her eyes and put a warning hand on her mother's arm.

'Don't say it!'

Caroline exhaled through her nose like a furious little dragon. 'I'm going to say it. I have to.'

'Oh God, Cress, I'm so sorry.' Sophy sighed. 'You know what she's like.'

'Caroline's lovely,' Cress said, because it was true. She and Sophy both regularly agreed that, when it came to step-parents and being a blended family, they'd won the lottery.

'Thank you, my darling, and you're lovely too,' Caroline said. 'Which is why . . .'

'Here she goes . . .'

'Yes, here I go, Sophy. Cress is lovely and you know what, I *never* liked that Colin. Never! Me and your dad always thought that he'd done nothing to deserve you and, quite frankly, you're better off without him.'

Chapter Twelve

The next day, Friday, was another day when Cress would have much preferred to stay in bed, the covers over her head.

But it was thirty-five degrees in the shade, far too hot to be mouldering between her sheets. The Northern line was unpleasantly sticky, and, when Cress met Sophy outside Chalk Farm station, both of their faces were glistening and their dresses already damp and crumpled.

'Horses sweat, men perspire and women barely glow,' Phoebe insisted as they spent their first five minutes on the clock standing in front of the big tower fan on the shop floor.

Despite the heatwave, Phoebe was still maintaining a crisp, form-fitting black dress, seamed stockings and heels, without a hint of puffy ankle, and a face full of impeccably applied make-up, though by lunchtime even her perfectly flicked eyeliner would be melting at the corners.

'I don't think she's even human,' Bea hissed as she sat behind the cash desk wafting an ornamental fan at her face. Phoebe had gone upstairs, so she was out of earshot.

As Cress set herself up for the day ahead, the skylight blinds pulled down but her workroom already stifling, she was already dreading her first fitting appointment; a very petulant teenage girl with an eighteenth-birthday party looming who wanted Cress to destroy a perfectly lovely silver lamé vintage dress, so it was short and tight 'and I look really hot on the 'gram.'

Just as she was scooping up her hair into a loose bun, she heard voices in the atelier and couldn't help but sigh heavily at the prospect of the day ahead.

'Cress?' Phoebe called out and, with a very uncharacteristic scowl on her face, Cress hurried into the main salon to find Phoebe with a tall woman who very much wasn't a petulant teenage girl.

She had her blond hair scraped back from her face and was wearing a loose blue dress, which even to Cress's non-judgemental eyes was very dowdy, and a pair of flat sandals that looked like they provided a lot of orthopaedic support and absolutely no style points whatsoever.

Cress was amazed that Phoebe had even let her breach the borders of the atelier – she was very fussy about who gained admittance to the inner sanctum – but Phoebe seemed very nervous, her hands fluttering at her sides.

'You remember that Ella is here for the day?' she said, her voice high-pitched and breathless.

'Ella?' Cress stared back at her blankly.

'Except, I've decided as I'm incognito that I should go by another name. I was thinking Jane. I'm sure there are some lovely Janes, Jane Austen for example, but it is a name that fades into the background,' the woman said in plummy tones that were kind of familiar but also kind of not.

'The film . . . you agreed to let Ella, I mean Jane, shadow you,' Phoebe prompted.

Cress blinked. Even her eyelashes felt sweaty. 'Oh my goodness, I didn't recognise you,' she blurted out.

Rather than taking offence, Ella grinned. 'I dimmed the star power, darling, and have come as a humble sewing intern.' Then she drew herself up to her full height, though Cress wasn't even aware that she'd been slouching, put her hands on her hips and shook back her head and then, despite the dowdy clothes, she was unmistakeably a BAFTA-winning actress and brand ambassador for a skincare line. 'And who is this gorgeous creature?' she added, her attention caught by Coco Chanel, who was in her usual summer position, on her back in front of a fan, stumpy legs splayed out so her belly and bits could get a good airing.

'That's Coco Chanel,' Phoebe said proudly. 'The most beautiful creature to ever grace the shop.'

That was really overstating Coco Chanel's very singular looks. In the wrong kind of light she looked more like a gremlin, but Ella cooed over her, and Phoebe was all smiles when she went back downstairs.

'So, you're here to shadow me,' Cress said a little helplessly. 'I've never been shadowed before so I'm not sure where to start.'

'Have you got any sixties dresses up here? That might be a good place to begin,' Ella suggested, and Cress took her into the side room full of their more expensive dresses so she could pull out a few samples.

The orange wool Courrèges dress, a brightly coloured, floaty Pucci mini and finally the jewel in their current collection: a Geoffrey Beene gunmetal and silver metallic silk lurex evening gown, which featured a multitude of handsewn silver metal studs and rhinestones scattered across the front and with an attached cape for full dramatic impact when its wearer walked into a room.

The very same dress that her first appointment of the day seemed to think Cress was going to turn into a micro-mini dress with spaghetti straps, she found herself telling Ella. Now that Cress wasn't fluttering with nerves around her, Ella was the sort of person that you ended up confiding in.

'So am I right in thinking that the film's set in swinging London and will be all about paper dresses and mini skirts?'

'Not so much!' Ella said, perched on the countertop, long legs swinging. 'In *Beat!*, to start with Julie, my character, is a model for a fashion house and it's all very staid and boring and parading stiff dresses to hatchet-faced dowagers and debutantes. She yearns to break free. So how, does *that*,' she gestured at one of the bolts of fabric on the shelf above her heads, 'become *that*?' And she indicated a delicate thirties, bias-cut wedding dress on Cress's dress form.

Cress tried to take Ella through the basics – from design to pattern to cutting to stitching – in between fittings, where Ella stuck to the sidelines as Jane, her dowdy, quiet alter ego. But the information didn't seem to be going in.

'What's the difference between centimetres and inches? The script is all in inches, it's very confusing,' she said at one point, but her eyes glazed over as Cress tried to explain about decimalisation, which had happened in 1973, and why a film set in the sixties would be using the old imperial measures.

'I really thought this was going to be like *The Great British Sewing Bee* and by the end of the day I'd be able to make a simple shift dress,' Ella announced sadly as they broke for lunch.

Ella seemed to be flagging, but, when she came back an hour late from lunch with her agent in a very exclusive Primrose Hill restaurant that Cress had never been to, she was newly energised and enthusiastic.

'The thing is, I just need to *look* like I know what I'm doing,' she said. 'Can I have a go at cutting up some material?'

She made a grab for a very expensive white silk brocade that Cress had specially ordered for a dress she pretty much needed to recreate rather than renovate.

'Do not *touch* the fabric,' she gritted in a voice that she didn't even know she possessed. It was a very scary voice that had even the irrepressible Ella backing away.

'Sorry!' she trilled.

'I'm sure you didn't learn to act overnight,' Cress began in more conciliatory tones.

'Well, I didn't really need to learn, darling. I got my first job in an ad for nappies when I was still in nappies. Apparently, I was a natural.'

'Well, sewing, fashion design, needs to be taught. You're meant to be shadowing me, so I want you to sit behind me while I put a new zipper in this green cocktail dress, and you can ask me questions but *you're not to touch anything.*'

Cress couldn't remember the last time that she'd been so stern with someone. Though it had probably only been a couple of days ago when she'd been screaming at Colin. At least with Ella taking all her time and attention, she hadn't thought about Colin for a good couple of hours.

Ella was on her best behaviour, though Cress couldn't help feeling that she was *acting* as if she was on her best behaviour. She watched intently as Cress replaced the zip, then turned her attention to a cotton summer dress from downstairs that needed re-hemming.

'Normally I'd hand-stitch a hem as it's the only way to make sure that the stitches are as invisible as possible but as this is such a busy pattern and I'll be sewing black on black, I'm going to do it on the machine,' Cress explained as she shook out the dress, which featured random items of fruit on a black background.

She could feel Ella's breath warm on the back of her neck as she watched Cress attach the black thread to her bobbin. 'Oh God, even that looks really hard.'

'It was much harder in the sixties when they didn't have state-of-the-art sewing machines and a computer-calibrated dial for setting the tension,' Cress told her and Ella groaned in what sounded like genuine despair.

Because she'd done so well during what had to be quite a boring day for a famous actress, Cress let Ella sew the last few centimetres of hem. 'Slow and steady. We're not aiming for speed,' she said, her hand on Ella's shoulder ready to wrest the woman away from her sewing machine if she decided to go rogue.

'I've got, like, proper first-night nerves in my tummy,' Ella gasped as she sewed the hem at a snail's pace. 'Look at me though! I'm actually sewing!' There was a pause and a sigh. 'Somehow I thought this would be more thrilling.'

When yet another bride came in for yet another fitting, Cress left Ella in the workroom with a metre of scrap material so she could practise stitches. As she pinned and made notes, she was on high alert for any odd noises coming from the workroom, like grinding or shrieking as Ella forced the sewing machine to do things that it couldn't really do, but all was well.

By now, it was nearly five. No more appointments and Cress expected Ella to push off, but she seemed happy to stay and even steam-pressed the black cotton dress under Cress's eagle eye.

When she wasn't putting her sweaty hands on expensive lengths of fabric, Ella was excellent company. All Cress had to do was name an actor and she had a piece of scurrilous gossip on them.

'. . . and that's why she's blacklisted from every branch of Cash Converters in the country,' she said of a national treasure. 'Miles worked on her last film, a period piece, and he said that they pretty much had to nail down everything on set and, even then, she tried to steal a pair of Chinese vases that were on loan from a museum.'

'No! I always thought there was something shifty about her,' Cress said in shocked delight. At the mention of Miles's name, she got a fluttery feeling that was nothing like the fluttery feeling she got when she thought of Colin. 'Have you known Miles long?'

'Quite long. About twelve years. We did a film together while he was still at drama school,' Ella revealed, to Cress's surprise.

'Miles was an actor?'

'In the loosest possible sense of the word. I love Miles to pieces but he couldn't act his way out of a paper bag. Then a few years ago I shared a flat with his now ex-girlfriend, but then we did a play together at the Royal Court and living with her and working with her too absolutely did my head in.'

Ella didn't know the meaning of discretion and, even though she knew it was wrong, Cress was here for it. 'So, you guys only date in the profession? Like, Miles only dates actors and film people.'

'I think Miles swore off dating actors after that.' Ella grinned, a mischievous glint in her dark eyes. 'I suppose it can be quite hard to be in a relationship with someone who always has to be the main character, quite literally. His last girlfriend worked for a branding agency and was very into yoga. It didn't last long though. She kept wanting Miles to get up at the crack of dawn to meet the new day with sun salutes, and he'd much rather have stayed in bed.'

Who could blame him? Not Cress, though she did feel a bit guilty that she was mining for gossip on Miles, especially as she was taken. Except, she didn't actually know what her relationship status was currently.

She and Colin were in uncharted waters. They were either still in a fight or broken up. Had she even really wanted to break up with him?

Cress was so used to thinking of herself as one half of a couple. She'd never had to worry about the relationship side of her life before, and could concentrate on growing her side business and finding time to read the allotted book for her book group. She didn't want to be single, which felt a lot like being adrift—

'Cress! I said, what about you? A gorgeous girl like you must have been scooped up ages ago.'

She snapped back from her introspective thoughts to find Ella looking at her with a keen and strangely perceptive look on her face.

'Actually, it's complicated,' Cress said, and it was the first time she'd explained her new relationship status to someone who didn't know her long and involved history with Colin and might just label Cress as single. Also, emotionally quite fragile. 'We've been together for fifteen years but apparently he doesn't want to settle down. After fifteen years it's not unreasonable to want your boyfriend to care more about you than his record collection, right?'

'Absolutely,' Ella said with feeling. 'My last-but-one boyfriend was a musician and he definitely loved his Fender Jaguar guitar more than me.'

'Oh, Colin isn't a musician, he works in IT.' Cress couldn't help but sigh at the thought of Colin in his underground bunker stroke office at the bank, staring at his monitors or whatever he did all day. Was he thinking about her? Or was he just in a mega-sulk because he'd revised and twisted the facts so that he felt as if he were the injured party? Or was he even relieved that Cress had given him an out by breaking up with him?

'Well, that sounds very dull. My boyfriend runs a cheese shop in Borough Market,' Ella revealed. 'We both love his Gouda with truffles more than we love each other, so it's worked out quite well. Are we done for the day?'

Cress nodded. 'We are. Feel free to head off and if you want to come back . . .'

'Of course I'm coming back,' Ella exclaimed, jumping down from the worktop. 'I'm still terrified of handling your sewing machine and I'm yet to be able to sew a completely straight line. I think I've got quite a long way to go until I can give a convincing performance as a fashion designer.'

Ella followed Cress down the spiral stairs, chattering away about how long it had taken her to learn to ride a horse.

'Sitting astride the beast was hard enough but they wanted me to ride side-saddle, it was for a period film, you see . . .'

In the shop the last customer of the day was having their purchase, an egg-yolk yellow fifties summer dress with a foofy skirt, carefully wrapped up by Sophy, who would then cash up. Anita was sweeping the floor. Bea was returning discarded dresses from the changing rooms back onto the rails. All was being overseen by an eagle-eyed Phoebe, who never missed a thing.

'No, Bea, that dress should go two dresses down on the rail. It's more of a fondant pink than a sherbet pink,' she said sharply.

All their dresses were arranged by colour, which looked fantastic on Instagram but was quite a nightmare to maintain, especially as Phoebe had very strong ideas vis-à-vis fondant pink and sherbet pink.

'This all looks very industrious,' Ella remarked now that she'd come to the end of her horse-riding story. 'Can I help?'

She didn't sound as if she wanted to help, and it wasn't as if she was on the payroll. 'No, you're all right,' Cress said, as the bell above the door tinkled and someone came in.

'We're closed!' Sophy and Anita all but shouted in unison.

Miles paused. One foot in the shop, one foot outside. 'Oh. Sorry.'

'No, they didn't mean you. You may enter,' Phoebe decreed.

Miles put both his feet in the shop. 'Happened to be passing.'

'Really?' Ella frowned. 'I thought you said you were spending the day doing pre-production stuff in Soho.'

Although he was wearing his usual dark glasses, Miles took them off so he could scowl more effectively at Ella. 'I spent the day doing that and now it's six o'clock and, as I said, I just happened to be passing and I thought I'd see how you were getting on.'

'Oh really, did you? How . . . kind of you.' Ella flung herself down on one of the pink sofas but in her usual elegant, long-limbed manner. 'I'm getting along fine, aren't I, Cress? Haven't managed to break anything or rip any antique dresses.'

Both Cress and Phoebe winced at the notion of any of their dresses being torn. It was odd but, all of a sudden, Cress didn't know what to do with her body. Her legs were crossed at the ankle, like she desperately needed a wee, and she was flexing her hands like she was gearing up for a marathon sewing session. 'It's been a very productive day. Ella even did some sewing,' she said. Her voice was also behaving oddly and sounding as if she'd just scaled the heights of Kilimanjaro.

'Very wonky sewing, but still . . .' Ella said.

Miles nodded. He also seemed as if he didn't know what to do with himself now that he was over the threshold. 'Right, then. Oh, sorry,' he said, to their last customer, who was now trying to leave the shop only to find Miles blocking the path to the door.

For want of anything better to do, Cress scurried for the safety of behind the till, where Sophy was now cashing up. Partially obscured by her stepsister, she could sneak a proper look at Miles, who was wearing jeans and a black and white striped t-shirt. His dark hair was still messy, like he (or someone else) had been running their fingers through it, and he was still long and lean and made Cress not know what to do with herself.

If only she could think of something to say. Something funny or clever.

It was as if now that Miles was here there was an awkward atmosphere and no one knew what to say. Miles stood near the door, arms folded. Bea's focus was on the last dresses to be returned to their rails, Anita now had the hoover out and Phoebe was frowning. Ella seemed to find the awkwardness amusing. The only person unaffected was Sophy, who was murmuring numbers under her breath as she attacked the keys of a big calculator. Then she tucked all the card slips in a plastic seal-top bag and looked up.

'Right then. Just going to put the cash in the safe, then I'm gasping for a gin and tonic. Who's coming to the pub?' she asked.

'God yes, pub!' Anita agreed. Even Phoebe was nodding.

It was a shop tradition that, after closing on a Friday, they all decamped to The Hat and Fan, just round the corner. Even though he was still in Australia and giving no indication that he might come back to London soon, Johnno kept a tab open for them behind the bar.

With a shy look at Ella, who seemed to have forgotten all about her role as insignificant Jane, Bea pointed the vacuum hose at her. 'Do you want to come to the pub?'

'My goodness, nothing would give me greater pleasure,' Ella said as if she was receiving an award. 'Pub, Miles?'

Miles shrugged. 'Yeah. I mean, why not?'

Chapter Thirteen

And so, with two new additions, The Vintage Dress Shop staff relocated to The Hat and Fan. It seemed as if half of Primrose Hill was standing outside the Victorian pub, clutching glasses and bottles slick with condensation, chattering happily now that work was done and the promise of the weekend stretched out before them.

Because most customers had spilled out onto the pavement, inside the pub it wasn't elbow room only as it usually was on a Friday evening. They snagged their favourite corner, two red velvet banquettes at right angles, and Phoebe despatched Anita and Bea to the bar with their order. 'Don't forget a bowl of water for Coco Chanel. But it has to be filtered. She won't drink tap water.'

'For a dog who'll eat any rancid scraps of food she finds on a walk, Coco Chanel is very fussy about what she'll drink,' Sophy explained in a whisper to Ella. Coco Chanel had also recognised Ella's star power, or maybe she was just jealous of the attention that a BAFTA winner might steal from her, but either way she was sitting next to Ella and, every time Ella tried to speak, she put a warning paw on her leg.

'She's quite terrifying, isn't she?' Ella whispered back, then turned her attention to Cress, who was just about to sit down in the opposite corner. 'No, Cress, come and sit next to me so we can talk about fashion, and Miles, you sit next to Cress, because you need to know about the fashion too.'

'You are *so* bossy,' Miles said, but he did as Ella asked and sat down next to Cress, who was very conscious that it was the end of the day and she felt unkempt and sticky. There hadn't even been time to assess how mop-like her hair was in the mirror before they left the shop and now, when she ran her fingers through her curls, they got stuck halfway.

'How did you manage to put up with her for several hours?' Miles asked.

'Oh, it was fine,' Cress said. She could feel the heat of his body, much more pleasant than the heat of the day that hung oppressively in the air. He also smelled very nice. Fresh and clean, but salty and woody too. Whatever aftershave he wore, it smelled expensive, understated.

'She was the perfect pupil.'

'I had a good teacher. Apart from the bit where you shouted at me for trying to put my grubby mitts on some fabric . . .'

'I don't believe for one second that Cress shouted at you,' Miles said with a conspiratorial sideways look at Cress, who was rolling her eyes at Ella's exaggerations.

'I spoke firmly,' she clarified.

'I bet you did shout,' Sophy said, pulling a stool nearer so she could join in the conversation. 'Once I bunged some of my vintage dresses on a standard cotton wash in the machine and you properly yelled at me. You nearly dropped the f-bomb.'

'I absolutely did not,' Cress insisted, though she had been very strident in her opinion that, if you were going to wash a vintage dress in a washing machine, then it needed to be on a delicates cycle and no hotter than thirty degrees.

She looked up gratefully to see Anita and Bea approaching with two laden trays.

They dispensed their wares. A bottle of lager for Miles, gin and tonic for Ella and Sophy, gin and slimline tonic – not from the mixer tap but from a bottle, with a slice of lime, not lemon – for Phoebe . . . 'and a vodka and elderflower tonic for you, Cress.'

'I thought you didn't drink,' Miles said.

'Yeah, I thought you didn't drink either.' Sophy gave Cress a surprised look, though she knew that Cress did drink. Or rather, as well as her Sunday evening cocktail in a can, occasionally she had a glass of white wine with dinner if she was in a restaurant. And *very* occasionally, when it was hot and she'd had a hell of a week and she was feeling kind of restless, then she might fancy an after-work drink that contained some alcohol. It wasn't a crime.

'Well, clearly you don't know everything about me,' Cress said, taking a sip of her drink, which was delicious and also so full of ice that surely it watered down any alcohol in it.

'I'm pretty sure that I do,' Sophy insisted. 'Like, I know that you can't eat fresh pineapple because it gives you terrible indigestion but you're all right with tinned pineapple.'

'That's kind of random,' Miles said and, while Cress appreciated how deeply embedded Sophy was in her life, she would also have liked to have had some mystery in front of Miles. Not have him think of her as a woman who needed to down a bottle of Gaviscon before eating a small tub of fresh pineapple. 'I don't do well with tropical fruit either. Pineapple, mango, kiwi; they all make my lips and tongue itchy.'

'Miles and his allergies. He's the male, twenty-first-century equivalent of a Victorian woman on a fainting couch,' said Ella – or tried to say, as Coco Chanel was now pressing her paw against Ella's mouth.

'Not true. I'm actually darkly dangerous and very sexy,' Miles said. Ella actually guffawed at this, though Cress had never heard anyone guffaw in real life before. Maybe it was something they taught at acting school. 'We shouldn't have to put up with this kind of slanderous talk, Cress.'

'We really shouldn't,' Cress agreed, clinking her glass against Miles's bottle of lager. 'Are you all right being so close to Coco Chanel?'

'Allergic to cats, OK with dogs as long as they don't shed too much,' Miles said with a self-deprecating grin.

Meanwhile Coco Chanel had stopped pawing Ella and had instead begun wiggling her entire body and making high-pitched snuffling noises. Her nose was an arrow quivering in the direction of Freddy, who'd just walked through the door.

Although Coco Chanel merely tolerated the presence of most people, treating them more as servants than anything else, she loved Phoebe – and she *really* loved Freddy. Though nobody was brave enough to point that out to Phoebe.

'Everyone all right for drinks?' Freddy asked when he reached their table. 'Hello, beautiful,' he added to Coco Chanel, who was up on her back legs, front legs wildly pedalling, until he picked her up.

Behind Freddy was Charles, Sophy's boyfriend, looking cool and knife-crease sharp in his cream-coloured suit. Sophy hadn't noticed him, but when Charles tucked a stray strand of her hair behind her ear she turned round on her stool, and she smiled. Not just a stretching of her lips, Sophy seemed to smile with her whole face; everything about her looked softer, even prettier.

Charles smiled back and he was looking fairly smitten too.

Cress couldn't even remember anyone, but especially Colin, looking at her like that. She was also quite sure that she'd never been so pleased, so happy, so right-in-the-world to see another person. She couldn't help but sigh, which made Freddy, who now had Coco Chanel tucked under his arm like a football, nudge her.

'No need to be so sad about finishing your drink. I'll get you another one. What you having?'

One alcoholic drink was Cress's limit. Especially when it was so long since lunch and lunch had been a heat-wilted salad and then a Solero.

She handed Freddy her glass. 'Same again, please. Vodka and elderflower tonic, lots of ice.'

When Freddy came back with more drinks, he and Charles were quickly subsumed into their little group, along with Phoebe, who took Coco Chanel out of Freddy's arms and made the dog sit on her lap. It turned out that Charles, who seemed to know everyone, had met Ella several times before, and Freddy and Phoebe were having a hissed conversation, which left just Miles and Cress to make small talk between themselves.

It wasn't hard. Though often Cress could get tongue-tied with strangers, she'd met Miles several times now and, although she was far from even tipsy, two – no make that three, because Charles had gone to the bar again – vodka and elderflower tonics *with a lot of ice* had loosened her up.

They mostly talked about films, or rather their favourite clothes in films, a conversation that Cress was only too happy to have. She even confessed to Miles that one of the first dresses she'd ever made was inspired by the scene in *The Sound of Music* where Maria fashions play clothes for the von Trapp children from several pairs of gold brocade curtains. 'Except I used an eighties floral duvet cover, then walked around in public in the skirt I made from it.'

'Can't be as bad as the leather jacket I bought after a month spent watching James Dean in *Rebel Without a Cause* on repeat,' Miles said. 'I saved up all my summer job money from working in an industrial laundry – don't ask, it was awful – but all I could afford was a jacket made from pleather, which later melted when I left it on the radiator.'

It was one of the most soul-satisfying chats Cress had had in a long time. She even got to tell Miles about the dress she was making for Tanya inspired by *Breakfast at Tiffany's* and how when Audrey Hepburn had died, Tiffany's had taken out an ad in *The New York Times* wishing goodbye to their 'huckleberry friend'. It was a little story that Cress had retold countless times and, each time, she cried.

This Friday night was no exception. By now, Phoebe and Coco Chanel had left, quickly followed by Freddy. Anita and Bea had gone into town, thrilled to be accompanied by Ella, and it was just Cress and Miles and Sophy and Charles, the last men standing.

'Their huckleberry friend,' Cress said again with a sniff. 'Like in the song "Moon River".'

'That is all kinds of beautiful,' Miles said, his eyes on Cress's now tearstained face as she tried to get rid of the lump in her throat by taking a big gulp of her drink.

'Why are you crying, Cress?' Sophy's voice was a sharp distraction.

Cress waved her away with a vague, fluttering hand. 'Huckleberry friend,' she muttered, because Sophy had heard the huckleberry friend story many times. Usually she had tissues on hand, but not this evening.

'Is that the only reason why you're crying?' Sophy asked gently.

Cress, with a put-upon sigh, turned to where her sister-friend was sitting on her other side. 'Yes. Why else would I be crying?'

She turned back to Miles, a far more pleasing sight than the concerned expression on Sophy's face.

'I always get a bit tearful when I'm watching *Casablanca*,' Miles said, because, unlike certain men of Cress's acquaintance, he was emotionally intelligent and in touch with his feelings.

'The bit where Rick makes Ilsa get on board the plane to Lisbon?' She might not have watched *Casablanca* as many times as she'd watched *Breakfast at Tiffany's* or even *The Sound of Music*, but she knew the film well.

Miles shook his head. 'No, it's the bit where they're in Rick's Bar and the Nazi soldiers are bellowing their way through a patriotic anthem and Laszlo, Ilsa's husband, orders the band to play "La Marseillaise" and everyone in the club starts singing and drowns out the Germans.'

'It's so stirring, it just really gets you in the feels,' Cress hiccupped because now she was tearing up again just thinking about it.

'But it's more than that. A lot of extras in *Casablanca*, in that scene, were actual French refugees, torn away from their homeland,' Miles explained. Now it was his turn for his voice to become thick with emotion. 'They didn't know what had happened to the people they'd left behind, if they'd ever see them or France again, so when they sing "La Marseillaise", their national anthem, they sing it with their hearts and souls.'

Cress was properly crying now. All those poor people. Completely uprooted. Not knowing what their future might be because it wasn't the future they'd expected. 'So sad,' she spluttered.

'Oh Cress, I didn't mean to make you cry.' Miles took her hand and, when that didn't have any discernible effect on Cress's tear ducts, he tried to brush the tears that were streaming down her face away with his thumb.

'You're such a nice person,' Cress told him, her hand reaching up to touch his face too. She could trace the line of his cheekbone with the tip of her finger. His skin was as soft as old, worn velvet.

'What's that about velvet?' Miles asked and Cress realised that she might have said the last bit out loud.

'Nothing. It's just your skin is so soft and you're so kind and you don't mind when I talk about fashion,' Cress said, holding Miles's hand tighter when it seemed as if he was about to let go of her.

'Well, I'll come to you next time I need a reference.' Miles had stopped looking at Cress's face, which was probably just as well as she was still crying softly. Now he glanced down at all the empty glasses on the table in front of them. 'Let's get another drink. I think probably you need some water. Yes, lots of water.'

'I'd quite like another vodka and elderflower tonic,' Cress insisted with a surreptitious look at Sophy but, *quelle surprise*, she and Charles were now snogging away.

It had been ages since Cress had snogged or been snogged. Proper, desperate, I'll-die-if-I-don't-know-the-touch-of-your-mouth-on-mine kissing. Probably not since she was an actual teenager, and even then Colin hadn't been keen on public displays of affection and Cress had been so shy.

Then again, even now Colin would never hold her hand when they walked down the street, or say that she looked nice, or save up for a future together.

All the things that Cress deserved.

'OK, I'm going to get you some water,' Miles said, trying to tug his hand free again, but Cress clung on to his fingers, all the better to slide her hand up his arm, then across his chest, his *firm* chest, so she could gather up – 'I really think you need some water, Cress' – a fistful of black and white striped cotton to bring him nearer to her so she could lean forward and try to mash her lips against his.

Cress wasn't a robot. She needed passion. She needed feeling. She needed Miles to kiss her.

She needed it so much that it was a while before she realised that Miles had his face turned away and was holding himself very still and the hands on her arms weren't there to pull her closer but to try to hold her back.

Slowly, very slowly, Cress retreated. She stopped trying to get at Miles's stiff and unresponsive mouth, removed her hands from his chest and slid back on the seat so there was a respectable amount of distance between them.

She slid so far that she made contact with Sophy, who wasn't kissing Charles any more and, when Cress turned her head, who was looking at her as if she was spewing ectoplasm from her nostrils.

'What *are* you doing, Cress?' she asked in scandalised tones.

'No, it's all right. Everything's cool,' Miles said quickly, standing up. 'I'm going to get Cress some water. I'm going to get everybody some water.'

It was then that Cress realised that all the crying she'd done before was just a dress rehearsal, because now she rallied for the real performance.

Big, ugly tears. The biggest, ugliest of all the tears.

It was all a bit of a blur after that. Or maybe it was because all Cress could mostly think about when she tried to replay the events of the evening was forcing herself on Miles.

She could remember standing outside The Hat and Fan crying all over Sophy as a lairy drunk man tried to pat her back as he told her, 'Cheer up, love, it might never happen.'

Then crying all over Sophy in an Uber on the way home.

And still crying all over Sophy as Sophy explained in hushed tones what had happened to Diane, who'd come down to answer the door as Cress couldn't find her keys.

She was still *still* crying as Sophy made her drink three massive glasses of water because 'You'll thank me in the morning,' washed her face, turned on the fan, then snuggled up to Cress as they lay on top of the covers of Cress's bed.

It was too hot to snuggle but Cress didn't even care.

Chapter Fourteen

Cress woke up early. It wasn't even five o'clock but the sun was bright and pouring in everywhere and she really needed several more glasses of water and also she really felt like she might die.

Sophy was fast asleep and didn't even stir as Cress came back to bed after a litre of water and a couple of paracetamol, which felt like they wouldn't even touch the sides of the headache that was already making its presence known. Her mouth felt like the driest place on Earth and she was never going to be able to get back to sleep.

Every time she shut her eyes, everything seemed to lurch in a very unpleasant way. But the horrible feeling in her stomach was no match for the horrible images that assaulted Cress when she thought about how she'd thrown herself at Miles, while he'd quite rightly shunned her drunken advances.

Oh, the shame! How Cress longed for a swift and painless death!

But it wasn't to be. Somehow she did manage to go back to sleep but it wasn't for very long because soon she was woken up by Sophy gently tugging her arm.

'Darling sister-friend, it's eight thirty, you really do have to get up,' she said softly. 'Also, can I borrow some clean clothes? I was meant to be staying the night at Charles's where I have a drawer.'

'Oh no. And yes, of course.'

Cress's head was properly thumping now, like a tiny person had a jackhammer jabbing into her skull, and she also felt like she was going to throw up if she made any sudden movements.

'Just think how much worse you'd be feeling if I hadn't made you drink all that water,' Sophy said as she investigated the contents of Cress's wardrobe. 'I know you probably feel terrible on so many different levels . . .'

'Many, many different levels . . .'

'But you will feel better if you have a shower and maybe something to eat.'

It was the thought of putting something, anything, into her mouth that did it.

Cress jackknifed off the bed, threw open the door and ran for the bathroom, almost knocking Aaron down the stairs in the process.

Then she threw up mouthful after mouthful of bile, which didn't make her feel any better but made her cry again, as Diane appeared to hold her hair back and rub circles on her back.

'I'm never drinking again,' Cress moaned as her mother wiped her face with a damp flannel.

'I think you're the only person to ever say that after a night on the sauce . . .'

'Oh God, don't mention sauce . . .'

'And to actually mean it,' Diane said. Probably because Cress had reached the age of thirty-one without ever being drunk and hungover (though surely this couldn't *just* be a hangover, because nothing that run-of-the-mill could feel quite this bloody awful), she didn't sound very angry. 'Clean your teeth, have a shower. You'll feel better.'

There was another hairy moment when Cress first wedged her toothbrush into her mouth, but she was pleased to wash the awful acid taste away. Then she had a very wobbly shower and though she still felt as if she might die quite soon, at least she'd be clean.

She staggered back to her room, where Sophy was once again contemplating Cress's wardrobe.

'You have so many dresses and I've hardly ever seen you wear any of them!' she said as Cress lay back down on the bed with a tiny, anguished groan. 'What are you saving them for?'

'I just like having them close at hand,' Cress said. 'I'm not the sort of person who wears vintage dresses. Everyone would look at me.'

'Only because they'd think you looked good and weren't in the same Zara dress as every other woman,' Sophy enthused as she rattled the hangers in a very loud and very unnecessary way. 'I'm going to wear this, and I might not even give it back.'

Cress peeled her eyes open to see Sophy holding up a sleeveless fifties sundress featuring mint-green flowers scattered on a white background.

'Let's pick you out a nice dress too. I always feel great when I'm wearing something gorgeous. This red dress would look good on you, especially with your tan.'

'Going to wear one of my smocks.'

Except Sophy had other ideas and Cress didn't have the strength to argue with her. Ten minutes later she came down the stairs in the red dress, which featured tiny black polka dots, a nipped-in waist and cap sleeves. She still didn't know if she was going to go to work; the thought of leaving the house and walking five minutes to the tube . . . Well, Cress didn't know if she was able to undergo such an arduous quest.

'Tea, toast,' Sophy said firmly.

'I can't,' Cress whimpered, but she did manage half a piece of dry toast and a couple of mouthfuls of tea to wash it down and though she still felt like she might die, as she said to Sophy, she no longer felt as if that death was imminent.

'Though it will be if you don't turn up to work on a summer Saturday when you're booked solid with wannabe brides and wedding guests,' Sophy said cheerfully as they left the house. 'Phoebe would hunt you down and kill you.'

'But I'm ill.'

'I'm sympathetic, Cress, I've been in your hungover shoes many a time, but also it was entirely self-inflicted.' She tucked her arm into Cress's as they walked along the tree-lined street, which did nothing to shield them from the sun, which felt hotter and more oppressive than ever before. 'Nobody could blame you for getting drunk last night. You'd had a hell of a week. I mean, you don't just come out of a fifteen-year relationship and carry on as normal.'

'There was nothing normal about last night, and I don't know if Colin I have broken up. We could just be on a break,' Cress said in a small voice. She came to a halt and wondered if she might throw up again. 'So why did I do it? The almost-kissing . . . I am *mortified*. The imminent death, I think it might actually be from shame.'

'Oh, Cress, it wasn't that bad,' Sophy said, but she didn't sound very convinced.

'It was. It was that bad. I can never face *him* again. I can't even say his name. And I can't face Ella either. She can't come back to the shop.' Cress wanted to sink to the pavement but Sophy tugged at her arm, so they resumed walking again. 'You'll have to talk to Phoebe and Freddy for me. Say that I can't have anything to do with the film people any more for personal reasons.'

'We'll see,' Sophy said, as they turned the corner on to Ballards Lane and Finchley Central tube station came into view. 'Now, you've got your water bottle, keep taking little sips of that and hopefully we'll get a seat on the train.'

It was one of the worst mornings that Cress had ever had.

'You look nice,' Anita had said in some surprise when she saw Cress arrive for work in a red dress. But then she'd peered closer at her, in her big dark glasses, pale underneath her tan, wobbling where she stood, and revised that opinion. 'Actually, no offence, but you look terrible.'

'Dodgy takeaway,' Sophy said loyally, which made Cress's stomach lurch so she'd had to run to the tiny work loo to throw up her toast and tea.

'She's not going to go home sick, is she?' Cress had heard Phoebe hiss in a horrified tone as she was rinsing her mouth out. 'We're booked solid today.'

Cress had unlocked and opened the door with shaky fingers – how was she going to operate her sewing machine? 'I'm fine,' she said in a croaky voice.

But she was far from fine. Within a minute of stepping into her workroom, she was coated in a film of sweat because it wasn't just hot today but muggy. Cress wondered if it might just be her, but Phoebe, coming up stairs with the first of that day's appointments, second fitting on a wedding dress, said that the forecast was for thunder and rain that evening and then hopefully the heatwave would break.

Cress had never understood the expression 'all fingers and thumbs' until, in her wretched state, she had to apply pins to a delicate 1920s lace dress without tearing it or puncturing the woman inside it. And she was expected to do this while asking if Natasha, her prospective bride, could move her arms freely and if she felt the waistband was *too* tight or just right?

There were more fittings after that. Come lunchtime, which was only half an hour, between brides and prom queens and wedding guests, she felt like she might join Coco Chanel, who was curled up in a sun patch in Cress's workroom, all fans on her, while she peacefully snored away.

It wasn't to be. Bea came up the stairs with a firm expression that wasn't to be denied. She looked exactly the same when there was a problem with the monthly stock check. 'Phoebe says that you're to come downstairs and get some fresh air,' she said.

'Oh, but . . .'

'Health and safety, Cress. Move your arse!'

Cress moved her arse as far as the little patio terrace at the back of the shop. Though the so-called fresh air felt just as hot and humid as it did inside. Sophy was dealing with a customer but Anita was waiting for her with another firm expression and –

'Is that for me? Because I can't . . .'

'Yes, you can. Full-fat Coke, a fried egg and bacon sandwich and a family-sized bag of Haribo Starmix. Scientifically proven to be the best cure for a hangover. We've all been there.'

Cress doubted very much that her friends and colleagues were able to come to work, and generally function, when they felt like they might die at any minute.

Anita clearly wasn't budging, though, so Cress showed willing and took tiny little sips of the Coke. She thought it would be too sweet for her but it did seem as if her body was craving sugar. After a few sips, she was embarrassed to let out an almighty burp, which made Anita grin and Cress blush. Then she realised that the gurgling in her stomach was because it was empty and she was hungry and, though she tried to take small bites, she ended up horsing down the sandwich, then wished that there was another one, because she was still starving.

She felt much better after that. Physically at least, and every time she felt she might be relapsing, she'd eat another handful of Haribo for the sugar hit.

But on the inside, she was very fragile. So fragile that she wanted the familiar after all the horrible new things that she'd experienced over the last twenty-four hours.

There was a part of Cress, a very large part of her, that was tempted to call Colin, to say she was sorry and to tamp down her irritation when he didn't say sorry too. Then they could just carry on like they were, like they had been for the last fifteen years. Their lives following the same narrow pattern that they always had, never looking ahead, never deviating.

But the irritation wouldn't be tamped down, now that Cress had let it out of its cage.

And when she wasn't thinking of Colin, she was thinking of Miles, and then her cheeks would heat up in a way that had nothing to do with the temperature.

She was on a break between fittings, and fixing the hook and eye on a dress from downstairs, but now Cress rested her hot hands on her burning face. Those very same hands that had *dragged* Miles towards her so she could try to *force* a kiss on him.

A series of chimes warning of incoming messages was a welcome distraction. Until Cress saw who they were from and then contemplated opening the skylight and throwing her phone across the rooftops of Primrose Hill.

But she couldn't resist knowing how bad the situation was.

It was quite hard to open her phone with a sweaty thumbprint, and then just seeing Miles's name again was enough for another hot wave of shame to engulf her. It took a little while before she could focus on his message.

How's the head?

If it's any consolation, I felt pretty rough for most of the morning.

> Anyway, next time we go out, it's mocktails for you.

Her hands were holding her cheeks again as if her skin wanted to slide off her face in sheer mortification.

Although Miles was properly cool – he looked cool. He had a cool job. He had cool friends – he was also very nice.

Very nice was an overlooked quality. Cress's friend Jacinta at her knitting club sprang to mind; she was always bemoaning how terribly treated she was by 'the bad boys' who were her type. Never seeming to realise the link between their 'bad boy' status and the way they breadcrumbed her, gaslit her, cheated on her and borrowed money without ever paying it back. 'Nice guys are *so* boring,' she'd say, when she was over her latest lousy boyfriend and was on the hunt for another man to make her life miserable.

But Miles wasn't boring. Not at all. Though what Miles was or wasn't was no concern of hers. It was very sweet of him to allude to a next time, but Cress was going to make sure that she never saw him again.

Her phone chimed again. Then again.

> Cress?

> Are you still alive?

She snatched it up because there was only one way to end *this*.

No. I'm dead.

Miles replied instantly.

That bad? I recommend a bacon sandwich. Kill or cure but usually cure.

Cress wasn't going to reply, but then it was kind of rude not to.

I did the bacon sandwich. Now I'm on the full fat Coke and Haribo starmix part of the treatment plan.

In that case, I'm confident that you'll make a complete recovery in the next couple of hours.

I hope so!

And that really was that.

Cress was relieved that her phone didn't chime again. But also, she was a little disappointed. She slipped her phone into her pocket and took the dress she'd just fixed downstairs.

It was almost closing time and the empty prospect of the rest of the weekend stretched out before her.

Usually she'd see Colin on a Saturday evening. Sometimes they'd even go out. Not out out, but to see a film or have a meal somewhere cheap and cheerful like Pizza Express, because as far as Cress had known they were both saving up.

But anyway, Colin was at Latitude Festival and really, what he was or wasn't doing this weekend was absolutely no concern of hers any more.

Sophy usually spent the weekend with Charles, and though Cress knew, without a shadow of a doubt, that Sophy would cancel her plans if she asked her to, she knew that was unfair. She'd already derailed their Friday night, and Cress did have other friends she could call.

Although she'd then have to explain what had happened with Colin and she wasn't ready to do that. The thought was just exhausting.

She'd go home. Order a very carby and delicious takeaway and watch *Breakfast at Tiffany's*. It was very much a *Breakfast at Tiffany's* kind of evening.

Cress slotted the dress back on the rail in between a royal-blue and an electric-blue frock. Then felt her phone vibrate just before it chimed.

It was another message from Miles.

I feel too wretched to stay home alone. *Breakfast at Tiffany's* is showing at the Prince Charles Cinema, if you fancy it. I know you've seen it a million times before but can I tempt you with air conditioning? Also, sitting in a dark room has to be good for a hangover.

Chapter Fifteen

It had been ages since Cress had seen *Breakfast at Tiffany's* on the big screen. As she explained to Sophy when Sophy had offered to cancel Charles and 'do whatever you want. I'm all yours. Especially if that involves chips of some kind.'

So Cress had falteringly explained that she was meeting Miles because the thought of spending the evening on her own, still feeling a bit grimy, wasn't a happy one. 'I have to see him again at some point, right? It might just as well be sooner rather than later.'

Sophy had given Cress a thoughtful look as Cress stood in front of the tiny mirror in the tiny shop bathroom and slapped some tinted moisturiser on her face, though it was sure to slide off almost immediately. It was yet to rain and Cress felt like she was very slowly being boiled alive.

'I think that's an excellent idea,' Sophy had said slowly. 'I mean, you've got to get back on the horse eventually.'

Cress turned to her with a horrified, half smeared with moisturiser face. 'But I was never *on* the horse.'

'You know what I mean. I've got a red lipstick that's a perfect match for your dress,' Sophy had said, even though, before she'd decided to change *her* life, she'd never worn a bright red lipstick.

Sophy was going into town too to meet Charles, so they took the 24 bus from Chalk Farm station together, as it was far too hot to even think about descending to the tube. Cress was glad of the company, even if she wasn't glad of Sophy's knowing looks.

As it was, she was terrified. She hadn't been on a first date in . . . well, in fifteen years. Not that this was a first date. If it was, it was a friend date and there was no need to be so very nervous, vibrating on the bus seat, because this was Miles and she knew him well enough now not to be scared. Although the circumstances of their last meeting were not . . . optimal.

Cress and Sophy got off the bus at Leicester Square. Cress longed to cling on to Sophy but instead she managed to say a breathless goodbye. And then they parted ways, Sophy off to Covent Garden to do something fabulous and quirky with Charles, and Cress to thread her way through the Saturday-night crowd and tourists to the independent cinema on Leicester Place where she'd first gone many years ago to a singalong screening of *The Sound Of Music*. The air was soupy and thick, heavy with the fragrant aromas coming from the restaurants of Chinatown, red paper lanterns strung between both sides of Lisle Street hanging gaily in the still evening.

Miles was already waiting outside the cinema, his back to her as he looked in the opposite direction. Cress knew a moment of blind panic but then she was walking towards him and he turned, just as she reached his side.

He was wearing dark glasses – Cress had expected nothing less and she was wearing hers too – but still he looked delighted to see her.

'You're still alive,' he said.

'Barely.'

He lightly touched Cress's arm, then leaned forward to brush his lips against her cheek. He went in for the double and Cress caught a delicious whiff of his salty, woody after-shave and wondered if she was having a relapse because she felt quite lightheaded all of a sudden.

'I already got the tickets,' Miles said, his hand on the small of Cress's back to gently nudge her out of the way of a crowd of tourists too busy taking pictures to look where they were going. 'Shall we go in? I'm one of those annoying people that likes to see the adverts and the previews.'

'Me too.' One of the few things that she and Colin used to argue about was that he never appreciated what a panic it was to have to find your seats just as the movie was starting, so it was a mad rush of trying to navigate seat numbers in the dark and apologising to people as you trod on their feet and spilled popcorn all over them.

'How much do I owe you for my ticket?' she asked Miles, but he shook his head.

'You get the popcorn and something to drink and we're evens,' Miles said. 'Are you going to have some hair of the dog that bit you?'

'Never drinking alcohol again,' Cress vowed. This was as good a time as any to launch into a heartfelt and bumbling apology for the wrongs that she'd done him but she didn't have a chance to even start with a simple 'sorry', as the small foyer was so crowded with people queuing for tickets and the tiny concession stand. She'd have to prolong the agony and wait until after the film.

As they waited, Miles took off his dark glasses and Cress could see instantly that he was fresh-faced, not even the littlest bit baggy-eyed and dehydrated.

'Have you really been hungover today?' she asked with narrowed eyes, which were still puffy and swollen. 'You didn't have *that* much to drink last night, did you?'

'I was a little peaky this morning,' Miles insisted. 'Like a sympathy hangover, because I knew you must be feeling rough.'

'It was my own fault.'

'Hangovers are always our own fault, but that doesn't mean we should have to suffer alone.'

Cress winced at what she'd put Sophy and her mother through. 'Yeah, you can say that again.' They'd reached the front of the queue and, though there was so much she wanted to say, *needed* to say to Miles, there was one matter that was more pressing than anything. 'Sweet or salted popcorn?'

Chapter Sixteen

In *Breakfast at Tiffany's,* a young man moves into a small New York apartment building and meets and is instantly fascinated by Audrey Hepburn's character, Holly Golightly. Holly is a good-time girl, who makes her money going on dates with wealthy men and asking them for fifty-dollar tips for the powder room. But underneath the glitter and the bravado, Holly is a lost soul with a dark past; but she still believes that nothing bad could ever happen to her when she visits the famous jewellers Tiffany & Co., to give it its full title.

Cress felt the same way, except that nothing bad could ever happen to her when she was watching *Breakfast at Tiffany's*. She couldn't even begin to know how many times she'd seen it. First, on a worn-out, crackling video tape on the big old telly they'd had when she was younger. Then on DVD on their sleeker, even bigger telly. She'd seen it in countless cinemas. She'd attended open-air screenings. Now, with streaming, Cress could watch it on her phone or her iPad, in bed under the covers.

It probably amounted to as many as a thousand viewings over the years, but the opening credits of a New York street, vast, and empty save for one yellow taxicab, pulling in to the kerb outside Tiffany & Co., while 'Moon River' played, always got to her. As Audrey Hepburn stepped out of the car, hair piled high in an intricate updo, and exquisitely clothed in the long black column dress that Cress was going to replicate for Tanya, she settled back in her seat. When Audrey opened the white paper bag she was clutching and pulled out a very flat croissant and a cup of takeout coffee as she stared at the jewels in Tiffany's window, Cress felt the same goosebumps that she got every time.

The way she thought about the film was different now. When she was younger, she'd thought Holly Golightly was a free spirit and she had longed to be just like her when she was grown up. Of course, now she could see how desperate and lonely Holly's life was. And that Mickey Rooney's character, the Japanese Mr Yunioshi who lives upstairs, was racist and extremely problematic, and Cress wouldn't have minded if he was cut from the film entirely. But still, the story of two lost people finding each other, and the dresses . . . Oh, the dresses, they always worked their magic.

This time, she was watching it with Miles. His body, all arms and legs and angles, folded into the seat next to her, his knee occasionally knocking into hers. Their hands collided in the massive bucket of popcorn because it turned out that they both liked two-thirds salted popcorn to one-third sweet. Occasionally Miles would whisper in her ear about a little detail that he loved and when Cress cried because she always cried when Audrey Hepburn sang 'Moon River' while strumming a ukulele on her windowsill, Miles gently squeezed her hand. And when Cress *really* cried because she always really cried at the last scene with the rain and Cat and the kiss, he gently squeezed her knee and kept his hand there as the final credits rolled.

It seemed as if there was an unbearable tension between them, but also a strange and comforting kind of familiarity.

Cress felt as if she could sit there for ever, tears still slowly rolling down her face, Miles's hand still on her knee, but then the curtains closed over the dark screen, the lights came up and the moment was broken.

They got to their feet, Cress scrabbling in her bag for a tissue and trying to steel herself for the apology she still needed to make.

Both of them were quiet as they walked down the stairs. It hadn't rained, Cress didn't think it would ever rain again, and as they stepped out onto the street it was like walking into a steamy fug.

She turned to face Miles with her heart sinking to the bottom of her sandals, and took a deep breath.

Miles looked up from his phone. 'Are you hungry?'

'Am I hungry?' Cress had been so busy planning her awkward apology and then a rushed goodbye that it hadn't even occurred to her that the evening might not be over. Or that she didn't want it to be over. Not just yet. She considered Miles's question. 'I've spent most of the day knocking back Haribo, then all that popcorn, but yeah, actually, I'm starving.'

'Me too,' Miles said. 'I know the perfect place.'

Even though the night was hot and sweaty, much like every inch of Cress's skin, Miles took her hand, and they crossed over Shaftesbury Avenue and then into the narrow criss-cross of Soho streets.

The streets got narrower and narrower, until Miles led Cress down a tiny alley and, just as she was starting to panic that maybe he was also a serial killer as well as an assistant director and was taking her to his murder lair, he stopped outside what looked like a very trendy bar.

Before Cress could say that she really needed something more substantial to eat than bar snacks and, also, one whiff of the barmaid's apron might make her hurl again, Miles gestured to a small flight of stairs.

'Best burgers in London,' he said.

Soon they were seated opposite each other in a booth in the basement burger bar, which was called – very appropriately considering the lessons Cress had learned about drinking too much – Mother's Ruin.

Usually when Cress was going out to dinner it wasn't a spontaneous affair and half the fun was perusing the menu online days in advance and debating what she was going to order. Having to do that in real time was quite stressful, but Miles didn't seem to mind.

Although Cress was sure that he'd have probably liked a proper drink, in solidarity with her now teetotal state he ordered a root beer, and Cress felt well enough now to switch back to Diet Coke.

They both ordered cheeseburgers loaded with all sorts of extras, then onion rings, deep-fried mac and cheese bites and fries to share. After the server had taken their order, Cress could finally broach the topic that she'd have got round to sooner the if she hadn't been distracted.

But she hadn't quite mustered up the necessary amount of courage so, as she opened her mouth, what came out still wasn't an apology.

'So, Ella . . .'

Miles groaned before Cress could say any more. 'So Ella is the most indiscreet person I've ever met. Never tell her anything. What dirt did she spill on me?'

'No dirt,' Cress assured him, because yes, Ella had been indiscreet, but she hadn't told Cress anything that outrageous about Miles. 'Except, she did say you used to be an actor.'

Miles rested his head on the scarred wooden tabletop, then covered his head with his hands. 'When she says actor, she means that in the loosest possible sense of the word.'

'Yeah, that was exactly what she said.' Cress poked Miles's shoulder with a finger. 'How bad?'

'So very bad. I'm not sure how I got into drama school, though the woman who interviewed me said that I had boyish good looks and they could teach me the rest.' Miles lifted his head briefly to preen, then collapsed again. 'Turns out they couldn't. Every year, I failed my practical exam but then they felt sorry for me so would move me up with all my friends.'

'You must have had some talent, in order to persuade them to do that.'

'Very good with the puppy-dog eyes, very bad at any kind of dramatic delivery,' Miles said, treating Cress to the most hangdog, forlorn expression, which was quite compelling. 'I did manage to score a film part after I graduated with a very low third, that's how I met Ella, but I was sacked on my second day. Again, they felt sorry for me, so they gave me some work as a runner, I stuck around, and the rest is history.' He took a sip of his drink. 'What about you?'

Cress shook her head. 'No acting talent whatsoever. When it came to school plays, I'd help backstage rather than tread the boards. Sophy was the one with the stars in her eyes.'

'Sophy? She wanted to be an actress?' Miles asked, as two servers appeared carrying two loaded trays.

'Not an actress, she was a ballroom dancer from the ages of seven to fifteen,' Cress revealed. 'I made her costumes, and on the weekends when I saw my dad, there'd always be a dance competition.' Cress couldn't help but smile at the memories. Sometimes she and Mike had hung out, just the two of them, but Cress had never minded going to one of Sophy's ballroom contests. It was a glamorous yet gritty world of sequins, fake tan and ruthless dance mums. 'Honestly, I've seen things at those dance competitions that would make your hair curl. I mean, if your hair wasn't already curly.'

Miles paused with a double-stacked burger on its way to his mouth. 'Your hair's curly too. If we had kids, they'd have the curliest hair imaginable.'

It was a throwaway remark, but it did something to Cress that meant she also had to delay delivery of her burger. Eventually, her nerve endings stopped tingling at the thought of a couple of ridiculously curly-haired kids and she was able to take a huge messy bite of her burger. Inevitably, she could feel relish and melted cheese dripping down her chin, but she wiped them away with her napkin.

In between bites, she told Miles of the murky secrets of the world of junior ballroom dancing. The ringer who turned out to be a very small-built 25-year-old. The tube of greasepaint left on a stair to nobble the knees of a rival. The copious amounts of tit-tape, glue and safety pins needed to secure the foofy dresses.

Eventually, their burgers were nothing but smears on a plate and they were both mindlessly working their way through the last of the fries and Cress had no more secrets left to share.

'Do you want pudding?' Miles asked, as the servers came to collect their plates.

Cress always wanted pudding but in this instance she was 'completely stuffed. I don't think I'll need to eat again until Monday morning at the earliest.'

'Me too,' Miles said, putting his elbows on the table, which was all right because they were no longer eating, then resting his chin on his steepled fingers. 'So, anyway, about last night.'

'Oh God, no!' Cress buried her face in her hands so she wouldn't have to look at him. All her good intentions to apologise and explain herself had been derailed and now she was too full of carbs and good cheer to want to go there. 'Can we just not?'

'We could, but I don't want it hanging over us. Because I do fancy you, if you were in any doubt,' Miles said evenly and, when Cress moved her fingers ever so slightly, he was looking straight at her.

'There was some doubt,' she admitted. 'Quite a lot of doubt actually.'

'I thought I'd made it quite clear,' he said and maybe he had but Cress didn't know what the signs were when someone fancied you. It had never really come up before. 'I wanted to kiss you, more than anything, but you were really drunk and it wouldn't have been right.'

'OK. Um, thank you.' She was going to have to say it, and there was no easy way to say it, and it would have been much easier if Ella had been indiscreet on Cress's behalf – but she hadn't, so . . . 'I'm so sorry, Miles. I've behaved really appallingly. In fact, I'm ashamed of myself.'

'Oh, come on, Cress,' Miles said with an easy smile. 'You weren't *that* bad.'

'I was,' she said sadly. 'Very bad because I have a boyfriend and we had a big fight, we never fight, and now I don't know if we've broken up or not. And if we have then I'm days out, like literally *four* days out, of quite a long-term relationship.'

Miles gave a start of surprise. 'Oh . . .'

'Hence the getting very drunk for the first time in my life thing,' Cress explained further, this time with a full-body cringe.

'How long-term?' Miles asked, his eyes never leaving Cress's flustered face.

'Fifteen years.'

'Fifteen years!' Miles took a swift gulp of his second root beer like he wished it were something stronger. 'That's longer than all of my parents' marriages combined.'

'It *is* a long time.' Cress sighed. 'Maybe too long. I don't know. I feel like I don't know anything any more.'

'Then I'm really glad we didn't kiss,' Miles said, which stung a little. 'I don't want to be the rebound guy and I really don't want to take advantage of you.'

Cress really was a terrible person. Not only was none of this fair to Colin, whom she was still furious with, but also she would quite like Miles to take advantage of her. She'd like it very much.

She couldn't tell him that though. It was a secret that she'd take to the grave. 'I'm really flattered. But I'm not . . . I mean, you don't throw away fifteen years together just like that. We could still work things out. When we've both cooled off a bit.'

It was impossible to know what Colin was thinking because he'd done his usual vanishing act. And Cress wasn't done with being furious with him. Though Miles had been a wonderful, beautiful distraction.

He was looking at her thoughtfully, kindly, which she didn't deserve.

'I'm so sorry,' she said again. 'I didn't mean to lead you on.'

'You didn't lead me on,' he insisted, which was very sweet of him but untrue.

'But last night . . .'

'Last night you gave me hope.'

Cress winced. 'It was very wrong of me.'

'And so, you know ten minutes ago, how I said I fancied you?' Miles asked mildly and without even a hint of condemnation.

All Cress could do was nod, though the memory of Miles saying that he fancied her was a very pleasing one, no matter how conflicted she felt.

'Well, I've got some bad news.' Miles looked at his watch, as Cress felt another hot then cold wave of shame engulf her. 'Come midnight, it will have been revoked because I'm friend-zoning you.'

Which was more than she deserved. 'Friends is good,' she said. 'You can never have too many friends. And again, I'm sorry for messing you around,' she added because even if she *was* officially single, she knew that she needed to spend quite a long time, months even, figuring out who she was now if she wasn't half of Cress and Colin.

There was nothing else to say except ask for the bill, which Miles whisked away as soon as it arrived and refused to let Cress go halves.

It felt as if the talk that had been inevitable had put a damper on the evening and the cosy, conspiratorial mood of before. But as they opened the door, it was to find that the world outside was damp too.

Not just damp but sopping wet, as the much-promised rain hammered down from the still-sultry sky. With a squeak, Cress swiftly retreated, barrelling back into Miles, who was behind her.

'It's raining,' she announced quite unnecessarily. 'Biblically raining.'

'Shall we wait it out?'

They huddled in the doorway and watched the sheets of rain bounce on landing, immediately causing huge puddles to form. It didn't seem to be easing in the slightest but there was something quite lovely about standing there, close to Miles, belly full, the glorious smell of petrichor rising up from the pavements.

'I think we're going to have to make a run for it,' Miles said in the end and Cress knew that he was right even though she wanted to stay in that moment.

With a deep anticipatory sigh, they ran up the basement steps and hadn't even reached the end of the alley before they were both drenched. Cress's feet were slipping and sliding in her sandals, her dress soaked to her skin in less than a minute as she pulled Miles into another doorway.

'I'm sure it will ease off in a minute,' she said, looking up at him. Raindrops were clearly even clinging to her eyelashes because he wiped them away with one unsteady finger and Cress realised how close they were. Their wet bodies were a whisper apart. Miles's hair was almost flattened to his head, which made his features even stronger; the clean lines of his cheekbones, his full lips. God, she couldn't stop staring at him.

'This is just like the last scene in *Breakfast at Tiffany's*,' he said, his voice husky over the relentless drumming of water hitting the hard ground. 'The alley, the rain . . .'

It was. It really was.

'We just need a cat,' Cress said.

'And a kiss.'

Miles took the half-step that meant they were pressed up against each other. Cress didn't care that they were both sodden and that her make-up must have slid right off her face. Didn't care that she might still be in a long-term relationship. Didn't care that they'd agreed to friend-zone each other. All that she cared about was Miles lifting his hand to cup her cheek and trace a finger over her lips, which parted on command.

It wasn't a kiss. It was a kiss by proxy. A promise of a kiss. Of what might be. Of what could be.

They stayed like that for long, long moments as the rain grew softer and softer until it stopped altogether.

'I did say that fancying you wasn't going to be revoked until midnight,' Miles said with an impossible smile.

Cress turned her head so she could graze the palm of his hand with her mouth. 'I expect it does take quite a while for the paperwork to be processed.'

PART THREE

Chapter Seventeen

It rained on and off for the rest of the weekend, which wasn't much fun. But it broke the heatwave, and, by the Monday after Cress and Miles's almost-kiss, then subsequent friend-zoning, it was a perfect summer's day.

The sun was high up in a blue, blue sky and as Cress and Sophy walked to the shop from Chalk Farm station there was a very mild but very pleasant breeze that ruffled the leaves on the trees and made them decide that they'd have lunch on the shop patio. Also, that lunch would consist of more than ice cream.

Cress's working conditions were much more amenable. It was no longer punishingly hot in her workroom and she was no longer treated to the sight of Coco Chanel, on her back, legs akimbo, having cold air blown on her down-below.

Not that Cress had much reason to leave her workroom. It was late July; they were *deep* into wedding season. Though the appointments had slowed down – people had chosen their wedding dresses or their dresses to wear to weddings by now – every day she had a huge amount of alterations and repairs to work through.

Cress would always rather be busy than not busy. It made the day go so much quicker, unlike her unhappy nearly-nine-year sojourn at the Museum of Religious Relics where time often seemed to have slowed down. Besides, every dress hanging up on the rail waiting for her attention presented its own challenges and triumphs, as she explained to Ella when she came in on the Wednesday for another tutorial in how to look like a convincing fashion designer.

'This needs the buttonholes tidied up and the buttons replacing,' she explained, holding up a lilac poplin shirt-waister dress. 'And it needs taking up a few inches, which means I can use what I cut off to re-cover the belt, which has worn thin in places.'

'That's a whole day of work,' Ella said pulling a face.

'Not even! A couple of hours at most, especially as you're going to replace the buttons while I work on the belt.'

Ella shied away as if Cress had dipped the dress in hydrochloric acid. 'Oh no! I'm not ready for that. I don't want to destroy a dress that's over seventy years old with my inept fingers. It's too much responsibility.'

'It's just enough responsibility,' Cress said firmly, as she rummaged on her haberdashery shelves for a box of jet buttons, because sourcing buttons in the exact same shade of lilac as the dress would be a thankless task. 'There's very low jeopardy involved when it comes to sewing on buttons.'

After a couple of false starts, Ella managed to sew on all twelve new buttons and even repair the belt tags, which were coming loose. 'Amazing!' She held the dress to her and twirled round. Even in 'civilian' clothes, her star presence couldn't be denied. It felt like she was taking up every spare atom of space in the workroom. Not that Cress minded. It was quite nice to have the company – and the gossip. 'This must be how Christian Dior felt after he designed his first New Look dress.'

'I'm sure he did,' Cress said, her mouth full of pins as she let down the hem on another dress.

'That's something else you're going to have to teach me,' Ella said, collapsing back onto her stool because she could never do something as simple as sit down. 'How to have your mouth full of pins and never swallow any. Never mind actually *talking* while they're in situ.'

'That is a very advanced skill,' Cress said as she extracted one of the pins from her mouth. 'Most sewers have a wrist pincushion on a piece of elastic. Probably much safer. I think it's more important that we focus on getting you familiar with a sewing machine.'

'You're actually much more assertive than I thought you were the first time we met,' Ella said slowly, her eyes seeming to miss nothing as she looked at Cress, who was sitting next to her on the other high stool and hunched over a zingy green satin wiggle dress.

'It does take me a while to warm up to new people,' Cress admitted and, even though most of her attention was on the hemline, she didn't miss Ella's sudden cat-got-the-cream smile.

'Well, I hear you've been warming up to Miles,' she said softly. Then turned to pull an imploring face at Cress. 'Come on! I've been here all day and you haven't said a word and I need you to spill the tea!'

'There is no tea to spill.' Cress hoped she sounded very firm about the lack of tea and not sad instead.

'You looked very cosy in the pub on Friday night . . .'

'There was a heatwave, it was too hot for any kind of cosying . . .'

'And then you went out for dinner on Saturday night.' Ella nudged Cress's elbow.

Cress's head shot up. 'Who told you?'

'Thank you for confirming it.' Ella's smile was very smug. 'One of my friends, she works the bar at Mother's Ruin when she's between acting jobs. She saw Miles and when she described the woman he was with – the woman he'd told me nothing about though I thought we didn't have any secrets between us – I knew it was you.'

'We're just friends,' Cress insisted, which had been the absolute truth since midnight on Saturday.

'Friends with benefits?'

'No, just regular friends.' Cress put down the dress because she wasn't giving the hem the attention it deserved and also, she could tell that Ella wasn't going to drop this until she was satisfied with Cress's answers. 'I'm in a fifteen-year relationship – or I'm not, but either way, it wouldn't be appropriate to be anything other than friends.'

'Either you want to be in your fifteen-year relationship, or you don't. It's very simple,' Ella said.

Cress shook her head. 'It's actually very complicated. What Colin's done; I'm not sure we can come back from that.' She sighed. Because it was the same old dilemma. 'But then again, we've been together so long – should we throw it away just like that?'

'What does your maybe ex-boyfriend think you should do?'

'I don't know because we're not currently talking. He can be very passive-aggressive when we argue and I'm still so angry with him that I'm not going to make things better like I usually do for the sake of a quiet life.' Cress glared at the green satin dress, though it wasn't the dress's fault.

'But surely the best way to get over someone is to get under someone else. Isn't that what they say?' Ella asked with a grin, because she was impossible.

Cress couldn't even remember the last time she and Colin had been intimate with each other. It was something that Sophy was always speculating about and Cress had always shut her down, though it was true that, with both of them living at home, it had been hard to find the time and space to be alone and in the right mood.

Much as she was flattered by Miles's attention, technically getting under him right now might be cheating, depending on her current relationship status. And Cress didn't want to be a cheater. It was so much better to just be friends. You knew where you were with friends.

Though since Saturday, Cress had replayed that cinematic moment in the alley with the rain and the almost-kiss until the memory was worn paper-thin.

'I'm not getting under anyone,' she said primly, wanting to shut down this conversation as quickly as possible. 'Now, I'm going to show you how to hand-stitch a hem.'

'That doesn't sound like something a glamorous fashion designer would do,' Ella said, backing away from Cress and the dress she'd been twirling only moments earlier.

'Even glamorous fashion designers started out with hand-stitching hems,' Cress said in the tone of voice that could even stop Phoebe in her tracks. 'We'll need a reel of lilac silk cotton thread and a very fine needle.'

'I hate very fine needles, they're so hard to thread,' Ella said because, as well as learning the tricks of the trade, she was also getting to grips with the minor annoyances and grievances that every sewer experienced.

After not even half an hour of hemming, Ella suddenly remembered that she had an appointment on the other side of London and, with vague promises to return, she was gone. Cress wasn't convinced that they'd ever see her again.

Besides, she was busy enough without having to mentor A-list actresses. Even though Cress didn't mind being busy – the taking in and out of seams, the letting down and letting up of hems, replacing buttons and zips and hooks and eyes, painstakingly repairing embroidery and beading – when she was able to work on Tanya's birthday gown, she got a tingly feeling all over. Much like the tingly feeling she got when she thought about the almost-kiss.

Tanya's gown was currently a toile, a prototype made in a simple cotton that hadn't been bleached or dyed. Cress would fit the toile on Tanya and only when they were both happy with it would she cut out her pattern pieces in the expensive black satin that she'd already bought.

There was something about making a dress from scratch, from a pattern of her own invention, that thrilled Cress like nothing else. Seeing her vision come to life on the dress form was intensely satisfying.

Phoebe was now on board with the whole notion of Cress making a dress for a customer and would often check on its progress. Sophy and even Anita too, when they were up in the atelier, which wasn't very often as Phoebe was very territorial over the high-end frocks, would wander into the workroom to see how it was progressing.

So, life was great when Cress was at work. But life beyond work was strange and unsettling without Colin in it.

It had been three weeks now since they'd split up and Cress still hadn't heard a word from him. Not a text or phone call to see how she was doing, or even if she had any plans to collect all the items she'd left in that one drawer in his bedroom that had only been allocated to her after fifteen long years together.

Of course, Cress could contact Colin, but she really wasn't sure what she wanted to say to him, other than to rehash all the sad facts that had led to their breaking up in the first place. Also, she was fed up with always being the first one to blink when they were having a disagreement.

Anyway, this wasn't a disagreement. It felt like the end, but also it felt strangely unfinished. Colin and Cress might have had their separate interests and friendship groups, but they'd always met up on Saturday nights, alternate Sunday lunches at each other's house, spent a couple of evenings a week hanging out. Now Cress had to fill those gaps as best as she could.

Most of that time was now taken up with a major sort-through and reorganisation of her other business. Or rather the rails of vintage dresses that she'd rescued from the rejects bin and lovingly repaired and rejuvenated. The superior-quality black cotton tote bags she bought in bulk so she could embroider fashion-related slogans on them. The shelves of deadstock vintage fabric, fixings and fastenings and dress patterns. It took up half her bedroom and all of the small box room that she'd commandeered.

Part of Cress didn't know why she was bothering. She could manage perfectly well on her wages and it wasn't like she was saving up for a deposit any more.

But like Sophy said, she had to find a new dream, and, in the meantime, she signed up for a stall at an outdoor vintage market in south London. It would make a change from selling her wares online. Also, Dulwich was far enough away that Phoebe would never find out. Not that it was any of Phoebe's business what Cress did on her Sundays, and she knew that Cress had a side hustle because she'd bought a couple of dresses from her. But still, it was the just the kind of thing that Phoebe would take issue with in a really personal way.

It seemed to Cress that this was a time in her life of quiet reflection and much industriousness. There were brief respites. Sophy refused to let Cress 'moulder away in your box room reorganising your collection of zips.' She insisted that Cress come round for dinner and then stay over at least once a week, in the flat she shared in Hackney with Anita and a very sweet man called Jimmy who worked in a vintage shop in Shoreditch. Though Phoebe was never to know about Jimmy, or that he worked in a rival vintage shop, under pain of death.

Diane had also designated one night a week as a spa night, where she and Cress did face masks and hair masks and painted each other's nails. Mike and Caroline were always inviting Cress round for a takeaway and movie of her choice and every day there were messages from Miles.

Sometimes it would be a YouTube link to a fashion-centric scene from a movie; the "Think Pink" song and dance routine from *Funny Face*, Molly Ringwald cutting up two perfectly lovely vintage frocks to make one ghastly prom dress in *Pretty in Pink*. There were photos of random cats and dogs he'd met on his travels and he signed off every message, 'from your friend, Miles'.

Cress knew that this state of affairs couldn't last for ever. Despite keeping herself in a constant state of motion, eventually she'd have to make a decision either with or without Colin. She could hold on to the past, which was the safe option, or let go, which would be terrifying, and grab the future with both hands.

But at ten to six on an August Friday evening all she wanted to grab hold of was her bed. Even the prospect of the weekend couldn't cheer her up because she still had to work tomorrow, and summer Saturdays were her busiest days. Even more frenzied than the run-up to Christmas and New Year. Every bride or purchaser of a frock that needed alterations, who couldn't get time off during the week, came in on Saturdays.

Just the thought of the sixteen appointments that awaited her tomorrow – Phoebe had managed to squeeze a couple of hydration and bathroom breaks into the schedule – had Cress feeling very frazzled as she packed away her sewing machine.

She was just pulling down the blinds over the skylights when her phone chimed with a message.

I'm just round the corner. Don't suppose you guys are heading to the pub and there's room for another one? Your friend, Miles x

Cress went from despondent to delighted in the space of a second. Maybe she did have time for a glass of something cold. After all, she didn't want to be one of those people who only lived to work.

Also, it was the first time that Miles had seen fit to use an x. Not that Cress was going to read anything into it – she used an x with all her other friends – but still, the sight of that one letter chased the last of her bad mood away.

> We are pub-bound. Just finishing up at the shop.
> Would be lovely . . .

Cress deleted 'lovely' – she'd recently read in an article that women relied too much on 'lovely' as an adjective because their default position was to be people-pleasing tools of the patriarchy.

> Would be nice . . .

No! Nice was even worse than lovely.

Worried that her non-answer might mean that Miles was now quite some distance from round the corner, Cress racked her brains for a suitable word to describe what it would be like if Miles could come to the pub with them.

> Would be great to see you. Cress x (Your friend.)

That single x felt very daring, though possibly she was reading too much into it.

Chapter Eighteen

Cress just had time to run some serum through her hair to separate her curls. A little mascara, a barely-there lip tint and some powder to take the shine off, then she was tripping down the stairs, Coco Chanel breathing hot doggy breath on her heels.

She wasn't a moment too soon either. Anita had paused from vacuuming to shout, 'We're closed!' at someone who was knocking on the door, even though it was two minutes to six, so technically they were still open.

'It's Miles,' Cress said quickly. 'He just happened to be passing.'

'Just happened to be passing,' Sophy echoed, as Anita unlocked the door. 'What a coincidence!'

'I don't know why you're smirking like that,' Cress said, making sure to hold Sophy's amused stare. 'There are a lot of reasons why Miles would be in the area.'

'Well, I can only think of one,' Sophy said, her smile growing wider as Miles stepped into the shop and gave a little wave to the assembled company.

'Hope you don't mind, I was just . . . like, had to see someone, a meeting . . .' He gathered himself, adjusted his shades. 'Cress said it was OK to crash your Friday pub outing.'

'Of course it is,' Cress said with a smile that she tried to dim a little, but it was so *lovely* to see Miles. Even lovelier that he looked so pleased to see her. 'Shall we go on ahead?'

Ordinarily, Cress didn't mind lending a hand to close up the shop but strictly it wasn't in her job description, and she had already left the atelier looking spotless.

'Oh, you are coming to the pub, then, Cress?' Anita asked in surprise as she vacuumed under the sofa legs. 'Because you said at lunch that you were too tired to do anything tonight but collapse face down on your bed.'

'Second wind,' Sophy said because she was a lot more tactful and subtle than Anita. 'We'll see you in there. Mine's a rosé if you're buying, Miles.'

'I'll get a bottle,' Miles promised rashly, then held the shop door open for Cress, who'd never been so pleased to step through it.

She waited until they were out of sight of the shop to put a hand on Miles's arm to still him for a moment. She didn't want to give him false hope, or to lead him on, but she also wanted him to know, 'This is such a lovely surprise . . .' She really needed to consult a thesaurus. 'I'm glad you're not avoiding me, after . . . after . . .'

'The alley in the rain,' Miles said and, though he had his shades on, he *sounded* as if he was arching an eyebrow. Then his hand was the faintest of touches at the small of her back as they started walking again. 'Anyway, we're safely friend-zoned now, aren't we?'

'Yes, safely and happily friend-zoned,' Cress said.

Friends was the only thing they could be. Though the longer that she didn't speak to Colin, the less she wanted to. Her anger with him was a fire in her belly that refused to fizzle out, which didn't bode well for them being able to work things out. But even if they did officially break up, Cress had read another article online that said it took a month for every year you were with someone to properly get over them. That would be fifteen months. A year and a quarter.

Cress hoped that she wouldn't still be this angry and, yes, this sad and confused, over a year from now.

By now, they were at The Hat and Fan, the usual Friday-evening crowd spilling out of the doors and onto the pavement, but Miles paused before entering.

'I'm asking this as a friend, but do you think you'll get back with him?' he asked softly over the excited hum and chatter, so Cress had to lean in to hear him.

Despite all Cress's soul-searching, Colin's silence – it had been three weeks now – said more clearly than words ever could that his life without Cress in it was going just fine, thanks for asking. So Cress would be fine too. Or rather, she would in up to fifteen months' time.

'I'm not sure,' she said. 'Even if we are broken up, when you've been with someone for that long it's hard to know exactly who you are without them.'

'My longest relationship was three years and I was a mess after that, so you're doing pretty well,' Miles said with a keen look at Cress, who now wondered if she should still be crying every day and unable to eat or sleep. Though the only time she had ever really lost her appetite was when she'd had norovirus. 'I hope I'm not overstepping. Just giving you some friendly support.'

'Isn't that what friends are for?' Cress hoped that the blush she could feel coming on was a delicate one and not one that made her look like a postbox. 'One day I hope I can return the favour.'

'I look forward to that. Shall we?'

He ushered Cress through the door of the pub and she wasn't going to drink alcohol, not ever again, but she definitely needed the comfort given by a bag of salt and vinegar crisps.

She was also delighted to see Freddy and Charles already in situ. They'd bagged their favourite corner spot and already had a bottle of rosé and a bottle of white chilling in an ice bucket. 'I got you an elderflower and sparkling water, Cress. And a gin and slimline tonic for Pheebs,' Freddy said with a sly grin. 'That's slimline tonic in a bottle, not from the mixer tap, with ice and a slice of lime, not lemon.'

'You know her so well,' Cress marvelled as she sat down.

'Oh, you have no idea,' Charles said, and before Cress could ask what he meant because he was smiling in a maddening way while Freddy stared down at his phone screen, even though his device didn't appear to be turned on, Miles said he was going to the bar and The Vintage Dress Shop staff suddenly descended on them.

It was a flurry of allocating seats, and, though there were drinks on the table, giving Miles a complicated crisps and bar snacks order and 'a bowl of water for Coco Chanel. Filtered, Miles, she can't drink tap water', but soon everyone was settled.

Cress was on the end of a banquette, with Sophy and Charles sitting next to her and Miles opposite on a small stool, which couldn't be comfortable but when Cress offered to switch places, he refused.

'I'm good and I like bumping knees with you,' he said, gently bumping his knee against her leg to prove his point. Which was fine. Friends bumped knees all the time 'How's Ella been? Has she driven you mad yet?'

'She's been learning loads,' Cress insisted.

'In between gossiping, I'll bet.'

'Hardly gossiping at all.' Although Ella had told her a scandalous story about the judge on a TV talent show that had left her reeling. 'She's successfully mastered sewing on buttons and semi-successfully hand-stitched a bit of hem. I'm sure in a few weeks she'll give every impression that she's a sewing maestro.'

'Talking of which, got a massive favour to ask you, Cress. I didn't want to bother you earlier because I know how busy you've been today,' said Anita, leaning right over Sophy. 'Quick, while Phoebe's taking Coco round the block.'

A favour that Phoebe clearly wouldn't approve of then.

Anita was rummaging in her slouchy leather bag, and pulled out a bedraggled black dress.

'No wonder you don't want Phoebe here. She'd kill you if she saw how you treat your frocks,' Cress said, taking the dress from Anita. In another life it had been an elegant, form-fitting black frock with a little starburst on the shoulder picked out in diamanté. In its current life, it was pretty much at death's door. 'Even I feel like I should at least glare at you. Crêpe, 1930s . . . Wow, you've completely destroyed the armholes.'

'It wasn't me. It's modern antiperspirant,' Anita said crossly. Then she assumed a less furious face as she remembered that she wanted a favour. 'This is my absolute favourite dress in the whole world. Which is why I've literally worn it to pieces. Don't even look at the side seams, you'll be too upset.'

Cress did look at the side seams and then held the dress up for Miles's inspection; he was watching this exchange with a look that was equal parts amusement and bemusement.

'I'm sorry, but this is beyond repair.' She shook the dress gently. 'You've *shredded* the lining, Anita!'

'OK, OK, don't go on about it!'

'For someone who wants a massive favour, I'd watch the tone,' Sophy advised. 'Also, you're actually resting your boobs on the top of my head.'

'Oh my God, I am. Sorry.' Anita retreated slightly and looked fearfully round the pub to see if Phoebe had reappeared. Then she batted her very long eyelashes at Cress. 'You're *so* good at working miracles on every dress that comes in, but I hadn't realised that you could make dresses too. Like, design them and make patterns and stuff.'

'Well, yes, I started by making dresses for my Barbies,' Cress admitted with a sidelong look at Miles, who didn't seem too perturbed by this confession. 'Then Sophy's dance outfits, and, when I did my degree in fashion conservation, sometimes it was about replacing and replicating garments rather than repairing them.'

'Which is what I would love you to do with this dress.' Anita clasped her hands together, eyelashes fluttering like she was in a force 10 gale. 'If you could make me another one. I'd supply the material . . .'

'This is synthetic crêpe, rayon; you'd be better off with crêpe cotton or a crêpe jersey if you wanted a heavier dress for winter,' Cress said, when she should have been saying that she didn't have the time to be making dresses as well as her day job and her side hustle.

'This is amazing! Thank you so much, Cress!' Anita cooed.

'I haven't said I could do it . . .'

'And I'd pay you for your time except I'm completely broke so I thought that maybe I could buy you your morning coffee every day for two months,' Anita said quickly as they saw Phoebe coming towards them. 'Stuff that dress in your bag before she sees it. Hurry up! Also, can you make sure the new dress has pockets?'

'We'll talk about it tomorrow,' Cress said, tucking the dress out of sight as Phoebe reached them.

'What's going on?' she asked suspiciously, eyes narrowed as if she'd sensed that there was a vintage dress nearby that had been poorly treated. 'You all look very guilty about something. What is it?'

Cress squirmed. She always cracked under pressure.

'Miles was telling us that we couldn't have walk-on roles in the film,' Sophy said calmly, because she was made of

171

stronger stuff than Cress and Anita, who now had a nervous tic pounding away in her right eyelid. 'Very unfair.'

'It's a health and safety thing,' Miles said vaguely, knocking his knee against Cress's leg again as a nervous giggle leaked out of her mouth. 'More than my job's worth.'

'But Jackie Coulter said that she thought I'd be perfect for a little role as a fit model,' Phoebe said, because it turned out that Cress wasn't the only one with a side hustle. 'She was going to send my details to the casting person.'

Miles shook his head. 'Jackie's a law unto herself.'

'It's not even a speaking role,' Phoebe protested. 'I don't see what it would have to do with health—'

'Pheebs! Is it all right if I give Coco Chanel a pork scratching?' Freddy called out from a couple of tables away. 'She's drooling on my jeans.'

'What?' Phoebe looked over to where Freddy was sitting with Coco Chanel on his lap, her front paws beseechingly pressed against his chest, two slavering trails of slobber hanging down from her jowls. 'No! She's not meant to have any processed food.'

Freddy glanced down at the packet. 'I think they're organic pork scratchings.'

With a growl of frustration, Phoebe hurried over to where her beloved was now whimpering, and Cress let out a sigh of relief.

'Saved by the pork scratchings,' she said. Then with a sigh of regret, because although Miles's knee was no longer knocking against hers but rather pressed against it now and they'd barely had a chance to chat about anything, she gathered her stuff. 'I'm going to have to go now.'

'But it's not even eight o'clock,' Sophy protested.

Cress had a quick glance to make sure that Phoebe wasn't still lurking. 'I've got so much to do to get ready for that vintage fair next weekend.'

'I'm giving you a hand this Sunday,' Sophy said because they'd already agreed that she'd come round for lunch and then help to weed out the items to sell and the items to keep. Cress might even get her to embroider a few tote bags, though it would probably be quicker to do them herself. 'It's just the Sunday of the actual sale that I can't do.'

'Did you say vintage fair?' Charles asked. He'd been lounging elegantly because everything Charles did was elegant, but now he sat up straight, his eyes glinting. 'Next weekend?'

'In south London. Dulwich,' Cress said. 'But I thought you two had other plans for that weekend. You even persuaded Phoebe to let you have Saturday off.'

'We do,' Sophy said. 'Two estate sales, and we're staying with Charles's parents.'

She was attempting to sound casual, but Cress knew just how giddy and nervous Sophy was about meeting Charles's parents for the first time.

'Unfortunately, estate sales trumps vintage fair,' Charles said a little sadly. He dealt in semi-precious stones for a living, though even only being semi-precious they still came with a hefty price tag. He was always heading off on buying trips to estate sales in big posh houses where someone had died and their personal effects were being auctioned off to pay for the death duties. It was also where he sourced some of the fancier dresses for the shop. 'My parents are also absolutely thrilled to be meeting Sophy and I don't want to disappoint them by postponing.'

He took Sophy's hand and pressed a light kiss to her knuckles, which made Cress feel a little starry-eyed on her sister-friend's behalf. What must it feel like to be with someone who was so delighted to be with you? Cress couldn't imagine.

'I'll keep an eye out for any tiaras,' Cress joked, but Charles's eyes were gleaming again.

'If you do come across anything that looks interesting on the jewellery front, you can always whizz me over a picture,' he said earnestly. 'I'll keep my phone on at all times.'

'Maybe Anita can help me next Sunday,' Cress said hopefully but Anita shook her head.

'I would if I could, but it's my cousin's engagement party and all my family will be gathering to celebrate that such an unpleasant person has managed to find a man who wants to spend the rest of his life with her – and to ask me why I'm twenty-nine and not yet engaged myself.' Anita pulled an anguished face. 'I would much rather go to a vintage fair. Much, much rather. In fact, I'd rather have major surgery without an anaesthetic and I'm hoping for a burst appendix before the week's out.'

'Bea?' Cress asked hopefully.

Bea shook her head. 'Ordinarily, I'd love to, but I'm going down to Margate to see my grandparents.'

'A couple of the women from my stitch 'n' bitch group live in south London, so they might be up for it,' Cress said as she stood up. 'And I'm working on Aaron to drive me and do the heavy lifting.'

'Mike might be able to help?' Sophy suggested.

'Mike is my plan B,' Cress said, and much as she'd like to spend the rest of the evening in The Hat and Fan with her leg pressed against Miles's, even a couple of hours sorting through her vintage dress patterns would be a couple of hours well spent. 'OK, I'll see you all tomorrow.'

Miles was on his feet too. 'Are you heading for the station? I'm going that way too.'

'That would be great.' Cress couldn't help but beam that she could say a proper private goodbye to Miles instead of leaving him in the pub to be harangued by Phoebe about her role in the film; and who knows what secrets Sophy might let slip if she had too much rosé?

It was still light outside at just gone eight on a mid-August evening, though the sun was soft and fading as it sank slowly and streaked the blue skies pink.

Cress walked just as slowly as the setting sun, Miles alongside her, and every now and again their hands would brush against each other. Every time they did, Cress would glance at Miles and he'd smile at her.

It wasn't until they crossed over the bridge and Chalk Farm station was in their sights that he spoke. 'So, I'm going to Belfast tomorrow to work on some pre-production,' he said.

'That sounds exciting.'

'It's really not. It involves a lot of permits and getting parking bays suspended and finding out that the authentic 1950s street you're meant to be shooting on actually has several satellite TV dishes installed.'

'You're right, that doesn't sound exciting at all,' Cress decided. This was the first time she'd seen Miles in a couple of weeks, but the thought of him not being in the same city as she was made her feel sad for reasons that she didn't want to explore too deeply. 'I thought making a film would be a bit more glamorous than that.'

'Well, it is more glamorous than the summer I worked in a soft drinks factory and came out a different colour every day depending on which drink was in production. At least there's no chance of my turning purple.'

'I think you could carry it off,' Cress said as they came to the crossing opposite Chalk Farm station. She was aware that both of them were talking low-key nonsense to eke out the moments before they had to say goodbye.

'Luckily, I have great mobile phone coverage in Belfast, so expect many messages, gifs, amusing links, etcetera,' Miles said, his hand hovering near the button to turn the lights to red so they could cross, but not quite making contact.

Cress flashed back to Charles kissing Sophy's hand and thought how lovely it must be to have someone who made you feel that special. 'I like getting messages from you,' she said, nervous but proud of her own daring.

'I like it too,' Miles said. 'It's funny, isn't it? A few weeks ago we didn't even know each other and now . . .'

'I feel like I've known you for ever,' Cress said. They'd moved a tiny distance away from the crossing by silent and mutual consent so they could stand facing each other, both of them shuffling nervously from foot to foot. 'But also, I feel like there's so much more I want to know about you.'

'Believe me, the feeling is mutual.' Miles took hold of Cress's hand, not to raise it to his lips for a kiss, but to thread his fingers through hers.

It was lovely but it wasn't enough. There was a part of Cress that wished that the circumstances were different. That she was simply . . . *single*. Unattached in a way that wasn't complicated or accompanied by a disclaimer. Then she could be free to be daring and brave and audacious enough to throw her arms round Miles and kiss him, while the sunset provided a glorious background.

But the circumstances weren't different. And throwing caution to the wind and her arms round Miles wouldn't be fair to him or to herself or to Colin.

'I should really be going now,' Cress said but she didn't make any attempt to let go of Miles's hand.

'You know, I'll be back next Saturday. I could go to the vintage fair with you. One of my friends has a big estate car I could borrow, and I'm great at heavy lifting,' he said suddenly, as if he'd been mulling the idea for a while. 'I'm deceptively strong. Wiry strong rather than ripped muscles strong.'

Cress felt a warm glow as if all of her had been dipped in caramel. 'You don't mind schlepping and carrying and trying to prop up my wonky clothes rail so it doesn't collapse?'

'Can't think of a better way to spend a Sunday.' A shadow crossed Miles's face. 'It's going to be an early start though, isn't it?'

'I'm afraid so,' Cress said, squeezing his fingers just a little tighter.

'There's not many people, maybe only five, that I'd get up early on a Sunday for but you're one of them,' Miles said, gently letting go of Cress's hand so she felt untethered. He took a step back and held his hand up to his head in a salute. 'I'll be in touch then. And I'll see you Sunday week.'

Cress nodded. 'I'm looking forward to it,' she said with even more added braveness.

The sunset was no match for the smile on Miles's face. 'It's a date then.'

Chapter Nineteen

Cress hadn't really been looking forward to the vintage fair. Or rather, she was sure she'd enjoy it once she was there, but she knew that she'd spend the days leading up to it worrying about the logistics and getting into a tizzy about what stock she should sell and what she should keep.

'Although what am I actually keeping any of them for?' she asked Sophy as the two of them put dress after dress on the sale pile.

'Some of these are gorgeous,' Sophy pointed out. She'd already nabbed two 1950s summer frocks for herself. 'I wouldn't sell them. Why don't you wear them?'

'Because I never go anywhere that requires a dress like this.' Cress shook out a beautiful grey silk dress adorned with big, blowsy, yellow cabbage roses from the pile of fancy frocks with very minimal repairwork destined for The Vintage Dress Shop. 'I buy them because they're beautiful but damaged and I can't bear to think of them being unloved and unappreciated, but once I mend them they end up unworn in my box room.'

'There's so many metaphors in that sentence that I don't know where to start. You could wear them if you wanted to,' Sophy pointed out – gently, because things had been a little tense between them that evening. Sophy had kept asking Cress if each dress sparked joy until Cress had reached the edge of her nerves and said that Sophy would be seeing sparks if she kept it up.

'But at the shop, I need to wear my work smocks because it doesn't matter if I stick my spare pins in them and they have big pockets . . .'

'There's still no reason why you can't wear a nice frock under your smocks, instead of a shirt and trousers.' Sophy bundled a huge leopard faux fur into a garment bag. 'I would never admit it to Phoebe but now I love wearing a pretty vintage dress to work every day. I leave the house in a good mood simply because I love the swish of my full skirt, or I imagine all the adventures that the previous owner of the dress might have had. Much more fun than those black sacks I used to wear.'

'Yes, but then everyone would be looking at me . . .'

'I think there are some people that like looking at you,' Sophy said, then pressed her lips together like she'd already said too much.

Cress knew what she was getting at and who she was referring to, but it wasn't a conversation she wanted to have. Not even with Sophy.

Miles was now in Belfast but he'd already secured a friend's very large car and had sent Cress an itinerary for Sunday morning. He'd even scheduled in a stop at a Greggs halfway to Dulwich 'because an army marches on its stomach and I'll be needing a steak bake by then'.

So, when Cress thought about Sunday, it wasn't just to panic about all the things that could go wrong. She was also greedily counting the hours that she'd spend hanging out with Miles, *as a friend*. Plus, if he was that organised that he'd put together an itinerary, he wasn't going to be the sort of person who borrowed a car whose engine would suddenly burst into flames in the middle of the Blackwall Tunnel.

The anticipation of Sunday made the week drag by. Until Tanya came in to try on the toile.

Cress had been worried (though really, when was she *not* worrying about something?) that the toile would look so different from the dress that she'd sketched out and the dress that Audrey Hepburn had worn in *Breakfast at Tiffany's* that there might be more tears from Tanya.

She was too worried to say anything once Tanya was in the toile and standing on the dais in front of the many mirrors in the main salon, so she and Cress could see what the fit was like.

'You have to remember that a white cotton toile is very, very different from a black satin dress,' Cress explained in a panicked rush as Tanya turned very slowly, craning her neck to see the toile from all angles. 'I mean, it won't be covered in blue chalk marks for one thing.'

Tanya's expression was unreadable. So different from the woman that Cress had first met who'd burst into tears. Now she wondered if Tanya was actually a professional poker player.

'OK, there's something I don't understand,' Tanya said at last.

Cress couldn't help but cringe a little. 'What?'

'I'm basically wearing a thin white dress tacked together and I can clearly see the outline of my bra and pants . . .'

'My fault, I should have asked you to bring a slip . . .'

'. . . but I look all right. I look really all right. I have a waist!' Tanya put her hands on her hips. 'I've never had a waist before.'

'I'm sure you have but you've probably never worn a dress that's been specifically made to your measurements.' Cress stepped up on to the dais herself so she could pluck at the muslin. 'See, I nipped it in here with these darts. And see these seams on the bodice? That will be actual boning when I make the dress. Comfortable boning though. It will accentuate that waist and, well, your boobs.'

'I have always had a cracking bust,' Tanya said, adjusting the breasts in question. She held out her arms and turned again. 'I think we can lose the sleeves. They're ruining the lines of the dress.'

'You want to lose the sleeves?' Cress queried because Tanya had been very adamant before about keeping her upper arms covered. 'If you're happy to do that, then I'm happy to do that.'

'When I'm walking out in the black satin version of this, no one is going to be looking at my bingo wings,' Tanya declared and now she was sounding a little sniffly as if the tears weren't far off. 'Between then and now, I'll work on toning up my triceps.'

Tanya was all smiles when she left, a very different woman from the one who'd first ventured into The Vintage Dress Shop all those weeks ago.

Whereas Ella always carried herself with the assurance and grace of a princess; but on Thursday morning when she turned up for more shadowing Cress ('What can I say? I'm a glutton for punishment'), she walked into the workroom and was rendered speechless. She even flinched.

'What the hell is that? Was it recently in an earthquake?' she asked, once she'd regained the power of speech, of the dress that was on the dress form, 'And why are you locking the door?'

Cress tried to assume an innocent expression but she was sure there was a muscle twitching in her forehead. 'We're working on a special project,' she said, approaching the the poor bedraggled scraps of black crêpe on the form that had once been Anita's favourite dress. 'I'm making a replica of this dress for a friend and you're going to make one too. We're going to start with unpicking this dress so we can trace our pattern pieces, then maybe we'll do a toile, I'm not sure. Then we'll get to the fun part where we pin the pattern pieces onto our fabric, cut them, sew them together and *voila!* A dress!'

Ella backed away. 'Oh no, I'm not ready for that. I know that I give off "can do" vibes but actually, Cress, there's lots of things I can't do. Isn't there some hemming I can be getting on with?'

'I'm sure learning to ride a horse side-saddle was harder than making a dress,' Cress insisted. She hadn't even got to the best bit yet. 'And not only will you be making a dress, you'll be doing it on *this!*'

Ella hadn't even noticed the bulky item on the counter shrouded in black cotton, until Cress pulled the material away with a flourish.

'What is that? Apart from something that should be in a museum?' Ella asked, her voice very screechy.

'It's a 1930s sewing machine. Works like a dream,' Cress said fondly as she stroked the hand-crank. 'I forgot I had this until I was sorting out my box room.'

'It's not even electric!'

'Yes, but it's probably easier to use than my modern one with all its bells and whistles, and it's also what your character would use.' Cress could feel her lower lip jutting out in a justified pout. 'I was feeling very pleased with myself and now you're raining on my parade.'

Ella immediately assumed a diva position, chest out, arms stretched wide. 'Don't tell me not to live, just sit and putter,' she sang, like she just couldn't help herself.

'You can sing while you sew, but you *will* be sewing,' Cress told her, as she began to unfurl a length of ivory silk she needed to replace the lining in a 1920s wedding dress. 'And tracing a pattern and cutting it out and everything else required. With no backchat.'

'You're being so strict. I'm not sure I like it,' Ella said. 'Also, you're handling that silk like it's part of you. I'm never going to be able to do that.'

'But you recognised that it *is* silk, so the information is going in,' Cress said proudly, but Ella didn't look convinced. 'Your hands will catch up soon enough.'

Still, it was the perfect way for Ella to learn how to be convincing as a trained fashion professional, though every time Cress heard Phoebe coming up the stairs she nearly had a heart attack at the thought of her bursting into the workroom and demanding to know what they were doing.

Phoebe didn't though. Her mind was very firmly on 'her brides' and matching the right woman with the right dress and, as long as Cress fulfilled her contractual obligations, Phoebe trusted her to get on with things. Which did make Cress feel a little bit guilty, but not guilty enough to tell Anita that she'd have to find someone else to remake her dress.

Then it was Sunday morning, after a fitful night's sleep of worrying about what could go wrong before, during and after the vintage fair. Cress really was the queen of the worst-case scenario.

But the sun came up, as it always did, and Miles, as promised, was pulling in to the kerb outside her house at precisely 7.59 a.m.

'A minute ahead of schedule,' he pointed out as Cress rushed down the garden path to meet him. He got out of the big estate car with its promised capacious boot space, especially as the back seats had been folded down. 'It's not very often that I'm up before six thirty on a Sunday. Unless some heartless director of photography wants to take advantage of the early-morning light.'

'I am *so* grateful,' Cress said, clasping her hands together, suddenly shy now that Miles was real again, with that lazy smile of his, and not just words on her phone screen. 'I can't thank you enough.'

'And I can't think of a better way to spend the day than a road trip with a . . . a new friend,' Miles said and then he was quite silent and still, just looking at Cress as she looked at him. He wore old jeans with rips in the knee and a black t-shirt with the same casual elegance that Charles wore one of his fancy suits. He wasn't wearing sunglasses for once, so Cress could see the warm, appreciative look he was giving her, and she was glad that she'd decided to wear a pretty dress, even though it was hardly practical for the amount of lugging stuff around that she was going to have to do. But she didn't care about that right now. All she cared about was the soft expression on Miles's face. They were having a moment on her boring little suburban street, a moment that was making her heart beat a little faster than usual.

'I missed you,' Cress said at last.

'I missed you too.' Miles took her hand and brushed his thumb over the back of it, causing a multitude of tiny brush-fires to ignite.

There wasn't any need for words but to just stand there, still, and revel in the nearness of each other.

'What are you two doing standing about like one o'clock half-struck?' Unfortunately Diane, always an early riser even on Sunday mornings, had been killing moments for as long as Cress could remember. She was standing in the open front doorway with her hands on her hips. 'You've still got all your boxes in the hall and I want to run the vacuum.'

'We're coming,' Cress called out and, with a little grimace at Miles, who smiled sympathetically, she turned to her mother. 'We're just going to load up now.'

'That's what the schedule says,' Miles said, following Cress up the garden path to where Diane was still standing like she'd been turned to stone. Only her eyes were busy, running Miles up and down like she was a barcode scanner. Starting with his bashed-in black and white Converse, the ripped jeans, the Ramones t-shirt, the polite smile on his face and his always tousled, always messy hair.

'This is Miles, my friend who's helping me out today,' Cress said, giving Diane a little shove so she'd stop gawping and also move out of the way. 'Miles, this is my mum, Diane.'

'Pleasure to meet you, Diane,' Miles said, shaking her mother's hand, which was proffered like she was a monarch receiving a dignitary from foreign shores. 'We'll be out of your hair in no time.'

'Always nice to meet Cress's . . . friends. Oh, there's no rush.' Diane folded her arms as Miles hefted the first of the plastic crates that Cress had packed. 'Shall I put the kettle on?'

'I don't think we have time,' Cress said quickly, because they were on a schedule and she hadn't really thought about *this* . . . Introducing her mum to Miles, whom she'd only briefly mentioned as a kindly friend doing her a favour – which was the absolute truth. And yet didn't even begin to come close to accurately describing Miles's presence in her life.

'Always time for a quick coffee,' Miles said with a smile as he lifted another crate, then winced. 'God, what have you got in here? Rocks?'

'Just some books.' Cress followed Miles out of the door with several garment bags hanging over her shoulder. 'We can get coffee on the way,' she hissed and he shrugged.

'As long as there is coffee in my near future, I'm not fussed,' he said. 'Your mum seems nice.'

Diane was nice. She was easily Cress's favourite mother and one of the best people she knew, but Cress was relieved she was nowhere to be seen on their next couple of trips from hall to car. Until she and Miles headed back for the last crate and Cress's collapsed clothes rails, only to find that not just Diane but now Aaron was loitering in the hall too, clad only in a t-shirt and his boxer shorts. Diane had clearly woken him up so he could have a good gawp at Miles too.

'Need a hand?' Aaron asked, though they very clearly didn't.

Again, Miles was unfailingly polite when Cress introduced them, and shook hands with her pants-clad stepfather while Cress glared at Aaron from over Miles's shoulder.

'Right, we'll be off then,' she said firmly, pushing Miles out of the door even though she could hear Diane shouting, 'But the kettle's just boiled!'

'You don't want to stay for coffee?' Miles asked as Cress herded him down the garden path.

'I think you mean, don't you want to stay to be thoroughly interrogated,' Cress said. 'I hadn't really thought about how Mum might react to a man who wasn't Colin coming round.'

Miles opened the passenger door of the huge car for Cress, though she could have done it herself. She didn't so much as get in the car as climb in. She felt very high up.

She scowled as Diane and Aaron stood on the doorstep and watched as Miles walked round to the driver's side. He lifted his hand in farewell and they both waved but made no effort to shut the door until Miles was in the driver's seat and pulling away from the kerb.

'Unbelievable,' Cress muttered under her breath. 'So sorry about that.'

Miles retrieved his ubiquitous Ray-Bans from the central console, as the sun was now making its presence felt. 'It's cool,' he said with a grin. 'At least I can say that I've met your parents now.'

Chapter Twenty

It wasn't really a road trip. Driving across London from north to south didn't really count, especially when one's journey was usually delayed by traffic jams, roadworks and emergency traffic lights.

But this early on a Sunday morning, they had a clear run through a London that was determined to be its best self.

'Do you want to go the quickest route or do you want to go the scenic route, which will add a whole seven more minutes to the journey?' Miles had asked as he plugged their destination into the satnav.

It was a no-brainer. 'Scenic route, please.'

They hadn't really talked much since then. Magic FM was on in the background and every time a particularly cheesy banger came on, Miles would turn up the volume. 'Total Eclipse Of The Heart' was a particular highlight as they embarked on a tour of all of London's greatest hits. From the glorious green open space of Hampstead Heath, through picturesque Hampstead Village, then on to Regent's Park and into town. They passed tourists queuing outside the British Museum in Bloomsbury, wound their way through narrow Covent Garden streets, then crossed the River Thames at Waterloo Bridge.

Cress never felt more of a Londoner, born and bred, than she did when she was able to glimpse the river that flowed through London like the city's lifeblood. The sun glinted off the water and though it was early, it was already busy with all manner of boats from waterborne taxis to pleasure cruisers.

Then they were in south London, which Cress didn't know so well. As they drove through Lambeth and Bermondsey, the sunny streets were slowly coming to life with people heading out to walk dogs or to get breakfast supplies or queue for brunch.

Just as Cress and her stomach both realised that they hadn't had breakfast yet even though she'd been up for a couple of hours, Miles pulled in to the side of the road.

'Are we stopping for your steak bake?' she asked, peering out. She couldn't see the familiar blue hoarding of a Greggs anywhere on the little high street of independent shops and artisanal cafés.

'I fancy something a bit more continental,' Miles said. He pointed to a pastel-pink shopfront that had the words Sourdough Sally written on it in a cursive grey font. 'What do you want? My treat.'

'It's absolutely not your treat,' Cress said, already reaching for her bag. 'You will not be spending any money today on food, drink or petrol. You're doing me a favour and not the other way round.'

Miles hand covered Cress's as it delved for her purse. 'We'll go halves on petrol.'

Cress shook her head. 'We bloody will not. Now, what do you fancy in the way of breakfast pastries?'

'Surprise me,' Miles said, sitting back in his seat because there was an uncharacteristically stubborn note to Cress's tone and he instinctively and wisely knew that this wasn't an argument that he was going to win. 'And a large coffee, please. Bit of milk, oat is great if they have it, no foam, no syrup.'

There wasn't much of a queue and Cress soon returned with a pink box full of sweet treats, which they decided to leave until they'd reached their destination so they wouldn't get pastry crumbs all over the borrowed car.

But they both sipped their restorative coffees as they completed the last leg of their journey through Peckham and finally arrived at their destination: Dulwich.

Like Hampstead, like Primrose Hill, Dulwich was another pretty London village, full of elegant houses ranging from small Georgian mansions to Victorian villas and huge red-brick Edwardian terraces. Like all of the most chichi areas of London, it was dominated by its own verdant green space, in this case Dulwich Common.

Their venue for the day was the large parish hall of a now-deconsecrated church that had been converted into loft apartments. At half past nine, it was a flurry of activity, with people unloading boxes and crates from the backs of vans and cars.

'We're going to take five minutes to finish our coffee and carb-load,' Miles decided when Cress flailed her hands as he parked the car.

'I'm panicking,' she admitted. 'I don't know why. I've become very used to dealing with the public since I started working at the shop.'

'Fear of the unknown?' Miles suggested through a mouthful of pain au chocolat and Cress could only nod glumly.

Every time she thought that she might step out of her comfort zone and have adventures, even if they were very low-key adventures with very mild jeopardy, she was reminded that she just wasn't built that way. Miles started unloading, while Cress hurried into the hall to locate one of the organisers and pray that the paperwork was in order and they hadn't given away her stall.

'Of course they hadn't,' Miles said, when Cress returned with lanyards for the both of them and a stern warning about not damaging the parquet flooring with any of her gear.

'After we've set up your clothes rails, we can put gaffer tape on the feet.'

All that organising and packing and sorting and Cress hadn't thought about gaffer tape.

Once again, it was Miles to the rescue. He rummaged in the boot of the car and pulled out a small toolbox. 'Got some gaffer tape in here. Never go anywhere without it.'

Their stall, or rather their three tables and enough space for two rails, was in a good spot between two other vintage sellers and just opposite a stall selling home-made cakes, brownies and other baked goods, so there was sure to be a lot of foot traffic.

Miles busied himself with the clothes rails, while Cress started unpacking her dresses. She might not have remembered gaffer tape, but she had brought her mini steamer to banish any wrinkles, and once the dresses that she'd painstakingly mended were hanging up and already attracting attention from the other stallholders and early bird customers, she felt much better.

'Right, what can I do now?' Miles asked and Cress set him to displaying her boxes of vintage buttons and trims on one of the tables, which she'd already covered with a length of fifties oilcloth in a colourful graphic design.

Cress sorted through her vintage patterns, arranged a stack of fashion books she was selling, carefully displayed her miscellaneous accessories including a velvet pillbox hat with a little figure of a robin perched on it, and stuck on the price tags she'd made the night before. Then on a corkboard she pinned a selection of her tote bags with their colourful embroidered fashion-related slogans like 'Florals? For Spring? Groundbreaking'; 'It's called fashion, Brenda'; and her bestseller, 'Go frock yourself.'

The last thing to do was make sure she had her pink and white striped paper bags to hand. 'Everyone who buys something gets one of my postcards, a couple of stickers and, if they're buying one of my repaired pieces, the information sheet on how to care for vintage clothes,' she told Miles. She'd ordered the bags, cards and stickers, all declaring that they were made 'With Love, by Cressida', when she'd first opened her Etsy shop several years before.

'People really love stickers,' she added as Miles studied the sticker, which featured a silhouette of a woman in a big foofy dress and Cress's logo, courtesy of her cousin Alyssa, who designed greetings cards for a living.

'I know you said this was a side hustle, but this is like a proper side hustle,' Miles said, his eyes drifting over the three tables, corkboard and the clothes rails that were Cress's empire.

If she wasn't saving up for a future with Colin, then Cress still wasn't sure exactly what goal she was working towards any more. Couldn't even remember why she'd thought that having a stall at this vintage fair was a good idea, especially when her stomach lurched with nerves as the first punter padded purposefully towards her.

She just had to survive the next few hours.

Cress didn't just survive, she thrived. After all, it was a vintage fair and she quickly realised that she was among kindred spirits.

People didn't just want to browse for vintage clothes and maybe harangue her for selling previously damaged items (though each garment came with a handwritten label detailing exactly what she had done to give the garment a new lease of life.)

No! They wanted to talk about how much they loved vintage clothes and commend Cress on her commitment to sustainable fashion. A couple of people even asked if she taught classes on repairing vintage clothes. Even better, a beautifully dressed woman in her sixties in an impeccable 1940s outfit, from the top of her stylish red velvet beret perked rakishly on her curled and rolled platinum-blond hair to her peep-toe black suede pumps, *did* run classes – on visible mending.

Instead of trying to darn holes and rips as inconspicuously as possible, Kathy made a feature of the repair work. She might use a contrasting thread or patch or even embroider a pattern where the damage was, and her next course started in September. Cress was definitely going to sign up.

After a couple of hours, her voice was hoarse from talking to so many people. She'd sold more than half of her dresses and accessories, all of the tote bags, her *Vogue* patterns and worn copies of French fashion magazine *L'Echo de la Mode*, and had even got rid of the leopard faux fur coat, even though it was itchy and far too heavy to wear for longer than half an hour, tops.

She'd also made fast friends with the vintage sellers on either side of her: a woman called Marianne who had a vintage shop in Kentish Town and her boyfriend Barnes, who was a tattooist; and Barbara, a sprightly septuagenarian who specialised in eighties fashion and tried to teach Cress, with little success, how to haggle.

While all this was going on, Miles was the perfect wingman. With the aid of his toolbox, some lengths of spare fabric and a supporting beam between Cress's and Marianne's stall, he was able to rig up a makeshift changing room. Once word got out that, apart from the very grumpy caretaker, he was the only person present with a fully equipped toolbox, he was much in demand with the other stallholders. But still, he always managed to be there when Cress realised that she'd run out of change or needed a bottle of water to soothe her parched throat, or even to tell a very annoying woman who seemed to think that Cress would mark down all her wares if she asked long and loud enough to do one. Politely but firmly.

He even managed to scrounge a couple of deckchairs so that Cress wasn't on her feet all the time. There were lulls when they were quiet, and he was the best person to chat nonsense with as they watched so many fabulously dressed people wander by.

It was just after three when Cress decided that it was probably time to start packing up. She didn't have much left to sell and the crowd had thinned as there was a vintage picnic starting on Dulwich Common at four.

'I don't know whether to massively reduce my prices or just save what I don't sell to put up in my Etsy shop,' she said to Miles, who'd just come back from a mercy errand with his toolbox and with a genuine RAF leather flying jacket from the Second World War he'd just bought.

'Maybe save your stock for another vintage fair,' he said, popping the sheepskin collar on his 'new' jacket.

'You think I should do another vintage fair?' Cress asked. She'd enjoyed herself much more than she thought she would, but she'd been treating the whole experience as a one-off.

Miles shrugged. 'Well, I'm game if you are. We make a good team, don't we?'

'We really do. I've got the vintage nous and you have . . .'

'Are you saying you're the brains and I'm the brawn?' Miles put a hand to his heart like he was hurt, though Cress hadn't been saying any such thing.

'Not just the brawn, you have a toolbox too,' she pointed out.

Miles took a step back as if she'd dealt him a mortal blow and Cress turned her head away to hide her smile and that was when she saw them.

It had to be a trick of the light. Or rather, in a parish hall full of vintage lovers, of course there were going to be women who looked like Phoebe.

But that didn't explain why the man she was with, the man *who had his arm round her,* looked just like Freddy.

Chapter Twenty-One

Cress knew her mouth was hanging open in a slack-jawed, very unflattering kind of way, but she just couldn't close it, so great was her shock.

Then the woman on the other side of the room who looked just like Phoebe turned the corner into their row of stalls and Cress let out an honest to goodness squeak and hid behind one of her clothing rails.

'You all right, Cress?' Miles asked with some concern, his hand on her shoulder. 'You look like you've just seen a ghost.'

'Worse than a ghost,' Cress croaked. She yanked hold of a handful of Miles's new flying jacket and pulled him behind the rail.

'It's not your ex, is it?'

'What? Ha! No!' The very *idea* that Colin would come to a vintage fair of his own volition, unless it was full of stall after stall of middle-aged blokes (always blokes) selling vinyl.

'Who then?' Miles shook Cress very gently. 'Don't keep me in suspense.'

'OK, there's a woman and a man walking in this direction . . . No! Don't look!' Cress grabbed hold of Miles's arm to keep him out of sight. 'I think it's Phoebe.'

'What's the problem?' Miles asked because he just didn't get it. 'I thought you and Phoebe were pals.'

'We are, but she's very territorial about vintage fashion and I know she'd be weird about me selling clothes at a vintage fair, and also the guy she's with looks like Freddy, and

why would she be with Freddy when she can't stand him?'
It was a very good question. It couldn't have been Phoebe.
Clearly Cress was delirious. It had been a long time since
that box of breakfast pastries and her blood sugar was obviously low.

She carefully peered out from behind the clothes rails,
only to catch another glimpse of the mystery woman. Except
there was no mystery about it.

It was Phoebe, coming closer and closer. There was no
mistaking her – or Coco Chanel, who was cradled in her
arms.

Their eyes met.

Cress cringed.

Phoebe glared.

'What are you doing here?' she asked, eyes narrowed suspiciously. Though really, did Phoebe's eyes narrow in any
other way?

Cress wondered if she could style this out. But she wasn't
doing anything wrong. It was a free country.

'I was just in the area . . .'

'Oh hey, Phoebe,' said Miles, stepping out from behind the
rail. 'Cress and I have been running a stall here. Pity you're so
late, we've sold all of the good stuff.'

'Selling dresses?' Phoebe could hardly get the words out.

'Not just dresses, blouses and cardigans and coats and
garments that are not dresses, so we couldn't sell them in the
shop anyway,' Cress said in a garbled rush, before she found
a small reserve of courage. 'Anyway, I gave you first dibs on
my fancier stuff but everything else wasn't shop-quality.'

'Even so. The shop has a reputation. I can't have my staff
selling inferior vintage . . .'

Phoebe was off on one of her rants and all Cress could
do was stand there and wring her hands – and also marvel
at what Phoebe was wearing. Come rain, come shine, she

was in her shop 'uniform' of fitted black dress, seamed stockings and high heels, her black hair always in an immaculate and shiny bob. But today her hair was caught up in a gaily patterned scarf and she was wearing a red and white short-sleeved gingham blouse knotted at the waist, with a pair of dark indigo denim pedal pushers and red wedge sandals.

Phoebe did Sunday casual. Who knew?

'. . . and there's a definite conflict of interest here, Cress, and, quite frankly, I expected better from . . .'

Cress's eyes were now firmly downcast as Phoebe read her the riot act . . . so she didn't see him approach, just heard a friendly and familiar voice cut through Phoebe's invective.

'Ah, there you are, babes. I wish you wouldn't wander off like that. This is why I always say that I'm going to get Coco a collar with a bell on it.'

Cress raised her eyes because there was no way she was going to miss this. Especially as *this* was Freddy putting his arm round a stiff-backed Phoebe, who immediately tried to shrug it off. 'Oh, hi, Freddy,' Cress chirped. She didn't have to fake the way her eyes widened in surprise. 'I wouldn't have expected to see you *and Phoebe* so far from home.'

There was a silence so spiky that it should have come with a health and safety warning.

Miles hadn't got that memo though. 'I never realised that you two were a couple,' he said, oblivious to all the tension. Or maybe he wasn't because, when Cress turned to look at him and signal the impending apocalypse with just her eyes, he winked at her.

Freddy shifted uncomfortably. 'Yeah, well, about that. I—'

'We're not a couple,' Phoebe hissed. 'We're here in a professional capacity only.'

'You just look very together,' Miles noted.

'You really do,' Cress managed to get out. Half of her was dying of mortification from being told off by Phoebe even though she hadn't done anything wrong. The other half of her was mainlining sheer glee. She couldn't wait to tell Sophy about this.

'Is this your stall?' Freddy asked, eyes darting nervously as if he was desperate to change the subject. He picked up one of Cress's information sheets. 'Oh yeah, it is. This is a nice idea. Telling people how to look after their vintage and what cycle to use in the washing machine. Maybe you'd let us print some off for the shop.'

'You can't just stick vintage in the washing machine along with your gym kit,' Phoebe said. Now Coco Chanel was giving Cress a disappointed look too even though, *again*, Cress had done nothing to deserve Phoebe and her gremlin dog's wrath.

In fact, there was no employment tribunal that'd find Cress guilty and if Phoebe wanted to sack her, for what? Selling vintage dress patterns, even though they didn't actually sell them in the shop? Then she was going to have a lot of very pissed-off brides who didn't have anyone to alter their wedding dresses. Besides, it was her day off.

'Actually, Phoebe, you *can* wash some vintage in a washing machine, if you put it in a mesh wash bag and do it on a delicate cycle,' Cress said, folding her arms and sticking out her chin.

'Not if it has a lot of beadwork,' Phoebe insisted.

'I don't know why you're getting so cross,' Cress said, and, under cover of the tablecloth, Miles took her hand and gave it a comforting squeeze. 'Why are you even arguing with me about the best way to take care of vintage clothing when we're on the same side? The side that doesn't want anything bad to happen to the vintage clothing.'

Phoebe opened her mouth to contest Cress's last point, then shut it when she realised that Cress was talking truth to power.

'I mean . . . Well . . . I'm just very surprised to see you here,' she said at last. 'In south London.' Her eyes narrowed again and Cress's heart sank. 'With Miles.'

Miles squeezed Cress's hand again. 'Oh, I'm just here in a professional capacity,' he said, eyes gleaming, and Freddy turned his head and disguised what sounded a lot like a laugh as a cough.

'Phoebe? I thought it was you! And Mademoiselle Coco.' Marianne from the next stall had arrived to save the day.

Also, she was at least five foot ten, had hair the same colour red as postboxes and London buses, more tattoos than Freddy, and was dressed in a skintight leopard print dress. In short, the sort of person who wasn't going to be having any of Phoebe's nonsense.

Phoebe stopped narrowing her eyes. In fact, she suddenly had one of her rare but wide smiles on her face, which instantly transformed her from imperious ice queen to a very friendly, very pretty woman.

'Marianne! I've been meaning to come and see you on my day off – but then I hardly ever take a day off because I'm not sure how the shop would manage without me,' Phoebe said, even though one of her staff was standing right there and was perfectly capable of getting through a normal working day without Phoebe's involvement and/or interference.

'You should come and visit. I've got a couple of dresses tucked away that I thought would be perfect for you, but there's a few things here that you might like too,' Marianne said as Phoebe finally moved out of Cress's orbit, homing in on Marianne's clothing rails like they were the mothership.

Freddy took Coco Chanel from Phoebe's arms and rolled his eyes. 'Sorry about that. You know what she's like. Bark far, far worse than her bite. So, you sold a lot today?'

It wasn't very often that Cress found herself in conversation with Freddy, but he seemed genuinely interested in her make-do-and-mend philosophy.

Then he wanted to know how things were going with Ella and all about Tanya's *Breakfast at Tiffany's* dress, because he was frighteningly well informed about what was happening at The Vintage Dress Shop. Or rather Phoebe, who was now hidden in the makeshift changing cubicle trying on dress after dress, must tell him everything.

By the time Phoebe emerged, still smiling, Cress, Miles and Freddy had packed up the rest of Cress's stall and Coco Chanel was fast asleep on one of the deckchairs.

'She really will fall asleep anywhere,' Phoebe said fondly, as Miles and Freddy carried the last plastic crates out to the car.

Now that Phoebe was in a better mood, Cress felt as if she could relax. 'What did you buy?' she asked, nodding at the gold carrier bag Phoebe was clutching.

Phoebe opened the bag so Cress could peer inside. 'A beaded cashmere cardigan, I love that Kelly green, and a velvet evening capelet. I feel like I might be entering my cape era,' she said a little wistfully. Then she turned her attention to Cress. 'I like that dress. I bet you've got a *huge* collection of dresses that I never get to see because you don't wear them at work.'

She was definitely in a better mood but, even so, Phoebe made it seem like Cress's decision to wear practical work smocks and also not draw unwanted attention to herself by wearing vintage dresses was a personal affront.

Cress tugged at the skirt of her grey plaid fifties dress, which had trellises of pink roses curling in and out of the two-tone grey squares. 'I'm not really a vintage dress kind of person.'

'That's what Sophy used to say and now she wears vintage dresses every day.' Phoebe preened a little. 'And the right size bra. One of my greatest achievements.'

'I hope you've never said that to Sophy.'

Was that another smile creeping onto Phoebe's face? 'Of course not. I haven't got a death wish. Shall I give you a hand with that?'

Cress was wrestling with her wonky clothes rail that didn't want to be dismantled, but Phoebe soon had it under control. Cress could see Miles and Freddy standing near the entrance and chatting away like they were old friends.

Whenever Colin had come into the same orbit as her friends, even Sophy who'd known him for as long as he and Cress had been dating, he was awkward and stand-offish. Yes, he was shy. Cress knew exactly what it was like to be shy, but being shy didn't mean that you never made any effort.

The only time that Colin had really met her friends and colleagues at The Vintage Dress Shop was at a vintage ball the year before. Cress had had to beg and plead and eventually agree to pay for their next week's takeaway before he'd agree to come. Then he'd been sullen and silent and hadn't said a word to anyone. This year, Cress hadn't even asked Colin and, though she'd pretended that she was sad that he couldn't be her plus one, she'd had much more fun flying solo. She'd even let Charles, then Freddy take her for a spin around the dancefloor. Cress knew that if she'd asked Miles to be her partner, he'd have entered into the spirit of things. Would have worn a dinner jacket and made an attempt to foxtrot. He simply slotted into her life in a way that was frictionless and easy.

But there was nothing frictionless and easy about the way she was starting to feel about Miles. Cress realised that it had been a while since she'd tormented herself with self-sabotaging thoughts that Miles was too cool, too handsome, too everything to want anything to do with her when she often felt like she wasn't enough. When he suddenly turned his head to look in Cress's direction, a hot, heady sensation overtook her, even though they were meant to be very firmly in the friend zone.

'Anyway, Cress, I'm sorry about before. About being so fierce. I just care about vintage clothes, about the shop, so much.'

The words that had just come out of Phoebe's mouth were worthy of Cress's full attention.

'Look, I love vintage style as much as the next person, actually a lot more than the next person, but they are just clothes. I love working at The Vintage Dress Shop, but it is just a job. It shouldn't be your whole life.'

'It's not my whole life.' Phoebe scooped up Coco Chanel and pressed kisses to her grumpy, scrunched-up face. 'This one is at least half of my life.'

It wasn't really what Cress had meant but at least Coco Chanel meant that Phoebe had *some* work/life balance.

'Well, apology accepted,' Cress said because life was too short and the argument she'd had with Phoebe was too ridiculous to still be fuming about.

'I'm so glad. Because I do consider you a friend and, as a friend, I'd appreciate if you didn't mention that you'd seen me and Freddy together outside of work.' Phoebe looked around furtively as if she expected the last stragglers and stallholders to be hanging on her every word. 'We were only here to look out for any possible stock for the shop and you know how people, and by people I especially mean Anita, talk.'

Cress had been so looking forward to telling Sophy about bumping into Phoebe and Freddy and how she'd been absolutely sure that Freddy's arm had been round Phoebe's shoulders very much not in a professional capacity. But if Phoebe was asking Cress not to tell, then she wouldn't. Not even Sophy.

'It's fine,' she said, waving a hand in a breezy manner. 'Your secret's safe with me.'

Phoebe and Coco Chanel shot Cress matching reproachful looks. 'It's not a secret, Cress, but to have people gossiping about me and Freddy, even though we're here on business, well, it would undermine my authority.'

It would take a direct hit from a cruise missile to even dent Phoebe's absolute authority at the shop, but Cress made the right noises and Phoebe was all smiles again as Freddy and Miles approached.

'There's a picnic thing happening,' Miles said. 'On the common. If you were up for it, I thought we could find a shop still open and get some picky bits.'

He was looking at Cress but then he shifted his focus to Freddy and Phoebe too, which was the polite thing to do, even if Cress didn't particularly want to spend what was left of her Sunday, and her time with Miles, with Phoebe. Yes, Phoebe was a friend, but she was very much a work friend.

Freddy shrugged. 'We'd love to, but we've got to get back to north London. Or civilisation, as I call it.'

It would also be the polite thing to offer them a lift, but Phoebe already had her hand on Freddy's arm. 'Actually, Marianne and Barnes said they had room in their car for both of us. They're skipping the picnic but also, there are several people here that I really don't want to picnic with.' She glared across the hall. 'That woman over there with the pink dress on, I called her out for selling 1970s reproduction vintage as original 1930s vintage at Goodwood and she's never forgiven me.'

'Well, let's get you out of here before she exacts her revenge,' Freddy said, and, as they walked away, for one brief moment before Phoebe said something and stepped away, his arm was very definitely round her shoulders.

Chapter Twenty-Two

Then it was just Cress and Miles. They'd been so busy all day that Cress felt as if she'd not had any proper quality time with him.

'Are you up for a picnic?' he asked, as he hefted up the wonky clothes rail, which was all that was left to be packed.

Ordinarily, Cress could take or leave picnics, which were never as much fun as advertised. They usually involved wasps and something leaking and making the crisps and sandwiches all soggy.

But it was a perfect summer's day and it was only four in the afternoon and she wanted nothing more than to lie on a patch of grass with Miles and possibly eat some strawberries too.

'I'd love a picnic,' Cress said with all the enthusiasm she could muster, which was actually quite a lot. 'Let's find somewhere to buy some delicious things. My treat.'

Even though he was carrying a clothes rail, Miles still paused to let Cress walk out of the door first. 'This whole "my treat" business, you know I'm going to fight you on that.'

'You won't win,' Cress said, lifting her face to the sun as they stepped outside. 'I know that I seem very mild-mannered but I'm a hair-puller from way back.'

'Always the quiet ones.' Miles nudged her with his elbow and, when Cress pretended to stumble, he took hold of her hand and didn't let go.

Although it was quite late on a Sunday afternoon, they found a very posh food shop that was still open and Cress spent a good percentage of that day's takings on fancy nibbles. It felt quite glorious to splurge on delicious food after years of scrimping for an imagined future with Colin.

Then they made their way to Dulwich Common and, though they never discussed it, Cress and Miles skirted around the vintage picnickers to find a quiet spot where they were almost hidden from view thanks to some bushes and a convenient dip in the ground.

After they had feasted on tiny savoury tarts, posh crisps, strawberries, then tiny sweet tarts, all washed down with sparkling pink lemonade, they lay down, side by side, on the grass.

The leaves of the trees cast shadows over them, but the sun still shone brightly through the foliage and Cress couldn't help but sigh. She was pleasantly stuffed, her head was overflowing with ideas to expand her little part-time business and she was so pleased to be with Miles. She couldn't remember the last time she'd felt so content.

'Do you ever have those moments which are so perfect that you wish you could save them in the Cloud?' She turned her head to look at Miles, who was looking straight at her.

'I'm having one of those moments right now,' he said softly, and he reached for her hand.

'Me too.'

There was something about holding hands with Miles – and it seemed to Cress that lately they'd been holding hands a lot – that must be as thrilling and butterfly-making as actual kissing. She tried to tell herself that she frequently held hands with her friends, but she couldn't remember the last time she'd held hands even with Sophy. Still, Cress imagined that she was putting everything she was feeling, the contentment and the conflict, into her fingertips, which she stroked along the back of his hand.

It wasn't enough. Miles took her hand and brought it to his lips so he could press a kiss, a hot, open-mouthed kiss, to the underside of her wrist, where Cress was sure her pulse was positively thundering away.

It was lovely but it wasn't enough. Also . . .

'Friend zone, remember?' she reminded him softly.

'Yes to hand-holding, no to hand-kissing?' Miles pulled a face but still managed to look handsome. 'I hadn't realised there were so many friend-zone rules.'

And then he placed her hand flat over his heart so Cress could match her own breaths to the steady rise and fall of his chest.

And that still wasn't enough, but it would have to do, even though it was probably another friend-zone violation.

Even the hand-holding was wrong, Cress knew that. She'd be furious if Colin was using this time apart to hold hands with another woman. But when Cress thought about Colin holding hands with a faceless mystery woman, she had a hard time believing that such a thing was possible. Colin hardly ever even wanted to hold hands with her.

She summoned up an image of Colin holding hands with Zooey Deschanel, his dream girl and 'free pass', and waited to feel even a flash of jealousy, but there was none.

Besides, she didn't really want to be thinking about Colin when she was with Miles, her hand protecting his heart from any harm that might come its way.

Cress couldn't say how long they stayed frozen in that perfect moment but eventually it was ruined by a very bouncy golden retriever that came bounding over out of nowhere. Cress sat up but it was too late. The dog had already stuck its nose in the bag from the posh food shop. Then, once it had wolfed down what was left of the savoury tarts, it very enthusiastically tried to lick Cress's face, without much success as she shied away from its attentions.

'Sorry! He's just being friendly,' said its owner from several metres away. 'Phineas! Come here!'

Phineas did not come, but instead rolled over on his back, his head now lolling on Miles's stomach, and wanted belly rubs.

'What a tart,' Miles said, obliging by rubbing circles on the furry belly with his long fingers. Cress actually felt jealous of the dog.

In the end, Phineas had to be retrieved by his human, who didn't even apologise for his dog scarfing the ends of their picnic or ruining their perfect moment.

'Coco Chanel has a lot more dignity and much better manners,' Cress said as she began to gather up what was left of the picnic debris.

'Coco Chanel is a cat disguised as a dog,' Miles pointed out, which was so obvious once Cress thought about it.

He stood up, groaned and stretched so a tempting slice of taut belly was visible as his t-shirt rode up. Cress tried to avert her eyes like a sheltered Victorian miss who'd never even been alone with a man, much less caught a glimpse of his forbidden flesh.

But when Miles held out his hand, she let him pull her to her feet so they were standing impossibly close to each other.

Even clutching handfuls of rubbish destined for the nearest bin, the tension between them was off the charts. All Cress had to do was reach up and all Miles had to do was lower his head and then kissing would be inevitable.

Her eyes were on a level with Miles's mouth, his firm lips, which seemed to quiver.

Could she be that brave?

Could she even remember why they shouldn't be kissing?

'Cress?' He made her name sound like a poem.

She raised her head to collide with the brilliant blue of his eyes. 'What?'

206

'Remember the friend zone?'

'Bloody friend zone,' Cress said with genuine exasperation. The feelings she had for Miles were growing stronger and deeper by the day. But she and Colin were unfinished business, which needed to be resolved. One way or another. She was going to give Colin another week, then she was going to clarify exactly what their relationship status was. Though Colin's deafening silence suggested that their relationship status was now null and void.

'You're being very patient with me,' she told Miles softly. 'A lot of people wouldn't.'

He stroked his hand down her hot cheek, which was another thing definitely not allowed in the friend zone. 'Some things are worth waiting for, aren't they?'

Even driving back across London couldn't break the spell.

The roads were clear; Cress longed for tailbacks and traffic jams and street closures, but no such luck. They didn't really talk much in the car, but the silence was full of promise, full of all the things they wanted to say but couldn't. Not just yet.

All too soon they'd reached central London. The minutes seemed to speed up until they reached Finchley and the satnav, annoyingly, mockingly, instructed Miles on the last few turns to Cress's house.

Dusk was gathering pace and Cress's skin felt tight from so much sun, though she was very conscientious about applying sunblock. She sighed as Miles pulled in right outside her house and turned off the engine.

'Right then, we'd better unpack,' he said heavily, as if he was dreading saying goodbye too.

Even unloading all those plastic crates was welcome because it meant spending a little more time with Miles. Cress went on ahead to unlock the front door and because she had ears on elastic, Diane popped her head round the living room door.

'There you are! We're just about to order a Deliveroo. Aaron wants Thai, I fancy pizza, you can have the deciding vote.' She looked beyond Cress to Miles, who'd just come in with one of the clothes rails. 'What would Miles like?'

'Oh, he's not staying,' Cress said. She turned to see the hopeful expression on Miles's face. 'I thought you'd have to get the car back.'

He shook his head. 'I can do that in the morning but if I'm intruding . . .'

'You wouldn't be intruding,' Cress said. 'Though you must be sick of me now.'

Miles grinned. 'Hardly. More like the other way round.'

'So, what's it to be then?' Diane asked impatiently. 'Thai or pizza – but if you don't choose pizza then I'll be very disappointed in you, Cress. Might stop letting you use the washing machine.'

'I heard that,' Aaron shouted from the lounge.

Cress was still full from the picnic earlier and it felt as if she'd been mostly eating stodgy carbs all day, but she sided with her mum. 'Pizza's great. Are you good with pizza?'

'I love pizza,' Miles said. By the time the pizzas arrived Miles and Aaron had finished unpacking the car and were now sitting on the sofa discussing football, while Diana nodded approvingly at Cress as they collected glasses and plates from the kitchen.

'He seems very nice,' she whispered. 'Very attentive.'

'We're just friends,' Cress whispered back. 'I mean, Colin and I . . . I don't know . . .'

'Where is Colin, anyway?' Diane body-blocked the kitchen doorway so that Cress was trapped. 'He should be begging you to take him back. When was the last time you heard from him?'

'You know very well that I haven't heard from him at all.'

'In one of his sulks and waiting for you to jolly him out of it, I expect.' Diane sniffed and what she was saying wasn't far off from what Cress thought herself, but she didn't want to be that person without a good word to say about her ex. Then it wouldn't reflect well on her that she'd spent fifteen years with someone who made her lip curl every time she talked about him.

Cress didn't hate Colin. She'd been angry with him, was still angry with him when she thought about all the lies, but they'd had some really good times. Though at the moment it was hard to recall any of them.

'I don't want to talk about Colin,' she said, squeezing past Diane and even resorting to a bit of elbow to shift her mother, who was the original immovable object, out of the way.

It should have been extremely uncomfortable; Miles properly meeting her mum and stepdad under the watchful gaze of the photo of her gap-toothed six-year-old self that had pride of place on the mantelpiece.

Instead of sharing the sofa with Cress like she usually did, Diane sat in one of the armchairs, Aaron in the other one, while Miles sat next to her on the sofa. It felt a lot like a job interview.

They asked Miles all the questions that Cress hadn't asked him because mostly they talked about fashion and film and their friend zone. Aaron and especially Diane didn't care about any of that stuff. They wanted to know how old Miles was (thirty-three). Where he'd grown up (in a small town called Lytham St Annes, near Blackpool). What he did for a job, which at least Cress knew.

'You earn enough from that to make a living, do you?' Diane asked. 'It sounds a bit unpredictable.'

'It can be feast or famine, but the more you work, the more contacts you make,' Miles said, his plate of two slices of primavera pizza resting on his knee. 'There's a lot of less glamorous but well-paid commercial contracts around. Recently, I directed a training film for a big firm of accountants and it paid more than I'd earned in the previous six months.'

'Do you own your own home?' Aaron enquired, while Cress pulled a face at him because they were both acting as if Miles had declared his intentions and it was their job to ensure that he could keep Cress in a style to which she'd like to be accustomed.

'I wish!' Miles said easily as if he didn't mind the interrogation. 'I share a flat in Shoreditch with a mate.'

'Does he work in film too?' Diane asked.

'No, he's an optician,' Miles said and both Aaron and Diane seemed to breathe out as if Miles couldn't be too bad or too flighty if he had a flatmate with a respectable job. 'Anyway, that's enough about me. I always like to know what people's favourite films are. I think it says so much about them. Diane?'

'Oh, well, gosh, I don't know,' Diane said, rearing back in her chair because the interrogator had become the interrogatee. 'Maybe *Dirty Dancing?*'

'Absolute classic,' Miles said. 'Did you know that Sarah Jessica Parker auditioned for the role of Baby?'

'I did not.' Diane nibbled on the edge of her pizza and Cress was relieved that she wasn't firing questions at Miles. 'Actually, my favourite film is probably *The Wizard of Oz.*'

'Another classic,' Miles noted.

'When I was little, about six, we went on holiday to Bognor Regis and stayed in this terrible guesthouse. We had to be out of there after breakfast and weren't allowed back until late in the afternoon and it rained the entire week,' Diane recalled. Cress thought she knew everything about her mother, had heard all her stories several times over, but this was a new one. 'So we went to the cinema every day, me, my mum, my little sister and my gran. The only film showing was *The Wizard of Oz*. Even seeing it six days in a row wasn't too much and now, when it comes on the telly, it reminds me of that holiday and how I didn't even mind that it rained or that the woman who ran the guesthouse was mean and now that I think about it, kind of racist. I just remember sitting in between my mum and my gran and feeling loved and eating Maltesers out of a special fancy box, when usually they came in a bag, and wishing that I had a pair of ruby slippers so I could click my heels and we'd be home. That was the last holiday we had with my gran before she passed.' Diane wiped the one tear that had appeared and smiled sheepishly. 'I guess that proves your theory that someone's favourite film explains who they are.'

'Thank you for sharing that,' Miles said softly.

'Oh God, I'm such a soppy old cow.' Diane flapped her napkin in embarrassment.

'Well, my favourite film is *Caddyshack*,' Aaron said proudly. 'What does that say about me?'

'That apart from marrying me, you have absolutely no taste,' Diane said.

'It is the worst film,' Cress added. 'The very worst film and he always tries to make us watch it, even though the only time that I did, it was the longest one hour and thirty-eight minutes of my life.'

'Though Bill Murray is good in everything,' Miles insisted, but Cress wasn't having it.

'Don't humour him,' she warned. 'Otherwise he'll think you're being genuine and next thing you know . . .'

Aaron pretended that he was getting up. 'Shall I go and get my DVD?'

'No!' Cress and Diane shouted in unison.

'Philistines,' Aaron muttered and, again, Miles's theory held and, just by knowing that Aaron's favourite film was the truly awful *Caddyshack*, he'd also learned a lot about their family dynamic.

It was far less awkward after that but all too soon Miles had to leave.

Cress was pretty sure that both Aaron and Diane were straining their ears to hear her say goodbye to him, so she saw him off as far as the garden gate.

'You have gone above and beyond anything I expected of you today,' Cress said as Miles lingered by the gate. 'I can't thank you enough.'

'It was a good day. I'm glad I got to spend it with you.' He twirled his key fob round one long finger.

It would have been the perfect opportunity for some more hand-holding, for standing really, really close to each other, but Miles stepped towards the car.

'Do you think you might be around to go to the pub on Friday?' Cress asked. 'I mean, if you happen to be in the area.'

'I think that might be highly likely.' He stood quite still, his eyes fixed on her face. 'Oh, Cress . . .'

She waited for him to finish the start of that promising sentence, but he turned away and pointed his key fob at the car, which beeped obligingly, and the moment was gone.

Chapter Twenty-Three

Not by even a flicker of an eyelash did Phoebe indicate that she and Cress had met over the weekend.

On Monday morning she was back in her imposing work uniform, so it was hard to remember that Cress had seen her in actual denim with actual Freddy. It was also even harder not to tell Sophy all about it, but a promise was a promise.

Not that Sophy noticed. She was glowing after her weekend away and meeting Charles's parents.

'They were lovely,' she said, when she and Cress had a quick patio debrief and coffee break. 'I thought they'd be like Charles. Beautifully turned out and all that. Maybe his dad would be in a dinner jacket and his mum in a ballgown – but when we got there on Saturday evening, they'd both forgotten to change out of their gardening clothes.'

'Did they make you feel welcome?' Cress asked, mindful of the trial Diane had put Miles through and also mindful that she was going to have to have a conversation quite soon with Sophy about Miles and feelings and friend zones, but probably not this Monday.

'Very welcome. They'd even asked Charles what my favourite foods were and they'd made roast chicken, with tiramisu for pudding. Also, Peter, Charles's dad, has this tool hire company . . .'

'Charles's dad has a tool hire company?' Cress echoed in disbelief. 'I thought he'd work in a museum or a university or something.'

'No, he started out as a builder and his mum was a nurse,' Sophy said. 'The apple, that is Charles, rolled very, very far from the parental tree.'

'I'll say.'

'Anyway, Peter has been in the hire business for decades now and he gave me loads of really useful advice about setting up my rental arm of The Vintage Dress Shop,' Sophy said with the determined glint in her eye that Cress always dreaded.

'I thought you'd given up on all that . . .'

'No, I hadn't. I was just waiting for all the dresses I bought in Australia to finally arrive after their very long cruise.' Sophy cracked her knuckles. 'I'm thinking that they'll be rental only, give them a bit of exclusivity. I know Phoebe will turn her nose up at them but they're good dresses, Cress. I'd gladly wear them.'

'Well, I'm happy that you're all about the vintage dresses now, and I'm saying this from a place of love, but hiring a cement mixer or whatever is very different from hiring a beautiful, possibly even vintage dress,' Cress pointed out.

'Oh my God, Phoebe's rubbing off on you,' Sophy groaned. 'I hear what you're saying, I really do, but *is* there much difference between hiring a cement mixer and a vintage dress? Both are valuable, in their own way. There's just as much risk involved in hiring out a cement mixer as hiring a dress that could get damaged. Peter said you wouldn't believe how many people rent power tools who don't have a clue how to use them. Which is why we'll have insurance. Freddy will sort all that out.'

At the mention of Freddy's name, Cress was sure that her face was twitching or she was displaying some other visible sign of the secret she was keeping but if she were then Sophy didn't seem to notice.

She was far too busy planning out her rental empire when she was at work and attending all sorts of glamorous summer season events with Charles when she was out of work to notice that Cress was feeling a little out of sorts.

Cress knew that she should get in touch with Colin, that they needed to talk, but she couldn't quite bring herself to send him a message. She was still so very angry with him, and this was all his fault, so why should she be the one to make the first move?

Or maybe she didn't want to contact Colin because even if they did manage to smooth things over, then could she really carry on seeing Miles? Although she kept insisting that they were just friends, when she was with him her feelings went far beyond friendship.

The only option was to keep busy. Very, very busy.

It was just as well that there was no shortage of work to do. Even though she hated locking up and Phoebe hated anyone who wasn't her locking up, Cress stayed late every night to work on Tanya's dress because her workroom at the shop was better lit and better kitted out than her box room at home.

Also her productivity during opening hours had slowed down because of Ella, who'd got herself in a real flap when she realised that she started filming in two weeks and she was still having trouble threading a needle.

'It's all your fault,' she'd pouted at Cress when she'd turned up on the dot of ten on Tuesday morning. 'You have to be stricter with me. You can even shout at me if you want. It's the only way I ever learn.'

'I'm not a shouter,' Cress had said as she'd retrieved the pattern paper from a drawer. 'I can't do confrontation. Raising my voice makes me want to cry. Now, let's have a go at sketching out pattern pieces and then cutting them out.'

Even though Cress wasn't a shouter, her volume knob did get progressively louder over the week as she and Ella worked on a replacement of Anita's precious dress and then a copy of the replacement.

Like any sewer, professional or keen amateur, Cress's mantra was 'measure twice, cut once'. But over the course of the week, she was forced to amend that mantra to 'measure at least five times, then cut but only under my close supervision'.

By Friday afternoon, they had two toiles of the dress, had adjusted the fit and had tacked the pattern pieces to black crêpe cotton and cut them out, ready to sew the actual dress.

Cress was physically and emotionally exhausted from the process.

'Have I broken you?' Ella asked worriedly as Cress slumped on her stool and rested her head on the worktop. 'On the plus side, I've learned so much this week and I really feel like I'm starting to inhabit my character. I've even had a stress dream about measuring twice and cutting once. I was chased around my old school by sentient tape measures.'

'You're not coming in tomorrow, are you?' Cress wished that her delivery wasn't quite so churlish but she just couldn't help herself. 'I mean, it would be lovely to see you, but Saturdays are always very busy. Lots of fittings.'

'I've got rehearsals all through the weekend,' Ella said. 'At some point, I've also got a wig fitting, and I have to have a medical for the insurance people.'

'I had no idea that being a movie star . . .'

'Very kind, Cress, but I'm just a jobbing actress,' Ella said, ruining this uncharacteristic display of humility by fluttering her eyelashes and making a haughty face.

'Honestly, I just thought you learned your lines, then turned up on set and winged it,' Cress confessed. She forced herself to sit up and felt a little thrill course through her when she saw it was five to six.

Five to six on a Friday afternoon meant the pub, which also meant Miles being conveniently in the area, though he hadn't messaged Cress yet.

'How dare you malign my noble profession?' Ella struck another pose, which turned into a stretch and then a yawn. 'I think actually you've broken me. Are we pubbing? I'm gasping for a drink.'

'We are pubbing,' Cress confirmed as she checked that sewing machine, overlocker and iron were all switched off. 'I'm gasping for a bowl of chips.'

The two of them made their way downstairs to where the others had finished restoring order to the shop and were assembling by the doors.

Cress looked through the shop window to see if she could see Miles but he wasn't there. There was just some bloke in a suit almost obscured by a huge bunch of flowers who was obviously waiting for his date to arrive.

Maybe Miles was already in the pub, Cress thought as Phoebe finally bustled in from the back office with the keys and Coco Chanel tucked under her arm like a designer clutch bag.

'There's still one minute on the clock, ladies,' she said. 'We don't actually close until six.'

'Please say you're joking,' Anita all but growled.

'Of course I'm joking,' Phoebe snapped. 'I'm not a complete dragon.' She stretched her lips into an approximation of a smile. 'Right, let's get out of here. I need a large gin and tonic, because you've driven me to drink, Anita.'

'No need to thank me,' Anita said sweetly, and Phoebe did laugh then and shooed them all out of the door and onto the street, where there was Miles. At last! He smiled as he caught sight of Cress, who smiled back.

'Hi,' she called out, and the bloke in the suit who was still waiting turned round at the sound of her voice.

Then he lowered the big bunch of pink and white sweet peas, roses and freesias tied up in brown paper and pink ribbon.

'Oh, hey, Cress,' he said.

Cress blinked twice.

Then she executed an almighty double-take because she couldn't believe what, or who, her eyes were seeing.

Back from his self-imposed exile and mammoth sulk, it was Colin.

PART FOUR

Chapter Twenty-Four

Cress couldn't believe that, after weeks of silence, Colin was suddenly there in front of her.

'You cut your hair,' she said at last.

Colin put a hand to the back of his neck, where his hair was no longer pulled into a ponytail. 'I thought it was time for a change,' he said uncertainly.

It had been four long weeks since they'd seen each other. Cress would have said that Colin's face was more familiar to her than her own – she'd spent longer looking at him than she ever had her own reflection – but now that he stood in front of her, pale and nervous, it was as if she were seeing him for the first time.

'What are you doing here?' she asked.

'Well, I missed you,' Colin said as if that should have been obvious. He thrust the flowers at Cress. 'These are for you. I made you a mix-tape too. I even got you an old Walkman off eBay to listen to it on. I know I could have just done you a playlist, but I wanted to do things properly.'

'You could have just called,' Cress said and she couldn't keep the sharpness, the anger, out of her voice. 'Much easier and quicker.'

'Don't be like that.' Colin pulled his brows together so he was the very definition of dejected. 'I've been miserable with-out you.'

Cress realised then that she hadn't been miserable without him. She'd been too cross. Too confused. Too busy. Too distracted.

'I'm still furious with you,' Cress said in the same tight tone that she hardly recognised.

Colin nodded unhappily in acknowledgment of that. 'Look, is there somewhere we can go to chat this out?'

Cress looked around helplessly. The others, by which she meant Miles, had very wisely left them to their own devices. It was a Friday evening in pretty Primrose Hill. All the bars and restaurants and pubs were full to bursting.

'Well, I guess we can go to The Hat and Fan, but it's going to be crowded,' Cress said and Colin nodded again.

They walked there in silence and Cress imagined they'd have to have a deeply personal conversation conducted by mostly shouting at each other. The thought of Miles and Colin in close proximity to each other was also making her feel quite nauseous.

Then as they got nearer to the pub, Cress saw Miles come out of the door that led to the saloon bar and fight his way through the pavement throngs.

Cress came to a halt and maybe it was her stillness that made Miles look up. He even took off his shades so that their eyes didn't just meet, rather it felt as if their gazes collided.

'Come on, Cress.' She turned to Colin, who was waiting impatiently at her side.

'What?'

'I thought we were going to The Hat and Fan, unless you wanted to go somewhere else?' he said, still brandishing that huge bunch of flowers.

'The Hat and Fan is fine,' Cress said, because Miles was gone in the time it had taken for her to glance across at Colin.

Though Cress had been sick at the thought of Colin and Miles meeting, of having to do *this*, whatever this was, in front of Miles, the flat, empty feeling knowing that he'd left wasn't much better.

But this wasn't about Miles. This was about Cress and Colin. Colin and Cress. And whether they were still an Us after these four long weeks of leading very separate lives.

When they finally made it into the pub, it was to find that The Vintage Dress Shop staff plus Freddy and Charles were at their usual corner banquettes. Sophy, bless her, had managed to annex a small table and two stools next to them and was waving at Cress.

'We got you both a drink,' she said. 'Hi Colin. You're a pale ale, right?'

'Yeah,' Colin said and though Sophy was always polite to Colin, if not exactly friendly, as usual Colin could barely do more than grunt at her. It really wasn't one of his more endearing characteristics.

'It's from a local brewery.' Sophy shot Cress a slightly manic smile, her eyebrows raised. 'Anyway, I'm sure you two have a lot to talk about without me rambling on.'

It was true, they did have a lot to talk about, but for long, long minutes they sat there in silence.

Every time Cress thought about speaking all that she wanted to say was, 'You lied to me,' and they'd already covered that.

Just when Cress thought they might just as well give up, Colin cleared his throat.

'So, I'm sorry,' he burst out. 'I've already said that I miss you but also this time apart has made me realise that I do want to be with you.' He paused and looked at Cress expectantly as if he was waiting for her to apologise too. But she hadn't done anything that she needed to apologise for.

'What does wanting to be with me even mean?' Cress asked. 'I thought we were working towards the next phase of our relationship – buying a place together, living together – but we can't do that, can we? Why should I use my savings to put a deposit down, even on a rental place, when you never saved a penny but let me think that you were?' The injustice of it all struck her all over again. 'You earn three times what I do, even with buying all those records you should still have been able to save something every month.'

Colin shifted uncomfortably on his stool. 'I can't keep saying I'm sorry.'

'Well you've only actually said it the once,' Cress pointed out. She folded her arms. 'It all feels kind of hopeless now.'

'But I have a plan,' Colin said, which was very unlike Colin. Usually it was Cress with the plans. They'd have barely ever left Finchley if Cress hadn't organised holidays, days out, even just a simple movie and dinner date, but now apparently Colin had a plan.

'I'm all ears,' Cress told him. She wasn't able to muster even the tiniest amount of enthusiasm.

He wedged a finger into the collar of his shirt as if it were choking him. 'I'm going to sell my record collection.'

It was the last thing that Cress had expected.

'You're *what?*' She felt like a cartoon character just after an anvil had dropped on their head. 'What do you mean, you're selling your records?'

Colin smiled faintly as if he were pleased by Cress's shocked reaction. 'They've come between us, haven't they?'

'They haven't come between us.' Cress was keen to correct that point. 'What came between us is that you bought them when you knew full well that I thought you were saving money for a house deposit, for our future.'

'Let's not get bogged down in all of that,' Colin said quickly. 'I've been doing some calculations and I reckon that if I sell them, I can recoup what I should have saved.'

Cress could feel the steely backbone that she'd inserted as soon as she'd told Colin that she never wanted to see him again begin to wobble. 'That is quite the grand gesture.'

Colin nodded and his smile widened now that he thought he was on safer ground. 'Not going to lie, I'm pretty pleased with myself for coming up with a solution to this problem. And yes, it is a problem of my own making.'

'It's . . . I'm having trouble getting my head around it,' Cress said. This was the last thing she'd ever expect Colin to do.

He took a sip of his microbrewed pale ale. He'd lost the ashen, nervous expression that he'd worn when he was waiting outside the shop and now seemed more sure of himself. 'Can you imagine how long it took me to process it then?' he asked. 'But then I began to realise that I could actually have more money than if I'd saved it in the first place. Especially with the interest rates being so low for the last fifteen years or so.'

'Well, I have some of my savings in an ISA. Mike said—'

'For instance, my original 1979 copy of *London Calling* by The Clash could be worth up to two hundred quid and I only paid thirty-five for it. The last track "Train In Vain" is only referenced in the run-out on side four and not mentioned anywhere on the sleeve or record, not even on the label of side four,' Colin said, his eyes now shining with missionary-like zeal. 'And the track listing on the back cover for the first track on side three – did I mention that it's a double album – "Wrong 'Em Boyo" has a credit to Stagger Lee, which isn't seen on all *London Calling* releases. It's got the printed inner sleeves with lyrics too. Some retail copies were sent out as promos and have a gold promo stamp at sleeve rear, which my one has as well, so it's quite the collector's item. Of course, I'll want to make sure it goes to a good home but . . .'

'Colin,' Cress said gently. 'I think that—'

'Then there's my 1972 original pressing of *Exile on Main Street* by the Rolling Stones still with the fold-out card sleeve including a set of twelve postcards with black and white text.'

'Colin, I can't—'

'That's easily got to be worth another two hundred, though it was a lucky find for me in a Cancer Research shop in Kenton. Or was it Kilburn? Either way—'

'Colin!' Cress really had to raise her voice to interrupt him mid-flow. 'Stop. Just stop!'

'But I thought you'd be pleased,' he said, his face resetting to unsure and sullen because he only really came alive when he was talking about his collection of vinyl.

'You're not going to sell your records,' Cress said, her voice thick with tears. 'I can't let you do that.'

He shook his head. 'No, I am. I've made my mind up.'

'You're not because they're part of you,' Cress said more gently. 'Like one of your vital organs.'

'But I miss you. You're always there and then you weren't.' Colin reached across the table to take Cress's hand but then thought better of it. 'I love you.'

This was the hardest thing that Cress had ever done. Harder than A levels. Harder than having her adenoids and tonsils taken out. Harder than a truly horrific abseiling activity to raise funds for a donkey sanctuary. 'You don't love me, Colin. Not in the way that I want to be loved. We're loving friends but we don't love each other like two people who want to spend the rest of their lives together. We're not in love.'

'It's been fifteen years, Cress. If that's not love, then what is?'

'I can't even remember the last time you kissed me,' Cress said, the tears threatening to put in another appearance. But it was the truth. Goodness, she couldn't remember the last time they'd had sex either, but she suspected that it was about a year ago, when they'd gone on holiday with Colin's parents and had a very unsatisfying quickie while Mary and Roy went to get fish and chips. 'And that's on me too. I never prioritised romance, I prioritised saving up and planning for a future with you rather than being present.'

'This is just nonsense, Cress.' Colin sounded panicked and like he was quite close to tears himself. 'I'm going to sell my records and we'll have enough for a deposit and we'll buy a house and we'll be happy together. We will.'

Cress sent an imploring look to Sophy but her stepsister and her colleagues and friends all had their backs to her, as if they were trying very hard to give Cress and Colin space and not listen in on their heart-wrenching conversation. She turned back to Colin, whose eyes were fixed on her, his face incredulous like he was looking, really looking, at Cress for the first time.

'This is not what I want. I don't want to spend the rest of my life in a small house in Tottenham, with you being sad and resentful because you've sold your record collection for me,' she said. 'I've been so fixated on this small, narrow life that I thought I wanted that I forgot to have any dreams.'

Colin folded his arms. 'Do these dreams involve the bloke that you've been seen with?' he asked sourly.

Her heart did a thoroughly unpleasant fluttering thing in Cress's chest. 'What bloke?' Technically she hadn't done anything with any blokes, but she still felt guilty because she'd wanted to do things with Miles. God, how she'd wanted to! Then the fluttering stopped and she could feel the righteous indignation start to bubble up all over again. 'Have you been spying on me?'

'No! I wouldn't do that,' Colin snapped, just as indignant himself. 'But Ayesha from next door was walking her dog last Sunday morning and she told Mum that she saw you holding hands in the street with some bloke.'

'He's just a friend,' Cress said quickly, though her face predictably enough was suddenly hot enough to fry eggs on. 'He was just saying hello before we went to sell some of my stuff at a vintage fair.'

'Right. So, that's what you're calling it then, is it?' Scepticism oozed from every word.

'I'm calling it nothing because nothing happened,' Cress insisted, even though that wasn't strictly true. Feelings had happened, but she hadn't acted on them.

'I suppose this is why you didn't get in touch after we had our argument.' Colin nodded as if all the pieces were falling into place.

'I didn't get in touch because I was angry with you,' Cress replied in a low, urgent voice. 'You were in the wrong. You lied. So why was it my job to contact you and smooth it all over?'

'Because that's what you do!'

'Well, I don't want to do it any more!' She wriggled her shoulders in annoyance. 'Oh my God, I bet you were just waiting for me to make things all right. You'd probably still be waiting if Ayesha hadn't seen me with Miles—'

'That's his name, is it? Miles.' Colin sniffed like there was something wrong and deeply contemptuous about the name. 'Look, I can forgive you.'

'Forgive me? Forgive me?' Cress's voice was so loud and high that it seemed as if everyone in the pub, certainly everyone on the next table, turned to look at her. 'I've done nothing that needs forgiveness, and FYI, all this time apart has made me realise that there are loads of things that I want to do with my life that don't involve you.'

'Oh yeah, like what?' Colin asked in a belligerent tone.

All those things that Cress had been doing to keep herself busy so she wouldn't mope or be cross had actually turned into activities and plans that she was excited about. 'I want

228

to grow my business. I want to maybe design clothes. I want to learn new skills. I want to be brave and try different things and have adventures and I want to kiss other people. I want to have kissed more than one person in the whole of my life. And when I've done maybe some of those things, I still want to have a family of my own, children. I'm sorry, I just want more than *this*.'

'Wow.'

They'd both been stiff-backed and angry but now Colin's shoulders slumped as all the fight went out of him.

'I really am sorry,' Cress said, a little less fiercely. 'I didn't even realise that I felt like this until we broke up. Because I was pretty sure that we were broken up.'

'But I didn't think we'd broken up,' Colin said sadly. 'I just thought we were having an argument.'

There were other things, hurtful things, that Cress could say. That over the last few weeks, she had hardly missed him at all. That she could see now how much they'd held each other back. That she'd met a different man, one who made her want to wear dresses. She might be angry, but that didn't mean that she wanted to be unnecessarily cruel.

'I think somewhere along the way, we stopped being a couple and neither of us realised it,' she said. It was her turn now to reach out to Colin, to try to touch him, but he flinched away from her hand.

'Mum said . . . she said that you could move in with us,' he offered with barely any hope. 'She said that when they die, the house will go to me anyway.'

It was a future too bleak to even contemplate.

'That's just not going to happen, Col,' Cress said softly.

'I didn't think it would.'

He took several long gulps of his drink and Cress sipped the Diet Coke that Sophy had got her. It had been sitting there for so long that the ice had melted and it tasted watery.

They sat there in silence. There really was nothing left to say. Colin concentrated on finishing his ale and when he was done, he placed his glass on the table with a soft thud that sounded final.

He stood up. 'Well, then . . .' He gestured at the flowers that lay on the table. 'Did you want to keep them?'

'Oh!' Cress looked down at the delicate pink and white flowers. 'Um, I thought . . . if you wanted to take them.'

Colin snatched them up. 'If you don't want them.'

'I didn't say that I didn't want them,' Cress said, eyes smarting again as she found herself embroiled in another tense exchange of words.

'Whatever! I'll see you around,' Colin said, trying to march off but the pub was so crowded that in the end all he could do was slowly inch towards the door, ensuring that their ending was just as awkward as their beginning had been.

Once Colin had disappeared into the night, Cress let out a very ragged breath. Her hands were shaking. In fact, all of her was trembling.

Then there was a gentle hand on her shoulder. 'Are you all right?' Sophy asked softly, and all Cress could do was shake her head.

Chapter Twenty-Five

Cress had been sad and angry when she and Colin had maybe broken up. But now they were officially broken up, her heart was broken too.

She realised now that somewhere along the way, she'd stopped loving him, but she'd liked Colin a lot for fifteen years. More than liked. Whatever the halfway point between liking and loving someone was. He was so woven into the fabric of Cress's life that she didn't quite know how to unpick him.

The rest of Friday evening had been a tear-soaked blur. A lot of crying and not even caring that she was crying in public. In the end, Sophy had hustled her out of the pub and into an Uber, though Cress had tearfully tried to insist that Sophy should stay in the pub.

'You're going to be fine,' she said as they sped through the back streets of north London. 'You've been very brave, Cress. It would be the easiest thing to stay as you were, like I did for all those years with Egan, but you've decided to take a leap of faith and I'm so proud of you.'

Cress didn't feel brave and she particularly didn't feel like someone who anyone could be proud of because, when her sobs had muted to panting and the occasional hiccup, it wasn't Colin she was thinking about.

'I saw Miles outside the pub. Did he say anything to you before he left?' she asked hoarsely.

'He decided that it was probably best not to hang with us,' Sophy said in a voice that was so neutral, it was beige. 'We need to have a chat about Miles, don't we?'

'Not now,' Cress choked out.

'Not now,' Sophy agreed. 'But soon.'

Sophy must have messaged ahead because Diane was waiting on the doorstep all ready to take Cress in her arms, then Sophy got back in the Uber to be reunited with Charles.

The next time Cress saw her sister-friend, it was some twelve hours later outside Chalk Farm station.

'You all right?'

'I'm alive,' Cress croaked, because an alcohol hangover was one thing but waking up after crying yourself to sleep at some time after half-one was very much another thing.

It felt as if all the moisture in her body had exited via her tear ducts and she was dehydrated, wearing her biggest, darkest glasses, and finding it hard to walk without wobbling all over the place.

'Have you eaten?'

'I can't even think about food,' Cress said but it turned out that her stomach didn't really care about the state of her heart and, as they walked past Sam's Café, a Primrose Hill institution, it let out an almighty rumble.

When they got to the shop, Phoebe was anxiously waiting at the door, much like Diane had the night before.

'You're here!' she said in surprise and also some relief. 'I would have completely understood if you'd called in sick.'

'Would you?' Sophy asked sceptically.

Phoebe gasped in outrage. 'Of course I would! I've even juggled around today's fittings. Put some of them back until next Saturday so you're not completely slammed.'

Although part of Cress wanted to be busy, madly busy, so she couldn't think of anything else, there was also the part of her, her hands especially, which were still quite shaky.

'I really appreciate that, Pheebs.'

'I don't know why people seem to think I'm some kind of unfeeling monster,' Phoebe said. 'I'm not even going to tell you off for bringing your breakfast into the shop so that everything, the dresses, are going to smell of bacon.'

'That sounded like a telling-off to me,' Sophy said but Phoebe, for once, refused to be drawn in.

'I was just about to suggest that Cress eat on the patio because I've put her ten a.m. fitting back by half an hour,' she said sweetly.

By the time Cress had demolished her bacon, sausage and fried egg breakfast roll and downed a large coffee, the shaking had stopped and she was ready to start work.

Even with fittings whittled down to more manageable proportions, she was still grateful to be focused on seams and bust darts and a piece of antique lace from a bride's great-great-grandmother's wedding dress that somehow had to be incorporated into her own, very sleek, very minimalist, very bias-cut 1930s wedding dress.

Her last appointment of the day was Tanya, who now felt more like a friend than a client.

'Phoebe tried to reschedule for next week but I'm off to Sicily on Monday for a fortnight,' she said, dumping her many shopping bags on one of the chintzy sofas in the salon. They'd probably never known the touch of an M&S carrier bag before. 'Joe, my fella, he says the holiday is the first part of my birthday celebrations.'

'You don't sound very happy about it,' Cress said, as she unzipped the garment bag that contained Tanya's dress. Not the toile, but a very rudimentary black satin dress that didn't have any lining or boning as yet.

'His family comes from Taormina. His grandparents and aunts and uncles still live there, so it's usually two weeks in his grandparents' house, which has no air conditioning and is at the top of a steep hill, with no road.'

'So no cars?'

'Have to lug the suitcases up,' Tanya said unhappily. 'Then it's two weeks of his family bitching about how I can't cook properly and that that's why he's never married me.'

'That really doesn't sound like fun,' Cress said, almost forgetting the sorry state of her love life with this little glimpse into Tanya's relationship.

'Which is why I've insisted that we spend the second week in a hotel with a swimming pool, otherwise I said that I'd push him off Mount Etna,' Tanya said. 'But if I did, I suppose the children and the dog would miss him.'

'Is he really that bad?' Cress asked as Tanya eyed the dress with some trepidation.

'He has his moments, I suppose,' she conceded. 'Though at least once a week, I dream of leaving him and the kids and just running away with the dog. Oscar, he's a bichon frise. Lovely temperament. Not like this little madam.'

Coco Chanel, the little madam in question, was splooted out in the middle of the floor. Cress thought she was asleep but as soon as Tanya started maligning her she opened one eye, then let off a series of revenge toots.

Once Tanya and Cress were able to open their mouths again without fear of asphyxiation, Tanya took the dress from her.

'I'm going to be honest with you, Cress. I've been trying on swimwear all afternoon and I'm not feeling my best self.'

'Remember, we're not having defeatist talk like that,' Cress reminded her, but her heart wasn't really in it.

Much like Tanya wasn't really loving the dress when she emerged from the changing room wearing it and a truculent expression. 'It's not how I thought it would be.'

'I've got a lot of work to do on it, but I just wanted to check the length and the basic—'

'I should have worn better underwear but I didn't want to be struggling in and out of a bra all day so I just wore a bralette.' Tanya frowned at her reflection in the many different mirrors. 'I think I'm too old for a bralette. The girls need more support.'

Certainly, Cress needed a lot more support of the emotional kind to be able to deal with this pity party. Whoever said that misery loved company was wrong. Cress was miserable enough without having to cope with anyone else's existential crisis.

'I haven't even started on the boning yet,' she said, as she unravelled her tape measure. 'Um, sorry to ask this, but I'm going to need you to hold the girls up to where you think they'll be when you have a bra on.'

'I don't need a bra, I need scaffolding,' Tanya lamented, and she didn't specifically say it but Cress could tell that she hated everything about the dress.

Cress had been through this before with countless women at countless fittings. When the dress was very much a work in progress, with so many alterations to be done, it could be quite hard to tell what the finished product would look like. So they feared the worst.

'You just have to have faith in the process. Faith in me,' Cress said when Tanya was back in jeans, t-shirt and the same truculent expression and they were downstairs in the now almost empty shop.

'I don't even know why I'm having a big fiftieth birthday party,' she said, as she stepped through the door. Then she paused and turned round. 'What is there to even celebrate except the relentless passing of time bringing us all ever closer to death?'

'OK, right, well, have a nice holiday, I'll see you when you get back,' Cress said with a feeble brightness, though she half

235

expected to get a message from Tanya before then saying that the party was cancelled and she didn't need the dress any more.

'Are you feeling better now?' Anita asked sweetly.

All day Cress had been treated like an elderly maiden aunt who couldn't take any loud noises or sudden movements. Now, after Tanya's visit, Cress didn't feel better. She felt worse, even though part of her was glad that she had finished things definitively with Colin. She didn't want to be heading for fifty and still feeling so discontented with her lot in life.

'I'm all right, I suppose,' she replied with very little sincerity.

'If you were up for it, I've got a date tonight and I'm sure that Ravi can scrounge up a mate for you,' Anita offered. 'Plenty more fish in the sea and all that.'

'It hasn't even been twenty-four hours,' Sophy protested, as she waited for a customer outside the changing cubicles.

'Yeah, but unofficially they were broken up weeks ago.' Anita patted Cress on the arm. 'Plus you've been very cosy with that Miles, haven't you?'

'No. We're just friends,' Cress said, turning to give Phoebe, who was at the till, a pointed look. If Phoebe had said anything about last Sunday . . .

'Of course Miles and Cress are just friends,' Phoebe said with heavy emphasis. 'A man and a woman can be friendly, you know, Anita. It doesn't mean that they're having a raging affair. Honestly, what will you think of next?'

'I still reckon you should come out with me and Ravi and whichever one of his friends is at a loose end,' Anita persisted. 'Ravi is well fit so it stands to reason that his friends would be really good-looking too.'

'It's not that I don't appreciate the offer, but it really is too soon,' Cress decided.

All she could think about was the scene outside the shop at almost exactly this time yesterday. When she'd been quite giddy about the thought of maybe seeing Miles again. How her stomach had dipped deliciously when she realised he was waiting for her.

But then she'd seen Colin and her stomach hadn't dipped but rather plummeted to the floor, Miles forgotten.

But he wasn't forgotten now. Not when his name was flashing up on her ringing phone.

'I need to take this . . . upstairs,' she said and raced up the spiral staircase even as Anita shouted after her, 'Don't be long! We're going to lock up in five minutes.'

'Hi, hello, hi,' Cress stammered when she was able to answer his call without anyone earwigging.

'Are you all right? You sound out of breath.'

'Just taken the stairs . . . too quickly.'

'Right. OK. So it's Sunday tomorrow,' Miles said and he didn't sound all right either. His voice was clipped and almost robotic.

'It is,' Cress agreed. 'Have you got anything nice planned?'

She winced at her use of the word 'nice', which was so basic, so inoffensive and so not what she really wanted to say.

'I'm going to Belfast on Tuesday for the final week of pre-production and then shooting starts the week after. I probably won't be back in London until the end of September,' he said and Cress felt her stomach both do the dippy thing *and* plummet to the ground.

'Six weeks is quite a long time,' she said slowly. She'd only known Miles for about six weeks but it felt longer. Yet it also seemed like no time at all, so for him to be gone before they'd had a chance to work out what they were, what they could be, could spell disaster.

'I suppose it is,' Miles said and Cress didn't think that during those six weeks there'd ever been such an awkward exchange of words between them. Not even during their first encounter when she'd thought him rude and arrogant.

Though she could hardly be surprised after what had happened yesterday evening.

'Look, about last night—'

'So, I think we need to have a chat—'

There were talking over each other. Then there was a long silence as they both waited for the other to fill it.

Cress tried again. 'I wanted to say—'

'I don't want—'

Cress shut her eyes and silently screamed. 'You go first,' she said firmly, otherwise they'd be interrupting each other for hours.

Miles sucked in a breath. 'We need to talk, so I was hoping we could meet tomorrow. If you're not doing anything.'

Cress's diary was empty. Or rather she'd planned to spend most of the day on the sofa catching up on *Love Island* and when that proved too triggering, watching some of her favourite films. Either way a lot of crying and a lot of ice cream was going to be involved.

'Nothing that can't wait,' she said. 'What were you thinking?'

Ordinarily she'd be quite thrilled to be spending time with Miles, but he sounded so un-Miles-like and also, even though she and Colin were now officially, irrevocably broken up, the circumstances weren't that different from how they'd been before.

Cress needed, no, *wanted* to mourn the fifteen years she'd had with Colin. She also really needed to figure out what she wanted to do with the rest of her life now it didn't have Colin in it. She hoped that Miles might feature somewhere in it, but it was still too soon.

'I could come to you or you could come to me, or we could meet somewhere in the middle?' Miles suggested, which sounded very metaphor-y to Cress.

'Middle sounds good. What's the median point between Finchley and Shoreditch?'

'It's probably in town, which will be rammed,' Miles said.

If she and Miles were Sophy and Charles, they'd have all sorts of fascinating, off-the-beaten-track places to explore but they weren't, so there was another horrible silence as they both racked their brains for a suitable meeting point.

'Let's just meet at Bond Street tube,' Cress said at last, and that was only because Anita had just bellowed up the stairs, 'Not to be insensitive, but bloody hell, haven't you got a home to go to? We're waiting to lock up!'

'Bond Street?' Miles queried, like he'd never heard of it before.

'Yeah, and then we can, I don't know, find a café or something,' Cress said. 'Is eleven too early?'

'Compared to last Sunday, that's a long, long lie-in.' For the first time since Cress had picked up the phone, it sounded as if Miles was smiling. 'I'll see you then.'

Chapter Twenty-Six

Even though Cress was sad – Saturday night *had* involved a lot of sofa-crying, as she had suspected – on Sunday morning, as she surveyed her clothes rails, the last thing that she wanted to wear was something black.

Yes, she was in mourning, but there was something about the prospect of seeing Miles that made her want to wear a pretty dress. She settled for a fifties dress in her favourite silhouette: boat neck, nipped-in waist, moderately swishy skirt. It was navy and featured a smudgy graphic pattern in black and a stinging orange.

Once Cress was on the tube, the odd bead of nervous sweat breaking out on her upper lip, she'd look down at the skirt of her dress and feel instantly calmed.

Though as she came up the stairs that led to the street and saw Miles waiting for her, she wanted to turn tail and run.

She didn't though. She waited for her fight-or-flight response to calm the hell down, then slipped on her favourite cat's-eye dark glasses and when Miles turned round and caught sight of her, she was able to summon up a smile.

He was wearing the usual scruffy jeans, though this was a pair she hadn't seen before. A faded, pale blue denim that was lightly scuffed in places rather than outright rips because Cress was sad enough and fashion-orientated enough to have Miles's collection of denim committed to memory. He was wearing a blue and white check shirt, the sleeves rolled up, and the sight of his forearms was doing things to Cress.

Dippy, swoony, swirly things, even though at the same time, yes, she was still sad.

'Hi,' she said, her voice so high-pitched that it seemed to come out as a yelp.

'Hi,' Miles said and then he leaned forward, a hand at her waist, which seemed to burn through the thin cotton of her dress, to guide her forward so he could kiss her cheek.

Cress pulled away, flustered by his touch, but he gently pulled her forward again so he could kiss her other cheek. It seemed to Cress that his lips lingered longer than they usually did, and his hand was still at her waist even after the kiss ended.

'I always do two, remember?' he said with the faintest hint of a smile.

'How could I forget?'

'Well, you've had a lot on your mind lately,' Miles said as if he wasn't really talking about two kisses on the cheek being industry standard any more. He slipped his shades on and moved his hand from Cress's arm to her elbow. 'Shall we?'

Cress had been walking unaided for years but the simple touch of Miles's hand on her bare skin made her forget, for a second, how to put one foot in front of the other.

Why did he keep touching her?

The thought made her feel like a jittery young girl from olden times who was never normally allowed out without a chaperone.

It was all right now for Miles to touch her *arm*. Even if it was giving Cress tingly feelings that still felt far too soon.

'Maybe we could get a spot at the rooftop restaurant at Selfridges,' she said quickly, as they stepped out onto the crowded Oxford Street pavement. It was time to assert some kind of control. 'If we're lucky, they might have a table free for a quick coffee before the lunch service.'

'I had a better idea,' Miles said, steering her a sharp left onto Bond Street itself, as if he knew of some other café that would do to have what Cress hoped wouldn't be another really awkward conversation. They were meant to have moved past that.

'I think there's a Le Pain Quotidien somewhere near here,' she said but Miles shook his head.

'I came with supplies,' he said, holding up a Gail's bag, which she hadn't even noticed.

'Oh! Well, I guess if we keep walking in a straight line we hit Green Park, or if we took a right, there's Hyde Park,' Cress babbled as they crossed over Brook Street and began to walk past the kind of designer real estate that made Bond Street a shopping destination for anyone with either money to burn or a really big overdraft.

Dolce & Gabbana, Armani, Mulberry, Smythson, Celine . . .

On any other occasion, Cress would have loved to linger as she stared in the windows at luxury goods she could never afford, appreciating the artistry of a sequinned cocktail dress or the exquisite stitching on a handbag.

But today all her focus was on Miles, who'd stopped touching her. Cress didn't think she'd ever been as aware of another being as she was of him, as they walked side by side.

'So, Friday night . . .' he said at last.

'Yes, about Friday night,' Cress said unhappily, because she'd been reliving that painful hour again and again and now she was going to relive it once more. 'That was Colin.'

'Yeah, I gathered that.'

'He turned up out of the blue,' Cress explained and she sounded faintly apologetic.

'As he's perfectly entitled to do,' Miles said. 'If anyone was out of place there, it was me. But we'd got into a little Friday-evening routine, I got ahead of myself.'

'I was always happy to see you,' Cress said. 'I was happy to see you then, until I saw Colin waiting for me. But I was happy to see him too. It sounds confusing, I know, that I could be happy to see two men, like I'm the sort of woman that keeps men dangling . . .'

'I don't think that at all.' Miles took Cress's hand to bring her to a halt just outside Hermès like they were about to go in, though even the very cheapest Birkin bag would still cost more than she earned in three months. 'I get it, I really do. Your life is quite complicated at the moment.'

'It's not quite as complicated as it was. Colin and I broke up.' Cress couldn't keep the throb of tears out of her voice. 'Officially. Properly. Definitively.'

'OK . . . I'm sorry.' Miles threaded his fingers through hers for a brief moment, then let his hand fall away. 'I'm sorry that you're sad. But I'm not sorry that you've broken up.'

Cress half sniffed, half laugh-snorted. 'So sorry, not sorry?'

'I think that just about sums it up,' Miles said. 'I can't imagine what it feels like to have broken up with someone you've been with for so long.'

'Weird. It hasn't really sunk in yet, I don't think,' Cress admitted. And right on cue, the guilt washed over her. 'And yet here I am with you, not forty-eight hours later.'

They started walking again. Past Chanel, past Dior, past Audrey Hepburn's beloved Givenchy.

'It's just I'm going away to film, and this was the only chance to see you before I left.' Miles sighed. 'I didn't want to leave things between us so unresolved. I know my timing could be better.'

Cress glanced over at him. Just looking at his face, the clean lines of cheekbone and jawbone, his riotous dark curls, the promise of his lips, gave her as much pleasure as looking at any of the diamonds in the window of Harry Winston.

'The timing . . . none of this is your fault,' she said. 'Honestly, Miles, I don't know how you put up with me and just how *difficult* this is.'

'Difficult does just about sum it up,' Miles said in a heavy voice, which immediately weighed on Cress. 'But then there's this connection between us. I haven't imagined it, have I?'

'There is.' Cress imagined it as an electrical charge. Invisible to the human eye, but she could feel it fizzing and sparking in the small space between them as they continued walking until, just as New Bond Street became Old Bond Street, there she was.

A grand double shopfront painted a dark, dark grey, its famous name picked out in gold, the flags in its trademark robin's-egg blue proudly flying in the gentle summer breeze.

The Mothership.

Tiffany & Co.

'We've arrived at our destination.' Miles held out his hand to Cress as if he were inviting her to dance a cotillion at a ball like a scene from a Jane Austen novel.

She let him lead her over to the windows, then he held up the white paper bag he'd been carrying all this time.

'I know the original can't be improved upon but I was worried that the coffee would be stone cold by the time we got here, so this is an iced latte,' he said, handing Cress a large cup. 'Also they'd run out of croissants, so I got you a cinnamon bun instead.'

'I much prefer cinnamon buns to croissants anyway,' Cress said, and now she was near tears for another reason. 'I can't believe you've arranged breakfast at Tiffany's for me. This is going to be a core memory.'

Miles shrugged. 'More like brunch at Tiffany's. It's no big deal.'

'It's a very big deal. Miles, this is amazing,' Cress said through a mouthful of flaky cinnamon dough. 'I can't thank you enough.'

'It was nothing.' Miles waved a hand to indicate the nothingness of it all, and he kept his face still when usually he had a smile at the ready. 'I only spent a tenner. Not even a tenner. Do you want to go inside? Only to look. I'm not buying you diamonds or anything when it's two weeks until I get paid.'

Cress held up the sticky hand that was clutching what was left of her bun. 'It wouldn't be the same if we went inside. This, here, it's perfect. Nothing bad can happen at Tiffany's.'

She didn't care that there were so many tourists getting in the way or that it was actually quite hard to sip and eat and walk. Audrey Hepburn had made it look so easy.

What Cress cared about was that Miles had done this sweet, thoughtful thing for her even though he didn't know what her relationship status was when they'd met at Bond Street station. He'd really thought about what would please Cress and gifted her an experience that she'd always remember.

Nothing could be better, not even if Miles had taken her into Tiffany and bought her a tiara. Cress would much rather have had a smile from him than a tiara, but his ready smile was nowhere to be seen.

Cress knew then that there was going to be Serious Talk that would probably lead to nothing good. Her simple, safe little life had derailed just before she met Miles and she couldn't expect him to keep picking up the pieces. Or pretending that they were in the friend zone when they both knew that they were far more than friends.

It was a conversation that was long overdue but it was a conversation that Cress wasn't ready for. Not just yet. For weeks, she'd suspected that she and Colin were broken up, but now that they were officially, irreconcilably broken, she had a lot of grieving to do. Thinking too, about what she wanted her life to look like. And though she wanted, *hoped*, that Miles might be in that life, Cress knew that she needed to be on her own for a bit while she planned her future. She couldn't and wouldn't plan her life around a boyfriend again. That had been a big mistake. Huge.

How to begin to put that into words in a way that wouldn't hurt Miles's feelings? Cress hadn't figured that out yet so, as they continued to walk down Bond Street towards Piccadilly, she needed to distract him. And she had the perfect story all ready to go, about the one and only time she'd ever entered the hallowed portals of Tiffany & Co.

Because she and Sophy had their birthdays a month apart, on a Saturday approximately two weeks between their sixteenth birthdays, Diane and Aaron and Mike and Caroline had taken the two girls 'up West' for a birthday surprise. First they'd gone to the big TopShop at Oxford Circus to spend their birthday money, which was more of a Sophy thing than a Cress thing.

Then they'd walked down to Bond Street, following much the same route as Cress and Miles had covered today.

'When we got to Tiffany's, we actually went inside. A man in uniform opened the door for us even though, now that I think about it, we really didn't look like their usual type of customer.'

'Then what happened?' Miles asked, the grim look to his face thankfully gone.

'I burst into tears. I mean, obviously,' Cress said and she could still remember how overwhelmed she'd been. 'I didn't really have a good nose around. It was just enough to be *in* Tiffany, and also, I've never really been that interested in jewellery.'

'So, you're really not annoyed that I chose a cinnamon bun over a diamond necklace?'

'Cinnamon buns are for ever,' Cress said. 'And so are keyrings, which is what our parents bought us at Tiffany. They were the cheapest thing there, though they still weren't exactly cheap, but the woman who was serving us made it into a special occasion. She put each keyring in a little velvet pouch, then a Tiffany's box, and tied it up with ribbon, and *then* a blue Tiffany's bag, which I used as my lunch bag for the next two years.'

'Of course you did,' Miles said with a really welcome grin. 'You're quite extra sometimes, aren't you?'

'Only occasionally,' Cress argued. 'I'm very low-maintenance most of the time, and look!' She rummaged one-handed in her handbag and pulled out her keys. 'I'm still using my Tiffany keyring!'

'So, without even fully realising it, I picked the perfect place for our date,' Miles said lightly, but the look he sent Cress, even with sunglasses on, was far from light. 'I know you need time, but when I'm with you it always feels like a date. That's what I wanted to talk to you about before I go away.'

This was Cress's cue to gently explain to Miles that she needed more time. That there needed to be a decent and appropriate gap between a fifteen-year relationship and even just *dates*.

'I know we need to talk,' she said. They were coming to the end of Old Bond Street now; she could see Piccadilly, bustling with buses and black taxicabs, in the distance. The day of their Tiffany outing, she and Sophy had been taken to Fortnum & Mason ('the Queen's grocer,' Caroline had kept saying) for afternoon tea. 'It's just so hard to find the right words.'

Today, Cress didn't think there'd be finger sandwiches and tiny, delicate cakes in her immediate future. She wasn't entirely sure what the future had in store for her.

'I don't want to rush this, but I have to get home quite soon,' Miles said. 'I have a ton of stuff to do before I go to Belfast.'

Cress couldn't remember things ever being this awkward between them except the first time they'd met when she'd thought Miles was pretentious and rude. Now she couldn't

247

help the disappointed sigh that leaked out of her mouth. 'That's a shame.'

Miles nodded. 'I didn't want to leave town with everything so up in the air.'

'I wish I could tell you that I'm not in a relationship any more and that I want to be more than friends,' Cress said. 'But it's too soon. I'm not ready.'

'So, you just want to be friends?' Miles asked, his voice flat.

'I know I want you in my life but I have no idea what that life looks like yet.' Cress put her hand on Miles's arm, his skin hot beneath her fingertips. She thought that maybe this was the first time she'd touched him rather than waiting for him to make the first move. She had to stop doing that. 'I always just drift into things. I let stuff happen to me. But now I really need to learn how to make my own decisions, be in charge of my own life.'

'I understand that, I really do, and I can wait, but I'm not going to wait for ever,' Miles said, his hand covering Cress's hand, which still rested on his arm.

'I wouldn't expect you to,' Cress said, even though she wanted him to wait. Not for ever, that wouldn't be fair, but long enough for her to get her head straight. Though she couldn't imagine that being mistress of her own destiny would mean that she suddenly stopped having these complicated, tender feelings for Miles. 'I can't give you a timetable though.'

'I understand that too, but it, well, it sucks.' Miles took his hand away, then moved his arm, so they were no longer touching.

'And I would understand if you fell in love with someone else,' Cress said, though she'd be absolutely devastated if that happened. 'Or if you just wanted to date someone who didn't come with huge amounts of emotional baggage.'

'I'm not planning to do either of those things. Not in the immediate future,' Miles said carefully. 'And you do have to take as long as you need to figure things out.'

248

But how long would that take? And would it be too long?

'It's probably good that we'll be spending a few weeks apart. We've both got some thinking to do.' Those were the words that came out of her mouth but in her heart she was thinking, *screaming*, please don't give up on us. Not yet.

'Yeah, you're right.' Miles nodded. 'I'm going to jump on the tube at Green Park. What about you?'

Cress couldn't bear the thought of either getting on a crowded tube or going home to brood. 'I think I'll head to Fortnum & Mason and have a mooch around.' If ever there was a time to buy a very expensive box of chocolates, as bougie comfort food, then it was now.

Time to say goodbye then. They were tucked into the doorway of what must once have been a very grand office block so they wouldn't be buffeted by the crowds. Cress pushed her sunglasses onto the top of her head because she wanted to get one last proper look at Miles.

He took off his sunglasses too, tucking them into the front pocket of his shirt. It seemed to Cress as if they were frozen in the moment, neither one of them wanting to be the first to walk away.

'This has been so lovely,' she said at last. 'Not the talk, not this horrible feeling that I might never see you again, but the rest of it has been lovely.'

'I'm pretty sure that you will see me again.' Miles lifted his hand to smooth away a strand of hair that was falling in Cress's face, then his thumb traced a path down her cheek to her mouth. 'I really hope so.'

'I can't think straight when you do that,' Cress said in a voice that hardly sounded like her.

'What, this?' Miles pressed his thumb against the pout of her bottom lip. 'I'm hardly doing anything.'

He was doing enough to cause havoc to Cress's nerve endings. She pursed her lips so she was kissing his thumb, and, even though it was a busy Sunday lunchtime in the centre of London, his eyes darkened as if it was just the two of them alone in a quiet room.

'Don't,' he said as if he meant do. 'Please don't make this more difficult than it already is.'

'I'm hardly doing anything,' Cress pointed out but he took his hand away and, before she could panic that she'd gone too far for someone who needed time, he leaned in closer.

'As we're saying goodbye, hopefully just for a little while, would it be all right if we sealed it with a kiss?' His voice was a purr, his eyes all pupil, and Cress could do nothing but nod, although there were several very good reasons why the last thing they should do was kiss.

But it wasn't really a kiss. It was a prelude to a kiss. Just the barest hint of Miles's mouth. Their lips not quite meeting, a gap, gossamer thin, between them. Then for one fleeting, all-too-brief second, Miles pressed his mouth to hers. It wasn't enough.

Then he stepped back and it would have to be enough. Though Cress couldn't even remember why they weren't kissing like their lives depended on it.

His hand stroked her hair one last time, his face tender, and then he pulled away. 'I'll wait to hear from you,' he said, then disappeared into the sunny Sunday afternoon.

Chapter Twenty-Seven

It was a week of goodbyes. Tanya went off to Sicily with an apologetic text message: Sorry for being such a negative nelly last time I saw you. Am sure the dress will be fine. Let's talk when I get back.

It was also time to say goodbye to Ella, who was graduating, not exactly with honours but with a decent enough version of the dress that Cress had also made for Anita. More importantly, Ella could now give every appearance of being able to design, drape and sew dresses, even if Cress still wouldn't let her near the pinking shears without supervision.

'I don't care if my seams are a bit crooked,' Ella said, as she twisted and turned in front of the mirrors in the salon to see what she looked like in her debut creation. 'I love it and I'm going to wear it to the wrap party.'

'What's a wrap party?' Cress asked, as she sat on one of the chintzy sofas with Coco Chanel in her lap. Despite her main character energy, Coco Chanel was very good at sensing when Cress was down then comforting her with the solid weight of both her body and her personality.

'Just a little bacchanal we have to celebrate when shooting is finally over,' Ella explained. She stepped off the dais with great care so as not to split the tight skirt of the dress, which had been made to Anita's measurements, and Anita was a good six inches shorter than Ella. 'But before that, we have to actually make the damn thing.'

Ella sounded a little unsure of herself, which was surprising.

'You're not nervous, are you? You're the most confident person I've ever met,' Cress said.

'I'm not nervous,' Ella insisted, wriggling out of the dress where she stood rather than heading for the changing cubicle. 'Darling, I'm bloody terrified. Standard behaviour before the start of a new endeavour. Though making a movie isn't quite so frightening as the theatre. I always throw up before opening night. Always.'

Cress looked up at Ella, who was now stripped down to her undies and miming someone being sick. 'I'd never have guessed.'

'Which is why I get paid the big bucks. Or however much my agent can negotiate above the standard Equity rate,' Ella said. 'Gotta fake it till you make it, right?'

It was something that Cress pondered once Ella had gone in a flurry of 'thank you, thank you, thank you's and kisses and promises to keep in touch. Maybe she should act more like the person she wanted to be: confident, decisive and, yes, sexy, until that confidence, decisiveness and even sexiness would become second nature.

Confidence was probably the easiest one of the lot. Cress looked in satisfaction at the dress she'd reimagined from the scraps of the frock that Anita had given her. The sartorial equivalent of a phoenix rising from the ashes.

Not just anyone could design and make a dress in two weeks, on top of their full-time job and assorted side hustles, but Cress could. She had talent and maybe it was time to start harnessing it for more than replacing zippers and taking up hems.

She texted Anita. Your dress is ready. Don't come up if Phoebe is lurking.

There was a brief pause, no more than ten seconds, then someone was thundering up the stairs as if they were being chased by wolves.

'Lemme at it!' Anita announced breathlessly as she arrived at the doorway of Cress's workroom. Her eyes locked on to the dress form, or rather the fitted, black crêpe cotton dress with a starburst of diamanté scattered over the left-hand side of the bodice. 'Oh my days!'

It was impossible to know how Anita felt about the dress as 'Oh my days!' was her go-to phrase for most life experiences, good and bad.

'What do you think then?' Cress asked with quite a lot of trepidation. She'd already forgotten that she was meant to be faking confidence.

'Can I try it on?'

'Knock yourself out,' Cress said a little huffily because some validation, even a thank you, wouldn't have gone amiss.

She waited for what felt like ages for Anita to emerge from the changing room. To Cress's trained eye, the dress fitted perfectly, as if it had been made for Anita. Which, actually, it had been.

Anita glided past Cress without a word. When she reached the salon, she hitched up the skirt of the dress so she could climb onto the dais and scrutinise herself in it from every angle.

Cress, with folded arms, watched her from the archway that led back to her workroom. She was in an agony that the first words out of Anita's mouth were going to be, 'Thanks, I hate it.'

But Anita was too busy staring at the pert curve of her bottom to speak.

'Are you some kind of witch?' she asked at last.

Which was kind of random.

'Um, no. I mean, I look at my horoscope sometimes but I'm not into all that tarot . . .'

Anita, despite the fact that she was in heels and a tight skirt, practically leapt off the platform and seized Cress's limp hands. 'What sorcery is in these fingertips?' she demanded. 'This isn't making a dress, Cress. This is magic!'

'You like it then?' It did no harm to clarify.

'Like it? I love it!' Anita did a little shimmy. 'It's just like my old dress, but better. I mean, it does things to my boobs and my booty that should be illegal and . . . and . . .'

'And?' Cress prompted.

'IT HAS POCKETS!' Anita shouted in triumph. 'You are a genius!'

Cress's confidence was back with a bang. 'Oh, it was nothing . . .' No, that wasn't what a confident person would say. 'I'm pleased that you're pleased. It did turn out pretty well.'

'What is all this noise going on up here?' said a cross voice that got louder and louder as its owner, Phoebe, made her way up the stairs.

Cress and Anita just had to time to share one look of horror before they scarpered. Cress to her workroom, Anita to the changing room.

By the time Phoebe appeared in the workroom doorway, Cress was bent over her sewing machine and, she hoped, looking the very picture of industry.

'What were you and Anita shouting about?' Phoebe asked, suspicion writ large over every millimetre of her face. 'And why is Anita even up here without my express permission?'

'Oh, just dress stuff,' Cress said vaguely as she didn't want to say anything that would incriminate Anita, or herself for that matter.

'Where is *she?*' Phoebe muttered under her breath as Anita slunk out of the changing room with her hand clutching something behind her back like an idiot. Cress would have left the dress hanging up in the changing room, but Anita clearly wasn't a criminal mastermind like her.

'Nothing to see here!' Anita trilled, which was exactly what someone would say when there was something to see, namely the dress she was trying to hide.

'What is that?' Phoebe snatched the dress out of Anita's hand with ease. Anita didn't even put up a fight. 'Why are you sneaking around with it?'

'Not sneaking around,' Cress said because Anita was opening and closing her mouth without any sounds coming out. Though usually Anita was skilled in dealing with Phoebe. 'I just made some minor alterations to one of Anita's dresses. In my own time.'

Phoebe held the dress up for inspection. Her eyes scanned up and down, left to right. Cress didn't doubt that if there was a wonky stitch or rogue piece of diamanté then Phoebe would find it.

'This is a brand-new dress,' she said at last. 'It's not vintage.'

Anita squirmed, which was actually quite similar to her earlier shimmy. 'It's based on a—'

'When I say brand new, what I really mean is that it's been very recently made by someone with impeccable sewing skills,' Phoebe said, her gaze coming to rest on Cress. 'Minor alterations, my Aunt Fanny!'

'Anyway, I'd better go downstairs,' Anita said quickly like the traitor that she was. 'Can't have Bea and Sophy holding the fort on their own.'

Then she disappeared with indecent haste, thundering down the stairs with as much speed as she'd thundered up them.

'What you do in your own time is, of course, your own business,' Phoebe said smoothly and also untruthfully because she made everything that happened in the shop her business too. 'But my spider sense is tingling. What aren't you telling me?'

'I did do the work in my own time,' Cress insisted. 'Except when Ella was here and I got her to shadow me by making her own copy of the dress too. But that was agreed! That I mentored Ella as part of my contracted duties. So . . . Oh, no, Phoebe, I'd leave that alone, if I were you . . .'

It was too late. Phoebe's gimlet gaze had now alighted on the sorry scrap of black rayon crêpe that Cress had foolishly left lying on the counter. She held it up so she could take it all in: the rotted underarms, the ripped seams, the scattershot diamanté. Then she held up the new, improved dress in her other hand.

By replicating Anita's ruined dress, had Cress infringed some kind of frock copyright? It wasn't as if Anita's dress even had a manufacturer's label on it; that was long gone. Still, it was just the kind of thing that Phoebe tended to get unfeasibly furious about.

It was a well-known fashion secret that a lot of the big designers, even the Paris-based ones, employed 'rag-pickers' who sourced vintage clothes for them, which they'd then redesign and parade down their own catwalks. Not even redesign sometimes. Last year a dress had cropped up in one of the autumn/winter collections that was pretty much a stitch for stitch copy of a 1960s dress from an obscure British fashion house they had on the rails downstairs. The designer had even copied the fabric, although in a slightly more vibrant shade of cobalt blue. Phoebe had kicked off long and loud about that.

'Right, I see what's been going on here,' she said now, but it was in a quiet voice, not her cutting, spitting-fury voice.

'I like to think of it as a homage,' Cress said quickly. 'Because the one I made is crêpe cotton, not rayon, and I added in pockets.'

'Pockets,' Phoebe said reverently, because talk of pockets often calmed her down when she was upset – in much the same way that Coco Chanel would stop having a hissy fit if you offered her a liver treat. 'I love pockets.'

'Who doesn't?' Cress murmured and now that the crisis seemed to have been averted, she could get on with what she was meant to be getting on with: replacing a silk-thread-covered hook and eye on an impossibly delicate oyster silk 1930s dress.

Phoebe perched on the spare stool, still holding both dresses as if she'd gone into a fugue state.

'I had a dress very similar to this one,' she said eventually.

'It's a pretty standard 1940s design,' Cress said. 'Quite fitted so it didn't use up too much fabric, which was on the ration.'

'My dress didn't have the diamanté but it did have a darling black velvet Peter Pan collar,' Phoebe said dreamily.

'Sounds lovely.' Cress was still trying to find alternative adjectives to 'lovely'. Without much success. 'Sounds nice.' Urgh! 'Sounds very you.'

'It was very me until it was destroyed by moths. Bastard moths!' Phoebe was getting ragey again. 'The bastard moth infestation of 2019. It nearly broke me, Cress.'

'Was your dress wool?' Cress asked even though she knew full well that the best thing to do was to change the subject.

'It was. My poor, poor dress.'

'Moths love wool so it's best to buy clothes that aren't 100 per cent wool but have some synthetic fibres in the mix,' Cress said, because she never knew when to quit. 'It's why I won't have vintage woollens in the house, even though I yearn for a vintage beaded cardigan.'

'I still have my dress in a sealtop bag in the freezer,' Phoebe confessed. 'Though Freddy says . . . Not that Freddy lives . . . Once Freddy just happened to be round mine and he needed some ice and he noticed that it was in the freezer.

Don't look at me like that, Cress! You know that occasionally I see Freddy outside of work.'

This was new and fascinating intel. Freddy round at Phoebe's. Not for the first time, more like the gazillionth time, Cress wished that she was able to share this knowledge with Sophy, but she couldn't. 'Putting a wool dress in the freezer *after* it's been attacked by moths is a lot like shutting the stable door after the horse has bolted,' she said instead.

'Oh, I know that, but I live in hope that I might find the same dress somewhere. But I never have,' Phoebe said woefully.

'I hate when that happens.' Cress squinted at the hook she'd just attached to the dress with tiny, tiny stitches to make sure that it was straight.

'I must have looked *everywhere*,' Phoebe said with heavy emphasis and when Cress reluctantly looked up it was to see that Phoebe was staring at her pleadingly. But being Phoebe, pride just wouldn't let her say the words.

Cress put down the oyster silk. 'Phoebe, would you like me to make you a replica of your dress? If you brought it to the shop, then I could take it apart outside on the patio and make the pattern pieces out there too . . .'

'Oh yes, I couldn't have the dress unbagged in the shop.' Phoebe wrung her hands. 'I'm convinced that there's still some bastard moth larvae embedded in its seams.'

'Maybe I'll wear gloves then when I'm handling it,' Cress said with a shudder. 'Unless it's very similar to Anita's, and then I could just add in the collar . . .'

'That makes sense,' Phoebe agreed meekly, though she never did anything meekly. 'Except this dress is gorgeous, but my dress is even more gorgeous.'

There was no point in arguing about it. 'OK, but you might have to buy me a hazmat suit before I handle your dress.'

'That's fine, anything,' Phoebe said, even though Cress had been joking. Sort of. 'I'm so lucky to be getting a Cressida Collins original made just for me.' She treated Cress to her most winsome smile, which made Cress feel as if they weren't quite done here. 'Also, just one last favour.'

'Do you want me to throw in my firstborn too?' Now that she knew Phoebe wasn't cross with her, and she'd agreed to do her bidding, Cress actually wished that Phoebe would go away so she could get on with her work.

'No! It's just a little thing really. My dress doesn't have any, but could you—'

'Pockets. You want pockets,' Cress surmised.

'Always, Cress. Always.'

'In that case, giving you pockets would be an honour and a privilege too.'

Chapter Twenty-Eight

Then it was time to say goodbye to Sophy, who was going on her first holiday with Charles. Though they'd already been away for more weekends than any other people Cress knew. Then Cress felt churlish for thinking such uncharitable thoughts just because she wanted Sophy to be there for her in her time of need and not sunning herself on the shores of Lake Como.

'I'll be back before you know it,' Sophy insisted on her last day in the shop. 'Unless George and Amal Clooney take a shine to us and ask us to stay on.'

It was a Tuesday, which meant it had been a whole week of Miles being in Belfast.

Cress assumed he was very busy doing important film stuff as, though they hadn't discussed whether they would stay in phone contact, they were still messaging each other but Miles's messages had slowed to a mere trickle. In fact, they were usually brief replies to messages that Cress had sent him. She was trying really hard not to read any sinister ulterior motives into them, but was mostly failing miserably.

'Will you be all right without me?' Sophy asked as they walked to Chalk Farm station together that evening. She'd been full of holiday plans and quite a few moans about having to get up at ridiculous o'clock to catch a 5 a.m. flight to Milan Malpensa airport, but now she seemed to realise that Cress was very quiet. 'You haven't once issued any of your usual dire travel warnings about deep vein thrombosis on the flight and which snakebites are fatal.'

'Probably because you're only taking a two-hour flight to Italy and there are no poisonous snakes native to Lake Como, as far as I know.' Cress held up her phone. 'I could google it though.'

'It's OK, let's not,' Sophy said with a shudder. 'You just seem out of sorts. Is it the Colin thing or the Miles thing?'

'There isn't really a Miles thing, and the Colin thing . . . I wish it hadn't ended the way it did,' Cress said. 'He was prepared to make this big sacrifice for me but then it morphed into an awkward argument in a crowded pub. We should have had a better goodbye.'

'Might be worth having one more shot at goodbye?' Sophy suggested but Cress shook her head.

'I think I've hurt him enough for now,' she said. But she was being cowardly. Not wanting to get in touch with Colin, because he was angry with her and it would be awful. 'Maybe I should get in touch with him. I realise that we weren't love's young dream, but we had a good thing for a long time. We both deserve a better goodbye than the one we got.'

Sophy waited patiently outside the station as Cress took a long time to compose what ended up being a very short message to Colin.

> I hate the way we left things. I hope you're all right. C

It wasn't much, but it was something to let Colin know that Cress wasn't cross any more and that she was thinking about him. Being Colin, he probably wouldn't respond, or, if he did, it would be weeks from now, but Cress felt a little bit better as she slid her phone back into her dress pocket. A moment later, it chimed with an incoming message.

Cress hoped it was Miles, but it was more likely to be Diane asking her to pop into Tesco when she got to Finchley Central to buy whatever items Diane needed to get through the evening. Usually either crisps or ice cream. Sometimes both.

But it wasn't Miles or Diane but, wonder of wonders, Colin.

> Thanks for the message. I have some of your stuff to give back to you. Are you around tonight? If so, meet at our bench at eight? No arguments, I promise. C

'Anyway, I'm sure you won't miss me in the slightest, you have so much stuff going on,' Sophy said as they crossed over the bridge that would take them to Chalk Farm Road. She didn't seem to realise that the message that Cress had just received had filled her with dread. Dread wasn't usually an emotion she associated with Colin. Even though he promised there'd be no arguments. 'You've still got to finish Tanya's dress and then *apparently* you're making a dress for Phoebe.'

'Yes, *apparently*, I am,' Cress said because that news had travelled fast.

'Can't believe you made a dress for Anita and now you're making one for Phoebe but where is the dress for your beloved sister-friend?' Sophy pouted. 'It wounds me. You could have made me an amazing sexy *La Dolce Vita* dress to wow George Clooney when we lock eyes on a crowded Lake Como beach.'

'I'll have to put you on the waiting list. My dresses are more in demand than a Birkin,' Cress said, her dread momentarily forgotten. 'Also, like you have eyes for anyone but Charles – and as if the Clooney would ever set foot on a crowded beach full of non-famous folk.'

'But if he did . . .'

'Obviously he'd fall in love with you at first sight, even though you're young enough to be his daughter,' Cress said.

They crossed over the road to the station and then ran to squeeze into a lift that was beeping, its doors about to close. Once they got down to platform level, it was almost time to say goodbye for ten days. They could hear a train approaching and had to run to catch it. Then it was a rushed, crowded minute to Camden Town, where Cress would change onto the High Barnet branch, while Sophy would travel on because she was staying at Charles's flat in Bloomsbury because 'have I mentioned that we need to get up at cock's crow?'

'Only once or twice. And don't forget to regularly apply your sunscreen. Especially if you go in the water. I know that you're now a redhead who tans but you can never be too careful.'

'Yes, Mum. And don't forget that you're an amazing person who is on the cusp of exciting new things,' Sophy said, giving Cress a quick but fierce hug as the train pulled into Camden Town station. 'And when I get back we are finally going to have an in-depth chat about you and Miles, plus you can show me the designs for the dress that you're going to make me.'

'I hope a less bossy Sophy comes back from Lake Como,' Cress grumbled as the train doors opened.

'I'm going to be even bossier as I implement my rent-a-dress scheme in time for the Christmas party season to begin,' Sophy vowed, and she laughed at Cress's horrified face as the train pulled away and Cress was left waving on the platform.

Cress squeezed past hurrying commuters to reach the High Barnet platform. There was only a two-minute wait for the next train, so she didn't have time to agonise over the words but sent a swift reply to Colin.

See you at the bench at eight. C

They'd always used to add an x, a kiss, after their initial but obviously they weren't doing that any more. For good reason, but it still made Cress feel sad.

When she got home, via a last-minute detour to Tesco for Kettle Chips for Diane, there was only time for a quick stir-fry for dinner, which tasted like ashes, before Cress was heading out again to meet Colin.

Almost equidistant between their houses was a small green on a corner where two roads met. There was a wooden bench where one could sit and watch the sights go by – not that there were many sights to be had on a quiet suburban street in N3.

During the earliest days of their courtship, when they were both under the parental cosh, plus had very little disposable income and a lot of GCSE revision, Cress and Colin had spent a lot of time on that bench. Cress thought that it might have been the venue for their first kiss, though she couldn't say for certain. The fact that she couldn't quite remember where and when their first kiss had happened was another thing that made her sad.

When she rounded the corner and saw that Colin was already at the bench, his hand raised in a tentative wave, she felt sadder still.

It was a matter of seconds to reach him but it felt to Cress as if it took for ever.

'Hi,' she said. 'No, don't get up!' Because Colin was getting to his feet like Cress was the Queen or something.

'Here's your stuff,' he said, handing over a large John Lewis bag. 'It was what was in your drawer.'

Cress didn't have anything to give back to Colin apart from the door keys, as he hadn't had a drawer at her house. They'd always stayed at his because he was too uncomfortable to spend the night under Diane's roof.

Cress opened the bag to check the contents, and on top of the small, neatly folded pile of clothes was a box from her favourite French patisserie, just round the corner from Colin's office in the City. It used to be that every now and again he'd surprise her with a fancy éclair.

'Oh, Col, you shouldn't have . . .' she said.

He shrugged. 'I was walking past after we messaged and saw that they had those caramel éclairs you like, so I got you a couple. Unless that breaks some rule of splitting up that I don't know about,' he added, his voice laced with real hurt.

'I don't know what the rules are,' Cress said, sitting down. She'd had some vague notion that the handing over of personal items would end up being brief and brusque, but those éclairs . . . 'I've never split up with anyone before. But I do know that I hated how we ended things in the pub.'

There was a moment of silence punctuated by a car backfiring in the distance. 'It was awful,' Colin said. 'It wasn't meant to go like that.'

'But secretly, deep down, you were kind of relieved not to have to sell your record collection,' Cress said very gently with an even gentler nudge of her elbow into Colin's side, which teased a smile out of him.

His new haircut, his sad hank of a ponytail gone, really suited him. He looked younger, especially when he smiled. He'd caught the sun too during this long summer and it was a bitter-sweet reminder of the boy that Cress had fallen in love with all those years ago.

'I was a bit relieved,' Colin admitted, sitting back a little as if, now that Cress was here and they weren't mad at each other, he could relax. 'But I think I'm still going to sell quite a lot of them. What you were saying about living a small life . . .'

'Everything I wanted to say came out wrong . . .'

'But you were right. I don't even know how I let my life get so small, so rigid, especially when I realise that actually I haven't been happy for a long time,' Colin said.

Cress couldn't remember the last time she'd heard him really get down deep with his feelings. 'I'm so sorry that you felt like that.'

He shrugged again. 'That's not to say I was unhappy. But us arguing, then breaking up, it shook everything up. I really had to look at myself and I've been existing, not really living. So, sod that!'

'I hope you're not going to do anything rash,' Cress said in surprise because this was very unlike Colin. But then again . . . 'Or maybe you should do something rash. Go travelling. Climb Mount Everest. Trek through the Hindu Kush . . .'

'Steady on!' It was Colin's turn to nudge Cress. He rolled his eyes. 'I get vertigo just going up the stairs. I don't see Everest in my near future. But, I think I kind of hate my job. Ten years in IT. Ten years of troubleshooting when really, ninety-nine per cent of people's computer problems could be solved by switching off and restarting.'

'Ninety-nine per cent?' Cress echoed. 'Not that many!'

'Yes, that many!' Colin said darkly. But then he brightened. 'I know this guy who's got a record shop in Holloway. It does all right. It could do better and he's looking to retire in a couple of years, so I'm thinking of selling some of my records, saving up, then taking over the lease from him.'

'Wow. That's a big thing,' Cress said, and she wasn't even riled that Colin would save up for a record shop but not to buy a house with her. 'Scary too.'

'Scary but exciting. When I haven't been cut up about you, I've been thinking of all the things I'd love to do with the shop,' he said. 'Derek doesn't even take part in National Record Shop Day or stock any new vinyl. Even Sainsbury's in Camden Town stocks new vinyl!'

'I think it's a brilliant idea,' Cress said. 'I could really see you with your own record shop. As long as you don't get an attack of the Phoebes and start hoarding the vinyl instead of selling it.'

'She's still doing that with the frocks?' Colin asked, which was sweet of him because he'd never really been that interested in the shop.

'She's not so bad, and I'm making her dream dress, so she has to be on her best behaviour.' All this talk of new endeavours was quite inspiring. 'In fact, I've started making dresses for people. Not just repairing them.'

'Maybe you'll have your own shop one day too?' Colin suggested.

'Maybe.' Cress didn't think she wanted her own shop, but her own ambitions were now much bigger than just saving up for a house and waiting for her real life to begin.

Her real life was happening every day and she didn't want to waste any more time.

She turned so she was facing Colin and she could take his hand and, for a second, she saw the hope flicker across his face. 'I need to tell you that you'll always be one of my dearest friends. Always. We know everything about each other, but we also know that we're just not in love with each other any more.'

'I do love you, Cress,' Colin said. 'But you're right. I love you like I love *Rubber Soul* by the Beatles. I could listen to it every day but it doesn't excite me in the same way that *The White Album* does.'

Cress wasn't exactly sure what the Beatles had to do with this but she got the general idea, because she and Colin knew each other that well. 'We grew apart without even realising it and there's no way round that.'

'I wish there was a magic solution. No other woman is ever going to put up with me,' Colin said with a little hint of desperation.

'There will be someone for you.' Cress hoped that she was right.

'And have you already found your someone?' Colin asked softly.

'I haven't . . . it's too soon . . . I'm taking some time to process everything, us not being an us any more, what I want to do with my life, but I do like him a lot,' Cress said because she had to be honest with Colin, she really owed him that.

'Well, I hope he makes you happy . . .'

'I think I need to make myself happy first. Same goes for you. You can't rely on someone else for your own happiness, right?' Cress sniffed. She thought she'd cried all the tears that she was going to cry for Colin, but it seemed as if she wasn't quite done.

She glanced across at him. He was scrubbing at his face with an impatient hand. 'I didn't think this would be so hard. I feel gutted.'

'Me too but I'm glad that we got to do this properly and, remember, friends for ever, Col.'

They both stood up and, without even words, they fell into each other's arms for one last, long, long hug until Colin broke free. 'OK, well, I'll see you around.'

Cress nodded. 'You absolutely will.'

She watched him walk to the end of the street, then turn to wave at her before he rounded the corner.

After everything, it had been a beautiful goodbye and they both deserved that.

Now it was time for Cress to figure out the rest of her life.

Chapter Twenty-Nine

There was no point in rushing the rest of her life. A few more weeks couldn't hurt for Cress to finish processing the past, assessing the present and manifesting her future.

Currently her present didn't have Miles in it and his messages were increasingly sporadic. It had been a month since she last saw him and she was forced to get updates on the filming of *Beat!* from Ella's Instagram. They were still shooting in Belfast but would then move to Eastbourne for a week, then to a studio in Bristol to shoot the last interior scenes. (Ella had put a call out on her Stories for 'cool places to drink cocktails and eat my bodyweight in dirty fries'.)

It did feel like she might never see Miles again. He could very possibly fall for a woman living in Belfast, Eastbourne or Bristol who didn't need time and was ready and primed for a relationship.

But Cress couldn't give in to catastrophising. She'd asked Miles for time and she was using it mostly to learn how to set up very strict boundaries. Once she'd made Phoebe her dress, then Sophy, back from Lake Como tanned and even more loved up, a very sexy ice-blue satin wiggle dress, everyone seemed to think that Cress had time to make them frocks.

Anita had at least eight best friends and had promised them all a dress made with love by Cress. 'I mean, I've seen *The Great British Sewing Bee*, Cress, how long does it take to knock one up?' she'd asked when Cress had confronted her about the WhatsApp messages she was getting containing Anita's friends' measurements and their dress requirements.

While Phoebe, who should have known better, it turned out had many dresses in sealtop bags in her freezer, victims of the Bastard Moth Infestation of 2019, and seemed to think that Cress had time to replicate them all with additional flourishes and pockets.

'We're not *that* busy in the shop,' Phoebe had pointed out when Cress had point-blank refused to recreate a really intricate number with a peplum and razor pleats. 'It's September! It's our quiet patch when all the summer weddings have happened and we haven't started the Christmas party panic. I'd hate to think of you upstairs in your workroom without even a button to sew on.'

'You're all heart but again, no,' Cress had said firmly, and Phoebe and Coco Chanel had been huffy with her for the rest of the day.

But when Tanya came in for the final fitting of her dress, she was far from the huffy lady she'd been before her holiday. She was even more tanned than Sophy and in high spirits. Joe had got pissed one night and asked her to marry him ('though I turned the silly sod down because after thirty years, he can do better than a drunk proposal when he's stripped down to his underpants') and both her kids were back at school.

Cress had had a sleepless night before Tanya came in because she felt like she was sitting a very important exam the next day. As she carefully inched the dress over Tanya's head, her hands were clammy and she could feel her heart positively pounding away.

Tanya disappeared from view as she was encased in black satin, but then her face emerged and she looked as nervous as Cress felt, her bottom lip caught between her teeth as Cress tugged the dress down over her hips.

'It's tight,' she said. 'I ate a lot of chips in Taormina.'

'It's fitted,' Cress corrected her but, as she inched up the hidden side zip with sweaty fingers, she sent up a prayer to every available deity that the chips hadn't undone all the painstaking work Cress had undertaken to get the fit just right. 'There we are. Zip's up. Now on the night, I need you to wear that strapless bra we talked about and the boning I've put in will do the rest. How does it feel?'

Tanya looked down at the dress. At herself in the dress. 'A bit like a fever dream, to be honest.'

It was quite hard to know if that was good or bad. 'Let's get your heels on, and are you ready for the dais?'

Tanya's nod was accompanied by a grimace. 'Ready as I'll ever be.'

She slid her feet into a pair of black suede heels that were almost as high as Phoebe's, then tottered out of the changing room.

Except Tanya didn't totter for long. Cress had created a side slit in the dress. So, maybe it was the slit, maybe it was the way that Tanya suddenly straightened her shoulders and lifted her head, but she seemed to glide into the main salon and float up the two steps that led to the dais.

Then she took a deep breath and looked at herself in the triptych of mirrors that had been the cruel enemy of many another woman who'd stood where she was standing.

'Don't forget that you'll have your hair up, make-up on, we'll sort out some statement jewellery—'

'Shhh!' Tanya put a finger to her lips to hush Cress's conciliatory babbling. 'Just give me a moment.'

Cress could hardly bear to look as Tanya slowly rotated a full circle. As far as she could see, the dress was flawless. Tanya looked exquisite. But it wasn't Cress's dress any more and Cress's opinion wasn't important. This was all about Tanya now.

Tanya completed her circle and stood motionless while she stared at her multiple reflections. Then she nodded her head. 'There you are, my darling,' she murmured. 'I've been waiting to meet you all my life.'

The moment was completely ruined by the snotty sob that burst out of Cress.

'Do not cry, Cress, otherwise you'll start me off and I've cried too many tears in this room as it is,' Tanya said throatily, as Cress snatched up a tissue.

Cress blew her nose. 'It's just . . . you look so beautiful.'

'Well, you're pretty bloody amazing at making dresses,' Tanya said, smoothing her hands over her hips in wonder.

'It's not the dress, it's *you*.' Cress wiped her eyes as she tried to explain properly. 'I'm not thinking of Audrey Hepburn in *Breakfast at Tiffany's* when I look at you. I'm seeing *you*. This beautiful, funny, intelligent woman who's finally putting herself first. I hope you can see her too.'

'I do see her,' Tanya said. 'I feel like the person I was always meant to be, except life kept getting in the way.' She held up the skirt. 'I think you must have sewn some magic into this dress.'

'No magic, but I think we both had a perfect vision of the dress and it all came together.' Cress blew her nose again. 'And if Joe doesn't propose to you, properly, when he sees you in the dress, then I'm never going to sew so much as a handkerchief ever again.'

'Quite frankly, the idiot doesn't deserve me,' Tanya said, twirling again. 'Honestly, in this dress, I'd marry me in a heartbeat.'

Tanya changed back into the jeans and casual top she'd arrived in. They had a chat about accessories and hairstyles and then she left with the dress packed away between layers of tissue paper in its special box. She walked out of the shop as if she was still wearing the dress. Head high, back straight, a glorious smile on her face.

That half-hour had probably been one of the most satis-fying thirty minutes of Cress's career. All the thoughts and plans and possibilities she'd been percolating as she imagined what her future might be suddenly came together into one brilliant idea.

Which was why, the next week, on a run-of-the-mill Wednesday halfway through September, Cress decided that she was going to take an early lunch.

'But it's eleven o'clock,' Sophy said when she tried to leave without a fuss. 'Far too early for lunch. Where are you really going?'

'To buy material to make me my peplum dress?' Phoebe asked half hopefully half belligerently.

The old Cress who'd worked at the Museum of Religious Relics and had been going out with Colin for donkey's years would have stuttered and stammered some excuse about a medical appointment, but this was Cress v.2.0.

'It's absolutely nobody's business but mine,' she said crisply, as she hitched her big tote bag up her shoulder. 'Let's just say that I'm going to see a man about a dog.'

Sophy and Phoebe sighed in unison. 'That really makes me miss Johnno,' Sophy said wistfully of her bioDad. Johnno was always going to see a man about a dog.

Actually, on a few occasions, the man that Johnno was going to see was probably the same man that Cress was about to see as she pressed the buzzer on a door just a few streets away from The Vintage Dress Shop.

'Freddy?' she said. 'I'm here as arranged. What floor are you on?'

Chapter Thirty

Cress had worked at The Vintage Dress Shop for well over a year but this was the first time that she'd had occasion to visit Freddy at his office, in a handsome white stucco building, which also contained a dentist's surgery, an architect's practice and, excitingly, a record label.

Freddy's office was on the second floor, no lift, and Cress was slightly breathless as she peered through an open door into a small room lined with filing cabinets. Sitting at a desk staring at a laptop, was a woman with rainbow-coloured hair, a rainbow-striped shirt and even rainbow-painted nails. She looked up, with a very stern demeanour for someone who was so colourfully exuberant, as Cress hovered in the doorway.

'Are you Freddy's eleven o'clock?'

Cress confirmed that she was, and the woman indicated a door in between the filing cabinets. 'Go in, he's expecting you. You don't want a drink, do you?'

Cress held up her water bottle by way of reply and was relieved to knock on the inner door and then enter Freddy's inner sanctum.

Compared to the colourful chaos of the outer office, here all was white minimalist calm. There was nothing in the room but a white desk and office chair and a couple of white leather cube-shaped armchairs arranged around a low glass table. And Freddy of course, his jeans and light blue Fred Perry the only pop of colour.

He stood up from behind his desk and gestured at one of the armchairs. 'Cress, to what do I owe the pleasure?' he asked, a serious look on his normally cheery face, as if he was only ever in business mode when he was in his office.

Though as Cress sat down, it occurred to her that she didn't really know what Freddy's business was. She knew that he was a solicitor by trade, but she thought of him more as a sorter-outer. Before he'd disappeared to Australia, Freddy had looked after Johnno's ducking and diving and wheeling and dealing. He was certainly very involved in the business side of The Vintage Dress Shop, tackling all the big admin things that were beyond Bea's pay grade or Phoebe's very narrow interest in anything that wasn't actually vintage dresses.

The rest was a bit of a mystery. Though once Anita had seen Freddy in a café with the members of a well-known indie band, and, when they were having Friday drinks in The Hat and Fan, Freddy was one of those people, like Charles, who seemed to know everyone. And everything, which was why Cress was here.

'I was hoping you could give me some advice,' she said, her grip tight on her tote bag, though it was Freddy, so no need to be nervous, except he was frowning at her like she'd overstepped.

'You're not going to hand in your notice, are you?' he asked.

'Of course not!'

'Has Phoebe done or said something heinous and/or offensive and you're intending to take her to an employment tribunal?' Freddy's face was still deadly serious.

'Tempting, but again, no,' Cress said and Freddy's grim countenance lightened slightly and he allowed himself to perch on the arm of the other armchair. 'I have an idea. A business idea and I don't really know anything about business but I thought you might.'

Freddy nodded. 'Go on, then.'

This non-smiley Freddy was quite intimidating, but Cress had come this far. She pulled her sketch pad and iPad out of her tote bag. 'Well, you know I designed a dress for a customer, then I ended up making new dresses for, well, everyone in the shop. And I loved it, the whole process, designing, choosing fabrics, sewing, seeing my vision become an actual frock . . .'

Freddy nodded again, but didn't say anything.

'Plus it's getting harder and harder to source decent vintage, we all know that, especially in a wide range of sizes, so there's definitely a market for good reproduction dresses, don't you think?'

Cress really wasn't loving business Freddy, who just made a 'carry on' gesture with his hand.

She turned on her iPad and then angled the screen so that Freddy could see it. 'So, I was thinking of starting my own line. Maybe a capsule collection of four dresses to begin with. The Anita, a 1940s-inspired, form-fitting dress in black and then in a pattern. The Sophy, a classic 1950s halter-neck dress, with swishy skirt, in a solid colour and a pattern. The Bea would be a tea dress, in two different colourways of polka dots, and then the Tanya, an evening gown inspired by *Breakfast at Tiffany's,* just in black.'

Freddy took the iPad from Cress so he could scroll through her designs, but he still wasn't saying anything. Luckily, for once Cress had plenty that she wanted to say.

'They wouldn't be cheap, I'd want to make them in Britain in the most sustainable way I can. But not ridiculously expensive. They'd go all the way up to a size 24. A limited production run to start with and then sell them via a website and hopefully with some bigger online retailers, like ASOS. Ha! I wish!'

That was it, that was the pitch.

'What do you want from me, then?' Freddy asked. Not suspiciously, but curiously.

Cress shrugged. 'I know all about the fashion side of things and I think I have a pretty good idea of what women like to wear, but everything else I haven't got a clue and I thought you might have, or you might know someone who did.'

Freddy handed back the iPad. 'A start-up like this is going to be pricey. Just in terms of production before you even get into marketing and logistics.'

Words like logistics didn't sit very well in Cress's vision of lots of grateful women wearing her dresses and feeling like the best versions of themselves. 'I have money saved up. Quite a bit. Well, it seems like a lot to me. I feel quite out of my depth,' Cress admitted, not that this confession was going to come as a surprise to Freddy. 'I could probably wangle a discount on bulk-buying fabric or sourcing deadstock fabric but finding a factory . . . would I have to employ people? How do I pay their national insurance? Oh my God, it is a lot . . .'

It felt like Cress's dreams had been crushed underfoot before they'd even had their moment. And yet Freddy had barely said a word. Now he smiled blandly.

'There's no need to look quite so devastated, Cress. You might decide that you'd prefer to go into partnership with someone who can handle the business side of things.'

'A partnership,' Cress echoed doubtfully. 'It would have to be with someone nice. Not some hard-headed person who says things like "time is money" and "don't bring me problems, bring me solutions".'

'Let's take Alan Sugar's name off the list then.' Freddy gave Cress a keen look. 'I definitely think your idea has potential. Lots of potential. Now, I'm not saying yes but I am saying that I'm always looking for new investment possibilities, and I'd certainly be up for doing a deep dive into costings and all that jazz. Then we can see where we are.'

'You'd want to go into business with me?' Cress asked incredulously because that wasn't at all what she'd expected. Which had been that Freddy would know someone who'd know someone and she'd have to go and talk to all these different someones and hope that, somewhere down the line, she'd feel confident enough to put her plan into action and risk her entire life savings.

But Freddy? Although Cress didn't really know that much about Freddy, she knew he was a good egg. He was Johnno's right-hand man and Johnno was Sophy's dad so Freddy was kind of like family. And he was the only person that Phoebe had any respect for. Also, business Freddy seemed like quite a formidable person to have in your corner.

'Well, let's not get too carried away,' Freddy said and Cress had never been so pleased to see his cheeky grin put in an appearance. 'This is a side hustle for now, you're definitely not going to quit the shop?'

'I don't think Phoebe would let me leave.' She and Freddy shared a conspiratorial look. 'She'd chain me to the over-locker.'

'True that. I'll have a think, and I'll need you to come up with some rough costs for fabric and notions, how long it would take an experienced machinist to make a dress, all that kind of stuff. Clara will email you.'

'Clara?'

Another grin from Freddy. 'You've already met Clara. The other woman in my life.'

Which meant that Freddy had *another* woman in his life and that woman was . . . 'Oh, by the way, talking of Phoebe,' Freddy added casually, though suddenly he wouldn't meet Cress's eye. 'Let's keep this between ourselves for now, until there's something worth mentioning. Though if things do progress, you know you're going to have to name a dress after her or both our lives won't be worth living.'

Cress left Freddy's office, after a cheery goodbye to Clara, who just grunted at her, in high spirits. She felt quite giddy with excitement and also with nerves about the unknown, but they were the good sort of nerves. Usually when Cress thought about the unknown and the future, it made her feel quite panicky. But now, as she fairly skipped along Regent's Park Road, she allowed herself a little fantasy of not just a capsule collection of four dresses but a whole range of dresses and – what the hell? Separates too. Maybe even some darling beaded cardigans made of a luxe yarn that was also repellent to moths.

She swung her arms, restless with expectation. Much as she loved her job, the last thing she really wanted to do was go back to the shop to sit in her lonely little workroom and sew buttons on stuff. For the first time in her life, Cress felt like skiving.

She didn't though. Like the responsible adult she was, she stopped off to get some lunch, splurging on a ciabatta sandwich from the really posh deli, then headed back to the shop. She'd only tell Sophy her news, she didn't want to jinx things, but there was someone else she really wanted to speak to too.

Not just about her plans for dresses but, even though five weeks probably wasn't enough time, Cress felt like a new person. She felt more in control of her destiny. And God, she really missed him.

As the Wedgwood-blue exterior of the shop came into view, she came to a halt and delved into her bag.

Cress wasn't a huge fan of speaking to people on the phone. This was why God had created messaging; but, as she pulled up Miles's number, she hoped that he would answer and she wouldn't have to leave a garbled message or, worse, revert to the Cress of old, take fright and hang up.

Miles answered on the second ring. 'Hello! This is a lovely surprise,' he said, sounding as if he was genuinely pleased to hear from her. 'There's not anything wrong, is there?'

'No, nothing's wrong.' Cress's voice squeaked ever so slightly. But she was determined to be brave. 'Just . . . things are good, really good, but I think of you all the time. I miss you.'

'Oh, Cress, I miss you too. So much.' Miles sighed.

Cress's current state of giddiness upgraded to sheer, dippy delight. She just needed to find a little more courage. 'I want you in my life. As more than a friend. Much, much more,' she said in a breathless rush. It was easy to admit that, now that she'd had the space to mourn her relationship. Yes, she was still sad, but a proper goodbye from Colin had given her closure and was helping her to heal. 'There's so many things I want to tell you. I can't wait to see you again. It's been ages since that Sunday.'

'Yeah, too bloody long.' There were voices in the background, a pause as Miles seemed to answer a question, and then he was back with her. 'Listen, if it's still too soon I understand, but I don't suppose you fancy skiving off work tomorrow?'

They were so perfectly in tune with each other. And yet. 'I can't skive off work tomorrow,' Cress said.

'Oh . . .'

'Because it's my day off so there would be no point in skiving, would there?'

'You sound happy, Cress,' Miles said softly. 'I like it.'

'I like it too. And what's happening tomorrow? Will you be back in London?' she asked hopefully.

'I won't. We're in Eastbourne but I've got a short shoot day, we'll be done by four, it's a whole thing with the tides and the light, but well, would you like to come down?'

'To Eastbourne?' Cress was already wondering what station she'd need to catch a train to Eastbourne. Maybe Victoria?

'We're shooting at Camber Sands tomorrow, because it's the only sandy beach in the whole of Sussex,' Miles said through what sounded like gritted teeth, as if the lack of sandy Sussex beaches had been causing him much aggravation. 'You'd need to get a train to Rye, it's the nearest station . . . I think you need to . . . I'll get someone to look up . . .'

'No need. I can sort out train times and routes to get me to Rye,' Cress said quickly, then she wondered if she was being too eager. But why not? Miles was missing her too. Miles wanted to see her too. There was every reason to be eager. 'Just tell me what time to get there and I'll see you tomorrow.'

Chapter Thirty-One

It was the most perfect of days.

Cress woke up five minutes before her alarm went off. Her hair decided to arrange itself in loose waves. She had no outfit panic but settled on a pretty black and white spotted tea dress, which she accessorised with her fancy trainers and a denim jacket.

She got to Finchley Central just as a via Bank train arrived and, when she arrived at St Pancras, there was enough time to grab a coffee and a pastry before she caught the train to Ashford International. Cress always panicked about having to change trains but changing onto the little local service, which would take her the rest of the way, was stress-free.

Twenty minutes later she was in Rye, the prettiest little town full of cobbled streets and half-timber medieval houses. Not that Cress was about to go exploring. She came out of the station, her feet and her heart practically skipping at the thought of seeing Miles again.

But there was no Miles waiting for her. Cress took her phone out to see if there was a new message from him, though she'd checked her phone just before she got off the train. She'd messaged him her arrival time last night and he'd replied, 'I can't wait to see you', and yet he wasn't here.

Cress fired off a quick message to say she'd arrived, and waited.

Fifteen minutes later, she was still waiting. Her anticipatory smile was replaced by a frown as she wondered whether she should google to see if there were any buses that ran from Rye to Camber Sands, though she didn't know exactly where they were filming and Miles hadn't replied to her message to say she'd arrived. Or the five other messages she'd sent him since then.

He was probably very busy with filming before the tide went in or went out or whatever. But he'd asked Cress to come and now she was here and blinking back the tears because she'd been too keen, too—

Her pity party was interrupted by the arrival of a black people-carrier suddenly screeching to a halt outside the station and narrowly avoiding ramming into one of the cabs that was idling at the taxi rank.

Cress peered through the open passenger window but it wasn't Miles, just a young guy, wearing a red beanie despite the warmth of the day, who turned and looked right back at her.

'Are you Chris?' he shouted.

Cress shook her head. 'I'm not.'

'No worries.'

He stayed parked there for a minute, staring at his phone, then leaned over to the passenger side again. 'Sorry. Are you here for Miles?'

'I am.' Cress dared to let hope flicker anew. 'But it's Cress. Not Chris.'

'Cress! What a muppet! Me! Not you.' He leaned further across to open the door. 'Sorry, I'm late to pick you up. Been having an absolute mare this morning with the council even though we had a filming permit. Whatevs. Jump in!'

He seemed legit, so Cress jumped in and shook the proffered hand. 'I'm Earl, production assistant and driver. Buckle up, mate, I'm going to lead-foot it.'

Earl didn't lead-foot it, Cress was pleased to note, but stuck to the speed limit for the ten minutes it took to reach

Camber Sands. As they drove past Rye Harbour and the marshlands, Earl kept up a steady stream of patter about the filming (going well apparently, apart from this unscheduled day having to film on an actual sandy beach), London (he'd grown up in Chelsea, not far from the Museum of Religious Relics, but 'on a council estate, mate. Cause I'm not one of those Eton types'), and how he'd been on a plant-based diet for the last year (but the on-set catering company and their bacon butties had been his downfall).

By the time they came screeching to another halt on a quiet road, the beach on their right and a whole collection of trucks, trailers and people milling about to their left, Cress felt slightly hysterical. There were big official signs every-where: Road closed! Filming in progress!

She got out of the car and then didn't know where to go. Or rather she wanted to hide because everyone looked so busy and serious and she was just here for a jolly. Miles must also be very busy and serious and probably regretting that he'd ever asked her to come.

Luckily Earl was there and he was still talking. 'Right, Cress, do you need a wee? Portaloos are just past that big grey truck.' Cress shook her head. 'Do you want coffee, tea?' She shook her head again because she really didn't want to have to use the Portaloos in front of all those film people. 'OK, then follow me. Are you ready for your close-up?'

Cress hoped that Earl was joking but she followed him as he went right towards the sea. There was a path through the sand dunes, piles of golden sand topped with green tufty grass, and right where the sand dunes became flat, white sand that stretched down to the shoreline, there was another flurry of people. A good-looking man in a slim-cut sixties suit was having powder dusted across his chiselled cheekbones as he sat on a camping stool, and next to him was—

'Cress! Hello, hello, hello!'

A blur of a woman in a white lace minidress came hurtling towards Cress and almost knocked her off her feet as she was wrapped up in a fierce, exuberant hug.

'It's so good to see you,' Ella exclaimed, pulling back a little to get a good look at Cress, who got a good look back.

'I hardly recognised you!' she said. 'Your hair!'

Ella patted her platinum-blond pixie crop. 'It's a wig, darling! And the bane of my life. Itches like you wouldn't believe.'

'Well, you look very glamorous,' Cress said, taking in the familiar features of Ella's face, which were both hidden and accentuated by the sheer amount of make-up she was wearing. From her sooty, sooty, long black eyelashes to the plump, rose-pink pillows of her lips. 'And I love your frock.'

Ella twirled. 'It's my wedding dress. In the film there's a montage of me designing and making the dress all by myself. You should have seen me handling a bolt of lace like it was my firstborn. You would have been so proud of me. Oh, this is Simon, by the way. Say hello, Simon,' she called out to the man with the cheekbones, who waved languidly in their direction. 'He plays a French film star, we've just eloped after I showed my first Paris fashion collection to great acclaim. It's all going to end in tears, alas, but for the moment we're on our honeymoon in the South of France.'

It was a lot to take in. Cress looked out at the almost deserted beach. The sky was a brilliant blue and the sand was like white gold as the sun shone down upon it. 'Who knew that the South of France was only an hour's train ride from St Pancras?'

'I know!' Ella gurgled and she seized hold of Cress's hands. 'Oh, it's so good to see you. We've been filming for what feels like for ever and it's lovely to remember that the real world, my real friends, aren't just a figment of my imagination.'

It was very touching to hear that Ella considered Cress to be one of her real friends and not just the very cruel woman who'd made her hand-stitch hems. The thought made her grin. 'I never go anywhere without a sewing kit, you know. I'm sure I could find you some hemming to do if you're missing the real world.'

Ella drew back with a theatrical shudder. 'Maybe I don't miss the real world that much.'

The make-up artist, with a holster full of brushes, tapped Ella on the shoulder. 'Let me take your shine away, then I think they're ready for you again.'

Cress was just about to ask where Miles was – she couldn't see him anywhere – but Ella was being ushered away. 'Pop yourself down in one of those deckchairs,' she shouted to Cress. 'We made sure to reserve you the best seat in the house.'

There was a row of blue and white deckchairs a few metres away and still no sign of Miles. With an apologetic smile that she just couldn't help, Cress scuttled towards the deckchairs and carefully lowered herself on to one at the far end.

There were quite a few people gathered at the shoreline, two of them wielding what looked like film cameras, not on big rigs like they were in the actual movies. There with other bits of technical-looking kit . . . And yet more people all taking it in turns to look at something on a MacBook that was being held by Miles.

Something in Cress's chest leapt at the sight of him but the rest of her stayed where she was, until she was joined by the woman with the make-up brushes, who sat down in the deckchair next to her.

'I'm Dawn,' she said with a friendly smile. She had close-cropped hair, all the better to show off her striking features, which didn't seem to need any of the make-up she had with

287

her in a little silver flight case. 'We're all dying to know who you are because we're all very nosy.'

'I'm Cress. A friend of Ella's . . . and Miles's.' Even saying his name made her voice catch, but Dawn didn't seem to notice. 'I gave Ella lessons in how to use a sewing machine and drape fabrics and generally look as if she knew how to design and make clothes.'

'That must have been fun and also exhausting,' Dawn said as if she knew Ella very well. 'First time on set then?'

'It is. There's so many people. What does everyone do?'

'Well, that woman in the back-to-front baseball cap is Claire, the director, and next to her in the red t-shirt is Art, he's the director of photography. Two cameramen, Ekow and Jules, then the one with the big furry muff is Olivia, who's one of the sound guys, then Miles you know. And here come our stars.'

Ella and Simon walked past the deckchairs and Dawn jumped up. 'Better check their shine,' she said, hurrying after them.

Cress applied sunscreen and though she really wanted to feel the sand between her toes, she kept her trainers on and revelled in the breeze coming off the sea, the salt tang in the air. Though it was almost the end of September, the days were still gloriously warm. It was so long since she'd been out of London and though this wasn't what she'd imagined when Miles had asked her to come down, it was proving to be quite fascinating.

She watched as Ella and Simon walked along the shoreline, both of them with bare feet, the waves just beyond them. They walked the same short path over and over again, reciting their lines, though they were too far away for Cress to be able to hear them *acting*.

But they were still acting. Every time they went back to their starting mark and someone called 'Action!' they changed things up. They'd hold hands or Ella would frolic, squealing as the waves lapped at her feet. They walked next to each other but without touching. And sometimes they did the same thing once more while they were filmed from a slightly different angle.

Cress knew then, though she'd suspected it before, that she wasn't cut out to be a film actress. She'd be rolling her eyes and asking if they were done yet after the fifth take. In reality, she'd actually lost count of the number of takes they'd done.

But even Cress could see that the tide was going out. In the time she'd been sitting there, an unbelievable two hours according to her phone, the sea was much further away than it had been, and the sky was now slightly overcast and there was a chill in the air.

Eventually they were done and began to disperse. Ella first, hurrying past Cress with a wave and a plaintive, 'So much to catch up on with you but I'm freezing and I really need a wee.'

Then the cameras and the sound equipment were packed away and, with his MacBook tucked under his arm, Miles began to head her way. Or rather he was aiming left of Cress but then he saw her sitting in the deckchair and he changed course. As he got nearer, his smile grew wider. He was wearing jeans and a thin-knit dark green jumper, inevitably with holes at the elbow and collar, over a white t-shirt. It was hard work walking over soft sand in sneakers but of course Miles made it look cool while Cress stayed seated because she didn't want to have to struggle out of the depths of the deckchair under his scrutiny.

'Cress, I'm so sorry,' he said once he was within talking distance. 'Please don't hate me.'

'I could never hate you,' Cress said. 'You haven't done anything wrong.'

Then he was in front of her, carefully putting the laptop down on a deckchair so he could hold out his hands to Cress.

There was no graceful way to get out of a deckchair, so Cress gave in to the inevitable and let Miles haul her up, which was all right because then she was in his arms. Properly in his arms for what felt like the first time. They hugged for a long time, his arms tight round her waist, his chin resting on the top of Cress's head as she buried her face in his neck so she could inhale great whiffs of his aftershave, which blended perfectly with the fresh sea-salt tang of the air.

Finally, they drew back a little so Cress could gaze into Miles's eyes, which had never looked so soft, so tender.

'I was going to be there to meet you but then the tide went out ahead of schedule and it was a mad crunch to get the shots we needed . . .' he said. 'I've spent most of today really over-identifying with King Canute.'

'It's fine,' Cress said. 'I did have a wobble at Rye station but then Earl arrived and everyone's been so lovely and also, Miles, I have conniptions if I have to unpick a seam and start again. All those takes? How do you stand it?'

'But every take's different. Not just what the actors are doing but the light, the position of the sun and in this case the bloody tide.' He smiled and smoothed the hair back from her face. 'Look at you. I can't believe you're actually here.'

'Well, I am,' Cress said and this would be the perfect moment for a . . .

'I'm dying to kiss you,' Miles whispered, his words echoing her own thoughts and sending a thrill coursing through Cress's veins. 'But not with this eager audience.'

Cress turned her head to see quite a few people looking at them with great interest. Dawn had said that they were all very nosy. 'But a proper kiss,' she said. 'I need full contact, Miles.'

'You're ready for a proper kiss, then? You don't need more time? Because if you do . . .'

What Miles was saying was sweet but Cress didn't want to hear it. She placed the tip of her index finger to his lips.

'No more waiting,' she said. 'Just lots of kissing. Quite soon, please.'

Miles nipped the tip of her finger, grinning when Cress gasped in mock outrage. 'I think lots of kissing could be arranged,' he said.

Then he retrieved his laptop and, with his arm firmly round Cress's shoulders, they walked back, through the sand dunes, to where the company looked like they were packing up and planning to head out very soon.

Miles deposited Cress in Ella's trailer, where she was put to work reattaching a zip on a skirt that had come loose from its moorings, while Ella removed her heavy screen make-up with handfuls of cold cream.

'We're going back to Eastbourne now,' Ella said, as she stared at her now bare face in the mirror. 'Still got three days of filming left.'

'Will you be done then?' Cress asked because it would be so good to only have three more days until Miles was back in London.

'Not by a long shot,' Ella said mournfully. 'Then we'll be in a studio in Bristol doing some interior stuff and even when we get back to London I'll have voice stuff to do in a poky little sound booth in Soho. Not as glamorous as you thought?'

It really wasn't. 'But I'm sure it will look very glamorous when it's all been put together.'

Ella struck a pose. 'And that, my darling, is the magic of cinema!'

There was a knock on the door. Then Miles's voice. 'Are you decent in there?'

'Never!' Ella declared. 'But you may enter.'

Miles stuck his head round the door. 'They're waiting on you, Els, so they can drive back to Eastbourne.'

'I'll be five minutes, tops.' Ella was already stuffing her belongings into a big slouchy leather bag. 'Are you coming on to Eastbourne, Cress?'

It was already getting on for five. If Cress went to Eastbourne, which would mean changing her return ticket, a ruinously expensive exercise, there wouldn't be much time before she had to head back to London.

But still, just getting to hug Miles in the sand dunes . . .

'Oh, Cress and I were going to hang out in Camber for a bit,' Miles said, with a pleading look at Cress, who needed no further persuasion.

'That's the plan,' she agreed.

Ella didn't say anything, which was very unusual for Ella, but she raised her eyebrows and muttered something under her breath, then gave a little laugh.

Then she was skipping out of the door with a wave and a 'Don't do anything I wouldn't do, darlings!', and it was just Miles and Cress.

'You don't mind staying on rather than experiencing the many delights of Eastbourne?' he asked, shoving his hands into the pockets of his jeans.

Cress had been to Eastbourne once and though it was a perfectly pleasant seaside town, it hadn't left much of a lasting impression on her.

'I think Eastbourne can manage without me,' she said, her voice a little huskier than usual.

'I have the production department's hire car, so don't worry about having to get back to the station,' he said quickly. 'We won't be stranded here.'

Cress had never seen Miles so nervous. He was practically twitching.

'I'm not worried,' she said. 'I'm not worried at all.'

Miles stilled and just looked at Cress standing there with a tinge of pink across her face from being in the sun all day, her hair a tangle of sea-salt curls. Cress didn't think anyone had ever looked at her so intently as Miles was.

Then he smiled. 'Though I wouldn't mind being stranded with you.'

Cress smiled back. 'Same.'

Chapter Thirty-Two

It did feel a little as if they were the last two standing as they watched the last of the fully laden people-carriers drive off.

Now that the sun had begun its descent and there was a sharp wind was blowing in from the sea, the beach was almost empty apart from one lone dogwalker with two exciteable Jack Russell terriers.

Cress and Miles decided to walk along the coast road until they found a chippy.

They held hands because they could do that now and Cress told Miles about her plans for her own reproduction fashion line. 'It might not come to anything, but nothing ventured and all that, right?'

Miles nodded emphatically. 'Absolutely right. No more vintage fairs for you. It will be the runways of Paris and Milan.'

Cress leaned into him. 'Hardly!'

'You never know,' Miles insisted. 'Have you thought of a name for your empire?'

'Really not an empire but I did wonder if I should just stick with my name, Cressida Collins. Because I have the same initials as Charles Creed, famous British couturier and Coco Chanel. That has to be a good omen.'

'We're talking Coco Chanel, iconic French fashion designer and not Coco Chanel, iconic French bulldog?' Miles asked with a muffled laugh as Cress dug him in the ribs with her elbow.

'You know exactly who I mean!' She let Miles pull her closer and wondered if this feeling, this contact high from being so near to him, being able to touch him, would ever fade. 'Though I was also considering Thank You, It Has Pockets! But I should probably work out if I can even afford to do this before I settle on a name.'

'You'll do it,' Miles said softly but firmly as if he had great faith in Cress, but then the glowing lights of a fish and chip shop came into view and their thoughts immediately turned from fashion to food.

Neither Cress nor Miles had eaten all day. Also, if you were at the seaside, with a beautiful sandy beach at your disposal, and you didn't get fish and chips doused in salt and vinegar and wrapped in paper to eat on that beach, then you were doing something very wrong with your life.

They retraced their steps and found a dip in the sand dunes, where they were hidden from the road and could see the shore stretch out before them, the ripple of the sea now a faint silvery suggestion in the distance.

Battered haddock and proper chippy chips with lots of crispy bits, even with a slight scattering of sand, had never tasted so good. Especially when washed down with a can of 7UP.

Cress couldn't remember the last time she'd felt so content. As she looked up at the glorious mackerel sky, the setting sun streaking the blue with pink and orange, she was keenly aware of Miles sitting next to her, their backs against the steep slope of a sand dune, so close, but still not close enough.

Cress had wet wipes in her bag, because of course she did, and once they'd both cleaned their hands she couldn't bear it any longer.

'If we don't kiss soon, then I think I might die,' she heard herself say, when she'd been thinking of doing something a little less dramatic, like snuggling even closer to Miles and staring at his mouth until he got the message. That always seemed to work in films.

Miles turned to her with a lazy grin. 'You might die?'

Cress nodded and she was blushing but blushing never killed anyone, unlike the lack of Miles kisses. 'Very possibly.'

'Well, we can't have that,' he said.

There was a lot of shuffling then to get in the right position, which could have ruined the moment, but it seemed to Cress that they'd been waiting so long for this moment that nothing could spoil it.

Then Miles was on his knees facing Cress and she tilted her face up towards the multicoloured sky and him. His hand cupped the back of her head, fingers threading through her tangled curls to bring her closer.

The first touch of lips upon lips felt almost unreal, like a dream that Cress had had for so long but never thought would come true. They drew back, then drew nearer for a kiss that couldn't be anything other than real, Cress's hands cradling Miles's face as he kissed her gently, like he was mapping out the contours and topography of her mouth so he'd know the way for next time.

These gentle, exploratory kisses seemed to go on for ever. Then Miles groaned, which made Cress's pulses quicken.

'I feel like that too,' she whispered.

'I hope not because my knees are actually killing me,' he said. 'The effort not to topple over . . .'

Cress pulled away from so she could laugh because they'd both got so worked up about this first kiss, about how romantic it should be, so worth waiting for, when really Miles could have kissed her by the bins round the back of the chippy and she wouldn't have cared.

'Please, feel free to topple,' Cress said.

Miles frowned and, before he could ask Cress what she meant, she grabbed hold of his jumper and pulled him down so she was lying flat on the sand and he was on top of her.

'Is that better on your poor knees?' she asked.

Even though the light was fading fast, Cress didn't miss the way that Miles's eyes darkened. 'Oh, you have no idea,' he said, then swooped forward to take her lips again.

These kisses were harder, stinging slightly from the salt and vinegar, and Cress much preferred them. Miles's tongue dipping into her mouth, his fingers plucking at the buttons of her dress to uncover her skin to the breeze and the touch of his hands.

They were straining against each other, Miles's leg hard between her thighs, Cress pulling him even closer until they came to a breathless halt.

'We can wait a little longer,' Miles panted against her neck. 'Not here. Not like this.'

He was right – the sand for one thing. It would get *everywhere*.

'We could book into a hotel,' Cress suggested. 'There has to be one near here . . . and then I could catch the train in the morning . . .'

'No, I don't want a night in some crappy little b'n'b and you worrying about the train times . . .'

'I wouldn't,' Cress said, but now that Miles had mentioned it, she *was* thinking about the train times.

He smiled as he rolled off her so they were both lying on their backs, and he linked his fingers through her. 'I get you, Cress,' he said because he did. Even though they'd only known each other a few weeks. It wasn't the same as knowing someone for fifteen years, but it was still deep and profound in its way. 'And tomorrow is an early shoot time, to catch the sunrise.'

'I know what you're saying is right,' Cress said as she buttoned up her dress one-handed. 'It still sucks though.'

Miles squeezed Cress's fingers. 'But when something feels this special, then it's not worth rushing it. Not when we have all the time in the world.'

Cress sat up. 'We're definitely not waiting *that* long.'

'It will be at least two weeks until I let you have your wicked way with me,' Miles said primly. 'Now, I'd better get you on that London train so you don't miss work tomorrow. Just between us, Phoebe *terrifies* me!'

Although she felt a little like crying at having to say goodbye and a fortnight of waiting, Cress was laughing as she staggered to her feet. 'It's been eighteen months that I've worked with Phoebe and she still terrifies me sometimes.'

They tried in vain to brush all the sand away before they got in the car but when they arrived at Rye station Cress still felt quite bedraggled, not that Miles seemed to notice.

He made a point of walking her to the station entrance and took her in his arms again. 'You look so beautiful,' he said, even though Cress knew that her hair was fifty per cent sand at this point and her dress was thoroughly crumpled. 'This is going to be the longest two weeks in history.'

They only stopped kissing when they heard the toot of the incoming train, then it was a hurried goodbye and a mad rush to reach the platform in time.

Cress's heart was still beating fast as she took a seat on the near-empty train, though she didn't know if that was from the kissing or the rushing.

Her phone chimed. A message from Miles.

Missing you already. xxx

She put a finger to her kiss-sore lips and stared out of the window at the darkened world. Cress's head was full of all the kisses they were going to have and all the dresses she was going to create. The plans she was going to make for things she hadn't even dreamed about yet.

Her future might look very different from how she'd imagined it only a few weeks before, but she couldn't wait for it to begin.

Epilogue

A month later

The function room of Barking Golf Club had never looked quite so glamorous as it did on this late-October night.

The theme was Old Hollywood and every horizontal and vertical surface in the room was swathed in white fake tulle with accents of silver. The party guests had all made a real effort too, even if, for some of the younger invitees, Old Hollywood translated as the shortest, tightest dresses they could find with cut-outs that highlighted underboob and sideboob. Or trousers so tight that 'you can see what they had for breakfast and why are they all showing their ankles? Don't young men wear proper-length trousers anymore?' asked the elderly woman who was sitting on Cress's right.

'It is quite chilly for autumn,' Cress murmured non-committally because she didn't like to judge other people sartorially and also because it was quite hard to concentrate on what her neighbour was saying when Miles had his arm round her shoulders, his thumb causing havoc in the dip of her collarbone.

It had been two weeks since he'd finished shooting and Cress had incurred Phoebe's wrath by spontaneously taking a week's holiday at seventy-two hours' notice. Even Phoebe's continued huffiness couldn't make Cress regret the week away in New York. Because yes, they'd gone to New York on a whim and Cress had to rethink everything she knew about herself because now she was the sort of person who went to New York on a whim.

Not that she and Miles had seen much of New York. They hadn't even made it to Tiffany & Co on Fifth Avenue. But they had spent an awful lot of time in their hotel room overlooking Central Park. As soon as the door had shut behind their porter, who didn't seem inclined to leave until Miles had tipped him twenty dollars, they'd fallen into each other's arms. Then shortly after that, they'd fallen onto the deluxe king bed, and stayed there for the best part of seven days. Cress might not have made it to the museum at the Fashion Institute, which had been the number one item on her New York itinerary, but it had still been one of the best weeks of her life.

Just the thought of it made Cress give a little rapturous sigh, even though the present was just as good as the memories.

'You look so beautiful,' Miles whispered in her ear because speeches were happening.

Cress did feel beautiful. It was so rare that she got a chance to really dress up or want to really get her glam on, but when Tanya had invited her to the famous fiftieth birthday she'd been touched. Miles was her plus one and though the thought of formal wear always sent Cress into a panic, she wanted to dress up for him as much as she wanted to dress up for Tanya and for herself too. New improved Cress was really leaning into the dresses thing.

That was why she was the first customer to borrow a dress courtesy of The Vintage Dress Shop's new rental service, which was almost up and running. It was a dark green 1930s velvet gown with shoulder straps, a fitted bodice and a skirt that fell in tiny, graceful pleats, an homage to Fortuny's iconic Delphos dress.

Cress had emerged from the changing room to be met with stunned faces from Sophy, Bea and Anita. 'Bloody hell, why do you have to be so gorgeous?' Anita had demanded and, though Cress didn't think she was gorgeous, she couldn't stop looking at herself in the mirror. She scrubbed up all right.

Phoebe had done Cress's make-up, though she was still cross about the week off and also newly cross that Cress was *renting* a dress; but she couldn't resist getting to work on Cress's face.

'I've been dying to get some liquid eyeliner on you ever since we first met,' she'd said, as she'd expertly given Cress cat-eye flicks.

Cress had decided that a strong eye was enough and she didn't need a strong lip too but Phoebe and her Lisa Eldridge Velvet Ribbon lipstick in a sultry red had overruled her.

And now Miles was looking at her in the same way that he'd looked at the prawn cocktail they'd been served as a starter. 'Soft, sleepy, first thing in the morning Cress is my favourite Cress, but I think Hollywood siren Cress might be my second favourite,' he said as they politely applauded Tanya's two teenage children, who'd just performed a very long off-key rap full of family in-jokes in their mother's honour.

'You don't look so bad yourself,' Cress told him, because Miles in a slim-cut, black suit with snowy white shirt and black tie, nothing holey, and his hair slicked back, was a revelation. A very handsome revelation. 'You need to get kitted out in formal wear more often.'

They smiled at each other, the other one hundred and forty-eight guests ceasing to exist. Cress was wondering how soon it might be before they could make their excuses and leave, when there was a squeal of feedback from the microphone as Tanya stood up to make her speech.

Cress couldn't stop herself from sighing in satisfaction because Tanya looked incredible. It wasn't just the black satin dress, which hugged her curves and put the bomb in bombshell. It wasn't her blond hair swept up in an elegant chignon or the ornate and bejewelled neckpiece she was wearing, borrowed from Charles, who said it was mostly paste and glass and not that expensive really 'but I'm begging you, Cress, don't let her or that necklace out of your sight.'

No, it was the way that Tanya carried herself, proudly, regally, confidently. It was a perfect match for her smile as she thanked everyone for coming. Then she took a deep breath as if she, despite her new inner confidence, was still a little bit nervous.

'I can't believe it's taken me fifty years to realise that I'm enough. That I don't need to be famous or rich or *married*,' she said with heavy emphasis as her guests hooted because they'd clearly heard many, many times about Joe's lack of a proposal after so long together. 'So, I'm glad that I've finally taken this opportunity to celebrate myself because I'll have a long bloody wait if I'm expecting someone else to do it. Now please raise your glasses in a toast to me because I'm fifty and I'm fucking fabulous.'

There were whistles of approval and applause, then raised glasses, and cries of 'To Tanya!' echoed around the room.

'We could go soon,' Cress whispered to Miles, who leaned in closer to steal a tiny kiss.

'Not now,' he said. 'They're playing our song.'

He was right, because the DJ – who'd been playing crowd-pleasers all night from 'Come on Eileen' to 'Blame It on the Boogie' – had turned it down a couple of notches and the opening bars of 'Moon River' rang out.

'Do you want to dance?' Miles asked and Cress could think of nothing better than shuffling around the floor with Miles, her huckleberry friend if ever there was one.

But Tanya and her partner Joe, sweating slightly in a white dinner jacket and bow tie that looked as if it was strangling him, had taken to the floor and it was their moment. Or it was Tanya's moment to revel in being the most beautiful woman in the room.

Cress could feel the prickle of imminent tears, though she really didn't want to smudge her make-up.

'You're going to cry, aren't you?' Miles hissed, handing her his pocket square.

'You can pretty much count on it,' Cress mumbled back, but then she joined in with the collective gasp as Joe suddenly dropped to one knee.

Was he having a heart attack?

No, he was retrieving a small velvet box from the inner pocket of his jacket, and the music stopped so everyone could hear him shout, 'Tanya, you know I bloody well love you. Will you make an honest man of me?'

He opened the box while Tanya stared down at the ring and then at the perspiring face of the man who she'd spent so much of her life with.

She looked so serious that for one moment Cress thought that she was going to turn him down or, worse, walk away without a word. But then she fanned herself, like she was about to faint.

'Will I marry you?' she mused. She made poor Joe and her assembled guests wait it out for an agonising ten seconds, then she grinned. 'Well, seeing as how you're wearing more than just your pants this time, yeah, why not? Let's do it.'

Then Joe stood up and tried to put the ring on Tanya's finger while she tried to fling her arms round him and they were bumping heads and giggling, and in its own way, it was the most romantic proposal that Cress could imagine.

Two people who, despite their differences, were made for each other.

Miles laughed and pressed his lips to Cress's shoulder and, when she took his hand, he entwined his fingers through hers and leaned closer to steal a kiss that she was only too happy to give.

It really was the perfect moment. And Cress couldn't wait for all the perfect moments that were yet to come.

Acknowledgements

Thanks to Rebecca Ritchie, Euan Thorneycroft, Harmony Leung, Jack Sargeant, Lucy Joyce, Gosia Jezierska and all at A.M. Heath.

And thank you to Olivia Barber, Amy Batley, Phoebe Morgan, Jo Dickinson, Katy Blott and Cara Chimirri at Hodder & Stoughton. The MVP award goes to Jacqui Lewis, copy editor extraordinaire!

An invitation from the publisher

Join us at www.hodder.co.uk, or follow us
on Twitter @hodderbooks to be a part of
our community of people who love the very
best in books and reading.

Whether you want to discover more about a book
or an author, watch trailers and interviews, have the
chance to win early limited editions, or simply browse
our expert readers' selection of the very best books,
we think you'll find what you're looking for.

And if you don't, that's the place to tell us what's missing.

We love what we do, and we'd love you to be a part of it.

www.hodder.co.uk

@hodderbooks

HodderBooks

HodderBooks